The Pessimist
and seven more plays of love

Paul R. Cooper

reallyreuben publishing
441 Pearl Street
Kingston, NY 12401

For Carol
who daily teaches me
what love is about.

Foreword

When I feel the urge to write a play, I don't think, *I'm going to write a play about love*. With honest intention I think, *I'm going to write a play about <u>life</u>*. My problem is that when I've finished, it turns out that my new play is in some way about love—love gained, love lost, love screwed up—or maybe all three at once!

I suppose this is due to a character defect on my part. It's not that I don't know that life can be a salad of horrors; one can't open a newspaper without tasting it. My failing is that—given a choice—I'd much rather see life as coherent, capable of meaning, if only we live fearlessly enough, and love deeply enough. So, despite my best intentions, a love play is what I end up trying to write.

Not everyone is pleased by this. A good friend of mine—also a playwright—says my fondness for happy endings keeps my work from distinction: to the extent that they end happily, *they lie.* Is he right? I tend to doubt it, but I fear I'll never know enough to change his mind. What I do know is what I like.

And that's what I write.

The Pessimist
and seven more plays of love

The Plays

How to Get a Good Husband

Scene: An auditorium. On the stage are a lectern and a microphone. Enter, on crutches, WENDY, an attractive woman in her middle twenties. A tote bag is slung around her neck. When she gets to the lectern, she leans the crutches on the side of it. She removes the tote bag from around her neck, and from the tote bag produces a 3-hole binder containing her speech. She places the speech on the lectern and opens up the binder to the first page. Then she adjusts the microphone to the proper height and angle. She addresses the audience.

Wendy: Is the volume okay? Can you hear me all right?

Pause

Okay. Good. Let's get started. My name is Wendy Isen, and the name of tonight's talk, as you know, is *How to Get a Good Husband.* That's the *original* title. But it's a bit misleading, 'cause it suggests that I'm an authority on the subject. Of course I *feel* like an authority, you know; I've given it a lot of thought and done some research. I work in a travel agency, and I see these couples coming in to plan their honeymoon. (I'm the honeymoon specialist.) And while I'm helping them with their honeymoon, I'm checking them out. Are they truly a team, will the choice be mutual, or does one of them decide for them both? And I wonder: will this marriage work? So I have some ideas on what makes a good couple, but I'm

1

hesitant to speak right now, because, the truth is, I'm not married yet. I'm *going* to be married—next week—to a great guy, and we've got a great honeymoon planned, and I'm sure that if I were giving the talk when I was originally supposed to—three months from now—by that time I would have had weeks and weeks of happy marriage under my belt—so to speak—and I'd be entitled to talk more confidently. But through some clerical error—wouldn't you know—the original date turned out to be unavailable. So they offered me tonight. And I said, what the hell. I mean, I *thought* what the hell. What I *said* was, "thank you very much, I'll take it." This was even though I had just broken my ankle a few days before. But I didn't want to postpone my life because of a little fracture, you know. Still, I have to admit that delivering a speech in this condition makes me a bit nervous.

Also, as I've said, I'm nervous about giving this speech before I'm actually married. Don't get me wrong—I feel that I'm ready to speak *now*—more or less. I feel that I'm choosing right—of course I do—and that everything will turn out fine, and if I give this talk again in a year or so, I'll be able to present myself as an authority on How to Get a Good Husband. But right now, maybe that title is a bit bold—I mean, I've chosen him all right, but I haven't actually *landed* him yet. You never can tell. Something may happen at the last moment. So I thought I'd change it to *How I'm Getting My Husband.* That way, I'm not laying down general rules; I'm just relating my experience. That's better anyway, regardless of how things turn out. So I told the house manager I wanted to change the title, but of course, the publicity had already gone out, and it was too late to change anything. Story of my life. Whenever I'd like to change my mind, it's always too late to change anything. People say I change my mind often, but I don't think I change it *that* often. And I'm not going to change it this time. My fiancé is a real find, a real catch, and I'd be crazy to want to change anything.

Oh, he's gorgeous! He works out every day, and it shows. He's a real hunk. Or maybe I should say, an *un*real hunk, since every time I see him—really get to see him if you know what I mean—I can't believe all that is mine. Or will be, in a week. He could be on the cover of GQ magazine—with his clothes on, of course. He dresses marvelously—has to, with his job: VP of Sales at Amalgamated Federal Bank. You should see him in pin-stripes! You should see him *without* them. He's eye candy all right; everyone thinks so. But *he* thinks that *I'M* eye candy. Loves to have me on his arm, he says, 'cause when people see him with me, his stock goes up. I'm gonna be his trophy wife, he says. And his name—are you ready for this?—is Adam de Brazza. What a name for someone so studly! I love it! And I'll be *Mrs.* de Brazza. I love that, too.

Nelson hates him. Nelson's my computer nerd. Well—he's not *my* computer nerd really, he's everyone's computer nerd. That's what he does; he goes around fixing things. Mainly fixes computers, but the truth is, he can fix anything that's broken. Handy guy to have around, and he's a good friend of mine. Trouble is, I think Nelson really hates Adam's guts. It started after I decided to buy a PC, even though Nelson advised against it. He wanted me to get a Mac. I chose the PC because that's what Adam uses; that's what his whole bank uses, you know. But Nelson—who fixes both PCs and Macs—says that the Mac is superior in all kinds of ways, and he wanted me to get a Mac, not a PC. But how would that look, husband and wife with different—you know—operating systems? Can you imagine the article in Redbook, *Can This Marriage Succeed?* Or in Cosmopolitan: *Is sex better with a Mac?* So I had to go with the PC for Adam's sake—for mine too, you know—and after the PC arrived Nelson didn't have one good thing to say about Adam. More than that, he's refusing to come to the wedding! I mean, you know, that's taking brand loyalty a little too far, don't you think?

Oh, I *know* what you think, that Nelson has a thing for me, and is jealous of Adam. I wouldn't have thought so. I would have thought that was stupid. Oh. Sorry, I shouldn't have said "stupid." It's a mean word, it's heartless; I try not to say it. I should have said, *clueless.* Which at least allows for improvement; like maybe you can learn something—or *try* to learn it, at least. Anyway, as I was saying, I would have thought that Nelson *couldn't* be jealous of Adam, and it's not because Nelson is gay or anything like that; in fact, he's had plenty of dates with all sorts of girls. He tells me about them—shows me their pictures. They're in his cell phone—he has a place just for them—and every couple of months or so, he opens it up to show me his latest conquest. Well, *he* doesn't call them conquests, but that's what I call them. Most of them are very pretty, but a few months ago there was one who was...well, frankly, to call her plain would be doing her a kindness. So I go, "what do you see in *her?* I mean, you seem to be able to get any girl you want, so why choose *her?*"

He just smiles at me. And he goes "because she has a lovely spirit, because she's kind and generous, and because it would silly to overlook a woman simply because she doesn't photograph well."

He talks like that—like a...like a *what:* A teacher? A preacher? Because he gets up and starts pacing the room, going "C'mon Wendy! Do you think that love is a business deal, where you say, 'I'm a 10, so I can love only another 10, or if need be, a 9, or in a pinch I might settle for no less than an 8 ½?'"

So I go, "well, that's what happens!" And he goes, "I **know** that's what happens: a guy says he loves a woman because she's beautiful, or because she's rich—it's the same thing— and it sucks. You don't want a guy to love you because of something. 'Cause what happens when you've lost that something: you've lost your looks, or your money?" he goes. "Is it ok for him to stop loving you? No, no! You want a guy who feels like that old song..." and—right then, believe me, people— he actually starts singing,

> *Imitating Nelson, she sings, as she sways, and snaps her fingers*

"I don't know why I love you like I do,

"I don't know why, I just do..."

> *(speaking)*

And then he grabs me and whirls me around, and he's singing ...

> *(singing)*

"I don't know why you thrill me like you do...

"I don't know why, you just do..."

> *(speaking)*

And I'm going, "Stop it Nelson, I'm dizzy!"

And he goes, "You—dizzy—is it possible?"

Of course he was trying to get a rise out of me—suggesting I'm a dizzy dame, or something. But I didn't want to rise to the bait, so I just told him that he had a beautiful voice. Which he does.

"Me?" he goes, "with a beautiful voice? Naah, it's all a delusion; pay attention to what I'm trying to *say*."

"Which is?"

And he goes, "I can't speak for anyone else, but as for me, I want to be *surprised* by how much I love a woman, and when that happens, when I'm actually surprised, then I'll *know* my love is right, and I can stop looking."

That has to be the smoothest line I've ever heard from a skirt chaser. Because, for years he's been busy as a bee, buzzing from female to female—lots of fun in the flowers, right?—but so far with no surprises. Poor fellow. But he keeps on trying. And there are lots of flowers left to sample; apparently there's a huge pool of women who can't resist him. He has that thin, wiry look, which some girls like. But not me! I mean, that's really the point, isn't it? I like the hunky, studly type. And Nelson's not it. He has always something going on that mind of his, but who knows what it is, and who can understand it? I mean, would you believe it: he once went on for thirty-two minutes about his latest sorting routine—I *counted* them: thirty-two minutes—all about sorting! Talk about boring! But when I complained, he told me he knew that deep down, I had the smarts to understand it. Is he kidding?! Give me a break— *please!* The only thing I understand about sorting is the sort of man I could get along with, and Nelson just isn't that sort. He must know it, too, because he's never made a pass at me, never even asked me out on a date...Tell you the truth, he has seldom given me *that look*—you women out there, you know the look I mean. It shows the man is interested, even if he's not available, or is too shy to say anything about it. No—very little like that from Nelson. He just keeps showing up to fix my computer. Even when I don't think it needs fixing, he'll find things that need tuning, like defragging the hard disk—is that what you call it? I'm a computer idiot, I *need* Nelson. So if he shows up and says, "let's clean the registry," I say, "fine, whatever. Do your thing."

So when the hard disk is being cleaned, and the registry defragged—or is it the other way around?—he talks to me sometimes about his love life, but more often about mine. Like that jazz musician I was dating: he warned me to be careful. And when I complained that it was none of his business, he said he was only telling me what my poor mother would have said if she were still around. Of course he was right about that. My father was a musician, and the grief he gave my mother! He shortened her life I'm sure—deserted us both before I was old enough to remember him. Mommy never talked about him much, but she often said in a hollow voice, "Wendy dear, never *ever* marry a jazz musician." Poor Mommy.

Beat

But I wasn't necessarily going to *marry* my jazz man! I was just having fun with him. Now that I think of it, it was probably the same sort of fun that Mommy was having with my father, before nothing was fun anymore. But I was luckier than Mommy. I found out about *my* jazzy delight *before* he had a chance to marry me and leave me. I found out about all his...his extracurricular activities. Oh, God. What could I have been thinking of, to date a musician? I should have known better. It's just that I love music so much—rock, jazz, even opera and symphonies sometimes. But I have to keep telling myself that as for the musicians *themselves,* let someone else marry them. I mean, though I love music a whole lot, I'd hate it if any of my boyfriends had music in them. Nelson sings a lot, but I try not to hold it against him. And besides, he isn't my boyfriend.

Nelson says I act as if my head isn't on straight. He says my priorities and values are all screwed up. Once he goes, "Wendy, your mind is like a hard disk badly in need of defragging." When he teases me like that, I have an urge to grab one of the sharp pencils in his pocket protector and stab him with it. But he smiles at me so gently that all I can do is grin back at him—when I can look at him at all. Sometimes he really bothers me. Like when I asked how he could waste time with a ditz like me, and he goes, "You, a ditz? I wouldn't say that."

"Well what *would* you say?"

He goes, "I'd say you're not yet fully conscious—yet. And as for wasting my time, I'd say that when you finally wake up, it will prove very interesting."

You see? Sometimes he talks like that—kinda condescending, you know—and it drives me nuts.

So when I met Adam de Brazza, I thought: finally—a man I can relate to, a man who I could bring home to Mommy—if she were still living. First off—he isn't a musician! And in every other way, he's perfect—he has a Princeton education, a great job, and in bed he's...*amazing!* Of course, he has to get out of bed *some*times other than going to work. Like every Sunday, he gets out of bed to escort his mother to Church, sits next to her in the pew, and has lunch with her when it's all over. Isn't that sweet? Nobody can fault him for anything—I figured that not even Nelson could find a thing to complain about. But I was wrong. For my nerd was very doubtful about him. He wanted to know whether Adam wanted me for my wonderful self—Nelson's words—or simply because of how I made him *feel*. But Nelson expects too much. I told him that. How many people could love with no thought of personal reward? I certainly was no saint in that department, I said. I was thinking how Adam made me feel in *bed,* but I didn't tell Nelson what I was thinking.

But Nelson simply gave me that gentle smile of his, as if he could read my mind. He said that while bedroom passions tend to cool with time, what has staying power are shared interests. Did Adam like the opera, he wanted to know. I   go, "Well, he *takes* me to the opera." And he goes, "sure he does, because you keep asking him to. But how much can he *like* the opera, when he sleeps right through *La Bohème?*"

Well, how on earth could Nelson know that—that's what *I* wanted to know.

Nelson goes, "because I happened to be there for that performance and had a seat in the upper balcony, where, through my new prism binoculars, I saw Adam de Brazza snoozing away in that box seat he bought just to show everyone he was there, and who with."

I was furious! Not with Adam—he'd had a hard day at the office, and you can't expect a busy man to stay awake *all* the time. No, I was furious with *Nelson*. What was he doing—stalking me?

"No such thing" he goes, cool as a flute. "I was there," he goes, "because I happen to like opera. I'll be there whether anyone asks me or not."

I'm beside myself. I go, "what *is* this, you want me to take you to the opera?!" But my nerdy Nelson says nothing, just gives me his trademark gentle smile, which is beginning to make me sick.

I start shouting at him. "Are you gonna sit there all day grinning at me like some dimwit ape? Can't you do something? Zipping those archives—or whatever the hell they are, does that have to take all day? Must I waste my whole Sunday on you?" I am starting to scream, but Nelson's voice never rises above his usual murmur. "I'm just trying to look out for your happiness."

I lose it—totally lose it, and start to shriek. "What business is it of yours to look out for my happiness? You're my computer nerd! Is this part of your job description?!" The smile fades from Nelson's face—finally!—and he goes, "I don't think I can do anything more today." He writes out the instructions for completing the archiving, tells me to call him if I need help with them, and lets himself out the door, which closes quietly behind him. He doesn't even slam it.

I am bummed out—totally. So when Adam finally comes home from work—he works six plus days a week—sometimes on Sunday, at that damned bank—he wants to know what was for supper, and I go "I haven't even planned it yet, let alone put it on the table." His face tells me that this is very serious. He goes, "You want me to take you out to dinner?"

I go "No! not yet, not until you sit down right here next to me and answer a question." His face turns white, as if he was wondering whether I was going to ask him about some affair he might be having in Chicago, where he often goes for business trips. And instead of sitting down next to me on the couch, he chooses a chair across from me, so that his fancy glass coffee table is between us. He sits down carefully, crosses his legs, and lays his hands in his lap as if he's protecting his...you know...privates. And he goes, "All right, my dear, what is your question?"

"What happens in *La Bohème?*"

"Is this a test?" He has his head cocked a little, to the side.

"Yes, this is a test. What happens in *La Bohème?*"

He clears his throat. "Well," he goes, "they meet in the first act, by the end of the last, she's dead."

"Yes, but what happens in the middle?"

He goes, "Oh, the usual: There's a lot of singing, and by the end there's a dead body or two lying around." He lowers his voice, and leans forward a little as if to make sure no one else can hear him.

"To tell you the truth," he goes, "I may have nodded off now and again. I guess you noticed that."

I'm looking away from him. "Well, Adam, I was so into the opera that I wasn't aware of just how much you slept through it."

"Then how did you know how much I slept?"

"A friend of mine was sitting in the balcony. He saw it."

"He?"

"Yes, he. Nelson the Nerd, if you must know. He told me right here in your apartment."

"What was he doing in my apartment?"

"Fixing my laptop."

Adam rises up to his full six foot three inches. "Listen to me, Wendy," he goes. "If you need any work done on that computer, bring it to the bank where we have certified professionals. Don't let that hack get his hands on it. Or on anything else in my house."

"Nelson is not a hack."

"I don't want him in my house."

"Perhaps you don't want me in your house, either?"

Adam seems to lose three inches of height. He pads over to me oh, so carefully, as if he were making his way through land mines. He starts cooing like a pigeon: "Darling, darling, what's come over you?"

What had come over me? I hadn't a clue. This hadn't gone the way I had expected. I was angry: Adam the hunk was now acting like Adam the asshole, and I was acting like Wendy the witch. Was he really like this? Was *I* really like this? But meanwhile he was whispering something: "Oh darling, this is our first argument, our first little tiff. And I'm glad that it's happening now because it gives us a chance to practice working things out."

How to Get a Good Husband

And you know what? He was right! If I was going to commit myself to this relationship, I couldn't let it be derailed by a stupid little tiff. No, no: "stupid" is too harsh. Maybe "misguided" is better? Maybe. But it sure felt stupid to me, so I went, "Great! Let's make up."

And did we ever! After hours of making up, when he lay gasping like a beached whale, and I had finally recovered my ability to think, I wondered how long this physical solution would work for us. If Nelson was right, if bedroom passions do tend to cool with time, what would Adam and I do to work things out in fifteen years? Thirty years? *Fifty?!* I shuddered. I didn't want to think about *that*. Things were working for us now; tomorrow would take care of itself, you know. Right?

The next morning, over breakfast, Adam told me that he was going to Chicago—again!—and would be there for a whole week. I made him promise that he would call me every single day. And on Monday, he left. I got along for a few days, planning honeymoons at the travel agency, and worrying all the while about *my* upcoming trips – first to the altar, and then to New Zealand—that's where Adam wants to honeymoon. And I was starting to have my doubts about both trips. But that's how I always am when Adam's away. When he's not here to reassure me, I feel a little...empty, you know. And thoughts like that were bubbling in my mind when I stepped off a curb the wrong way, broke my ankle, and ended up in the emergency room where they admitted me because the orthopedist wouldn't be available until the next day. And I lay there in the bed, feeling a lot of pain, and a lot of panic, because here it was 9:30 pm—past the time Adam was supposed to call home; what if he had called me and I wasn't there? I got a nurse to give me my cell phone (the hospital phone wasn't set up yet), and I called home to poll my voice mail. He hadn't called—or if he did, he left no message. So I decided to call **his** cell phone—which he had said was a big no-no because I might interrupt a business meeting or something—and I got him. From the background noises, it sounded like he was at a restaurant or something, and he said he was having supper with a business associate. He sounded a little pissed that I had interrupted him, but I told him what had happened to me, and that I missed him very much and hoped he would come home soon. He said he was sorry for my accident, that he felt very bad about it, but that he couldn't come home right away because of business, you know, but would return just as soon as his business was completed. I forget what else he said, because the drug they had given me was beginning to make me feel woozy, and I murmured something or other, rang off, and conked out.

When I woke up I felt someone holding my hand. Adam! I turned to look, and it was…Nelson? I felt groggy, and blinked my eyes. He was still there. I go, "Nelson, my laptop's at home."

He goes, "I know. "But *you're here*." He's still holding my hand.

"Nelson, how did you find me?"

For answer he brings my hand to his lips, and kisses it.

"Nelson, what are you doing?"

"Expanding my job description."

I take my hand away. "Nelson, I'm engaged to be married."

How to Get a Good Husband

"There *is* that complication," he goes. "But he doesn't love you. Not like I do."

"You love me?"

"Yes."

"You love me? Really?"

"It surprised me too," he goes, "and it's damned inconvenient, but there it is."

Now I'm wide awake. "Nelson, it's more than inconvenient; it's downright embarrassing. I am in love with Adam...and I'm...and I'm..."

"Not in love with me?" he goes. "I know it's too soon for that, and I don't ask that. I ask simply that you think it over, give me a chance."

"Nelson, I'm getting married in two weeks!"

"So?"

"Adam, I mean Nelson, you're very sweet; you're the best friend a girl could want...but..."

He goes, "No. I'm not your best friend. The best friend a woman could want is her husband. That's what I want to be to you. Nothing else comes close."

And he gave me a look, but it wasn't really *that look* that I mentioned before. This look said, "I'm yours, if you'll have me."

Oh my god, what could I say? That the hall, the caterer, and the honeymoon—the fabulous honeymoon to New Zealand— were all booked? That *I* was all booked? It was totally true, of course, but now, somehow, it seemed beside the point. Which was that I had given myself to Adam, and it didn't seem right to take myself back just because Adam was in Chicago too busy to look after me. And while I was thinking all this, I saw that, O my god, Nelson was leaning in to kiss me, and I wondered which was more embarrassing—the fact that this scrawny little nerd was leaning in for the kiss, or the fact that I wanted it! Somehow, I managed: "Nelson, we mustn't. Please don't do this—have pity on me." And he stopped. Thank god. And I go, "Nelson, for both our sakes, we mustn't see each other until the day of my wedding to Adam."

He goes, "Wendy, if you insist on marrying Adam, I can't be there to watch you throw your life away on this stuffed shirt. Yes, he's got plenty of money. A lot more than I do. If you marry me, we can't honeymoon to New Zealand. Jersey City will be more like it. Not that it would make much difference— we'd be in bed a lot of the time. But *in* bed or out of it, you'd have someone who really cares for you. It's your call. Let me know." And with that, he kissed my hand again, turned, and walked out the door.

Now I felt really empty.

But in a few more days, Adam came home, his clothes all smelling of cigarette smoke. And my emptiness—at least the physical part of it—was relieved, you know. So I went back to putting the finishing touches on my wedding day plans, and on rehearsing this little talk—on how to get a good husband. You see, what I was going to say was, that you have to keep your eye on the main chance. You want a guy who will satisfy the two main requirements of a husband, which are—and I've really given this a lot of thought, people, so please pay attention—the two main requirements of a good husband are first, to satisfy you in bed, and second, to support you like a queen.

Now wait, now wait, it's not as stupid as it sounds—oh God! I don't mean stupid, that's so snarky. I mean crazy, it's not as crazy. You know what I mean; hear me out on this. Start with sex—which is where I always start. Years ago, if a woman let out that she had strong sexual urges, she appeared little better than a slut, you know. Well, today, thank God, we all know that's bullshit. Right? We all know that sexual pleasure is for women as well as for men. Right? So it follows that we women should insist on our pleasures, for the men are always insisting on *theirs*, aren't they? Are you following me on this? Men expect us to be desirable, and to *remain* desirable for a long time. We all know why they marry us. For their...creature comforts—if you know what I mean. And if they want these comforts, the least men can do is support us royally, so we can *preserve* these comforts for as long as possible. Because let's face it, we women bear more of the burden than our husbands. No matter *what.* We are the ones who bear *the children*, for heaven's sake, and we're the ones who bring them up. And as for housekeeping—forget about it! You won't catch a man doing much of that. No wonder that women age much sooner than their husbands. That's what happens! For the sake of our families, we sacrifice our youth and our looks. So it stands to reason that we *get as much for that sacrifice as we can*. Plenty of money, and plenty of sex—supposing we have the strength to enjoy it after the kids come along. It all stands to reason, doesn't it, and it's logical, isn't it, that given everything I've said, Adam would *have* to be the right choice for me, wouldn't he? He's got plenty of money, plenty of sex appeal, *and there's not one note of music in him*—what more could a girl want? I mean, most girls would envy me, right? They'd wish they were in my shoes, right? *Right?*

A long pause

Wrong! It's wrong! What am I talking about? What *have* I been babbling about? Am I some prize to be offered to the highest bidder? God knows I'm no prize, unless I'm the booby prize, and this whole thing's *not* right; it's stupid! Yes, I don't mind saying it, *it's stupid! STUPID!!* What could I have been thinking? Did I suppose that by avoiding a musical flake like my father, I'd live longer than my mother, who died too soon? But by god, if I marry Adam de Brazza, I might die the day after!

I gotta go. My plans have changed. I gotta tell Adam that I've changed my mind. I'll simply tell him, I've changed my mind, I'm sorry. I'm really sorry, but that's what happens. And I gotta tell Nelson the Nerd to go ahead and expand his job description. By a lot!

> *As she says the following speech, she stuffs her notebook into her bag, slings her bag over her shoulder, and gets set on her crutches*

Many of you may have come here hoping to learn how to get a good husband. Maybe there is a way, but as to what it is, you know, I haven't a clue.

> *She turns and begins to exit, then, midway to the exit, she stops and turns to the audience*

I gotta go.

BLACKOUT

How to Get a Good Husband

THE AMULET

Act One

Scene: A room in the Castle. On the back wall is a row of royal portraits—Kings and Queens. They all are in period costume. The central portrait—that of a Queen—could be mistaken for that of a sexy movie star in a costume drama, as might appear in a fan magazine. At rise, two liveried servants— PRUDENCE and TURCO—are gazing at this central portrait. Prudence is a female in her mid-twenties. TURCO is a male of similar age. PRUDENCE is carrying a portrait of another royal woman. The woman is smiling. TURCO & PRUDENCE gaze back and forth between the central portrait—of the Queen who looks like a movie star—and the painting carried by PRUDENCE.

Prudence: Well, shall we do it? Come on.

Turco: Not so fast. Queen Isis is going to be angry about this.

Prudence: Of course.

Turco: She's going to storm in fury.

Prudence: You could say that.

Turco: I *am* saying it. The sun will go behind a cloud, rumblings of thunder will be heard, and a cold wind will begin to blow. Lightning will flash, the rain will pour down, and everyone will run for cover.

Prudence: That's going too far.

Turco: What's too far?

Prudence: The cold wind. The thunder and lightning. The rain.

Turco: Too far?

Prudence: Absolutely. People may run for cover. But there'll be no cold wind. No lightning. No rain.

Turco: Ah, but people will run for cover *as if* there were lightning and rain.

Prudence: *(trying to be patient)* Turco, it's not the same thing. Queen Isis may storm, but nobody's going to get wet.

Turco: If she throws her coffee at them, they'll get wet. And burnt, too.

> PRUDENCE *throws up her hands.*

Prudence: Oh God! Are we going to switch these pictures or not?

Turco: You're so coldblooded, Prudence.

Prudence: I see things as they are. Unlike you.

Turco: How can you say that? I have a very firm grip on reality.

Prudence: You do, do you?

Turco: Yes, and I can prove it.

Prudence: Go ahead.

Turco: Well, I can see that our arrangement is unequal, unfair.

Prudence: How so?

The Amulet

Turco: Well, I'm supposed to take down Queen Isis' picture, and you're supposed to put up the dead queen's picture—right?

Prudence: Right.

Turco: Well, that's unfair to *me*. Puts me in a very bad position.

Prudence: No worse than me.

Turco: It's a lot worse. By taking down Queen Isis, I create the vacancy which you then can fill by putting up her dead rival—

Prudence: (*interrupting*) Which will make Queen Isis equally mad at me.

Turco: No, no—don't you get it? If I don't take down, then you can't put up. My deed creates the *opportunity* for yours. Hence I get more of the blame.

Prudence: Forgive me, but this is stupid. Taking down or putting up—each act would be equally blameworthy, if it came to that.

Turco: You really think so?

Prudence: I do.

Turco: In that case, will you give me Queen Marianne's picture? That way, you can take down, and *I'll* put up.

Prudence: Fine, fine—anything so long as we get the job done, for Heaven's sake. Here, you take Marianne's picture.

PRUDENCE hands the picture to TURCO

Okay. Now I will do the dastardly deed and remove the live Queen.

She takes down QUEEN ISIS' picture.

It's done. Okay Turco, your turn. Put up the dead one.

TURCO just stands there, looking at the space made vacant.

Turco: I'm not so sure about this.

Prudence: You're driving me crazy! Look, idiot, what's worse: to anger Queen Isis, or to anger the King? Because I tell you that if His Majesty asks me why his orders weren't followed, I'll tell him the truth!

Turco: You would do that, Prudence?

Prudence: In a heartbeat.

Turco: You don't *have* a heart.

Prudence: You want me to perjure myself?

Turco: Well, no, but at least you could—

Prudence: *(looking off-stage left, then interrupting)* They're coming. If you want the King and Queen to catch you here red-handed that's your problem, but I'm leaving.

She begins to exit, stage right

Turco: No, no—wait...

He puts up MARIANNE'S picture, so hurriedly that it hangs badly askew, then he runs after PRUDENCE, exiting stage right. From stage left enter KING EDGAR and QUEEN ISIS. They both see the badly hung picture.

Edgar: Good God! This is terrible!

He adjusts the picture

24

The Amulet

Isis: Shocking! Those responsible should be impaled on a stake.

Edgar: Rather severe punishment, don't you think, for sloppily hanging a picture?

Isis: What are you talking about?

Edgar: They should be reprimanded for sure, but they scarcely deserve impaling. They were simply following orders.

Isis: Whose orders?

Edgar: Mine. I thought that under the circumstances, it was more appropriate to hang Marianne there rather than you.

Isis: More appropriate?!

Edgar: Yes.

Isis: *Why?!*

Edgar: Because, Isis, everyone on this wall is dead. Poor Marianne is dead. But you—as you've doubtless noticed—are not. But if you insist on being up there with them, you could join them.

Isis: On the wall?

Edgar: Absolutely. All you have to do is commit suicide.

Isis: That's all?

Edgar: You could slit your wrists, or eat cyanide, or even leap into the Moat. Your choice. I'm not fussy.

Isis: Very kind of you.

Edgar: I try to keep an open mind. All the same, the requirement for membership in the Royal Wall Society was and continues to be that you have to be dead. We have to uphold standards.

Isis takes this in.

Isis: My darling Edgar. Why didn't you tell me this when you brought me here on our wedding night, and I suggested that you put Marianne in the cellar and replace her...with *me?*

Edgar: I must have been engrossed in something else.

Isis: *(with a suggestive smile)* You certainly were, big boy.

Edgar: I don't know what I could have been thinking of.

Isis: You don't?

Edgar: It was so long ago.

Isis: *(suggestively)* I could remind you.

Edgar: No time. I'm going away.

Isis: Going away!

Edgar: Yes, going away.

Isis: One of your endless wars?

Edgar: And *while* I'm away, I want Anna and Jane to be able to look upon the image of their mother.

Isis: *I* am their mother.

Edgar: You are their *step*mother, Isis. I want them to remember their *birth* mother. Therefore her picture must remain on that wall. If I come back and find it gone, I'm going to be...very unhappy.

Isis: Heaven forbid that *anything* should make my lord unhappy.

The Amulet

Edgar: Heaven needs a little help from you.

Isis: Oh, my lord! What can I do? Actually, I know what I could do, but you've said you've no time for it.

Edgar: Isis, try to elevate your mind, and think of something nobler than the barnyard.

Isis: When the chief cock is standing near me? Or perhaps you're not standing; that's the problem. *(reaching for his privates)* Let me see if I can—

Edgar: *(interrupting)* Isis, there are limits!

Isis: What's happened to your sense of humor? You used to find me amusing.

Edgar: Isis, some things are just not funny, and increasingly I'm finding you're one of them.

Isis: Oh! Not only am I not funny, but now I'm a *thing?*

Edgar: Look, Isis: If you can just remember that in my absence, *you* are responsible for my children's well being, I will be happy.

Isis: I hear you. Happy now?

Edgar: As happy as I *can* be—under the circumstances. Let's change the subject. Where is Turco? Where is Prudence?

Isis: Prudence is with the children, as usual. As for Turco, he's probably in the next county. Afraid of me—and with good reason.

Edgar: I promised him my protection. *(calling)* Turco!

> *TURCO enters with a quick loping trot, his arms pumping. Then he stops so suddenly that his whole frame vibrates.*

Turco: Your Majesty!

Edgar: Where are the children?

Turco: They're playing hide and seek with Prudence in the Maze Garden, one of their favorite spots. But finding them is no trivial task. They *could* be in the grape arbors, they love grapes so much. Or at the Coy Pond, feeding the fish, or in Avenue of Ancestors, mimicking the statues, or in the Garden of Roses—

Edgar: *(interrupting)* Yes, yes, thank you, Turco, all that's good to know, and you did well. But all I need to learn is where they actually *are.*

Turco: Oh. Sorry. Shall I get them?

Edgar: Yes, please do.

Turco: *(bowing)* Your Majesty.

>   *TURCO starts off in his loping trot*

Edgar: Oh, and Turco...

>   *TURCO stops suddenly, vibratingly*

Turco: Yes, Your Majesty?

Edgar: You don't have to run; I can wait the extra minutes, so it's all right to walk—you understand?

Turco: Oh, Your Majesty! I'll do my best.

>   *He takes a couple of sedate steps, then resumes his loping trot*

Edgar: *(to Isis)* An eccentric fellow, that one.

Isis: Sometimes a bit *too* eccentric.

The Amulet

Edgar: Don't you lay a finger on him, Isis. He has my protection.

Isis: My dread lord! I wouldn't dare incur your displeasure.

Edgar: I hope not, for both our sakes.

Isis: What has happened between us, my lord, to make you feel that you cannot leave the castle without danger of my destroying everything in it?

Edgar: What's happening is that I...seem to be waking up.

Isis: In that case, it were best to keep dreaming.

Edgar: Really?

Isis: Oh yes, *much* better—were it not for the nightmares.

TURCO lopes in, then vibrates to attention, and bows.

Turco: Their Royal Highnesses are coming, Your Majesty!

Enter PRUDENCE, ANNA, & JANE. As they enter, all three are smiling and holding hands. ANNA is fifteen; JANE is about half that age. During the scene that follows, PRUDENCE & TURCO stand to one side, smiling.

Prudence: Princess Anna and Princess Jane!

JANE runs, arms outstretched, to the King, who has knelt to receive her.

Jane: Daddy!

Edgar: *(wrapping his arms around her and kissing her)* Jane. My little one.

Anna: *(with a deep curtsey)* Your Majesty.

Edgar: *(extending an arm toward her)* Come here, you scamp!

> *ANNA smiles broadly, and runs to him. With one arm around his older daughter, and the other around the younger, the King kisses both his children.*

Jane: *(a bit embarrassed)* Oh, Daddy.

Anna: *(brimming with pleasure)* Majesty!

Edgar: *(to ANNA)* So formal, so soon! Is your little head full of policy, too?

Anna: Maybe just a little, Father.

Edgar: Still. You can call me Daddy.

Anna: I love you, Daddy!

> *She kisses him on the cheek.*

Edgar: That's my girl. Now you look after Janey when I'm away.

Anna: You're going away? Oh, no!

Edgar: Our neighbors won't leave us in peace, so I'm afraid we'll have to persuade them to.

Anna: Don't we have diplomats for that?

Edgar: Smart girl. Yes, we've tried diplomacy, with no luck. Turns out the sword speaks the only language some neighbors understand. So…I have to go.

> *To TURCO*

Turco, will you summon the Captain of my Guard?

Turco: At once, Sire.

> *TURCO lopes away*

The Amulet

Anna: Daddy, I don't want you to go.

Edgar: That makes two of us.

Jane: I don't want you to go, either!

Edgar: That makes three of us, then.

Isis: My liege, *none* of us wants you to go.

> *EDGAR rises*

Edgar: Then I'll stop counting.

Anna: Father, what if you don't come back?

Edgar: I'll come back.

Anna: But you always put yourself in the thick of the fighting.

Edgar: Don't worry, Anna. I'll come back.

Anna: But what if you don't?

Edgar: Then you know what will happen: you will reign as Queen; and next in succession will be Jane, here.

Isis: And if neither survives you?

Edgar: What a thing to say!

Isis: Just a thought.

Edgar: A bad one. Look: All this is too complicated to discuss now. In the unlikely event that I should fall, I intend for my will to be read aloud.

Anna: *(near tears)* I don't want to be Queen. I'm too young to reign over anything. If something should happen to you, a slew of pretenders would see Jane and me as mere fledglings in the nest. Who would protect us?

Isis: Why *I* would protect you, my dear one.

Pause while ANNA looks at ISIS

Anna: We'd need more than you, Your Grace. Even though the country is well disposed to us, we'd need a regiment of statesmen to advise us on the exercise of power.

EDGAR takes this in.

Edgar: Heavens. I see there's more than just a *little* policy in that head of yours, my precocious one.

Prudence: Forgive me, Your Majesty, but "precocious" is hardly the word for Her Royal Highness. She's brilliant.

Edgar: If so, she got it from her mother, the late Queen. She didn't get it from me, more's the pity.

Anna: *(to Edgar)* I hope you'll love me anyway.

Edgar: Always. And I'm glad *someone's* smart around here. Someday, the Kingdom will be the stronger for it.

Anna: I don't think I'm *that* smart.

Edgar: Don't worry, Anna. The regiment of statesmen you've described has already been formed, sworn loyalists to me and to you. May God grant that we won't need them any time soon.

Anna: You've *got* to return, Daddy.

Edgar: Look at me, Anna: I promise you: I *will* return. You *shall* see me again. I swear it.

Anna: Please don't swear to anything you can't control, Father. These things are in the hands of God.

Edgar: And now you're preaching sermons to me?

Anna: I'm sorry.

The Amulet

Edgar: *(taking an amulet from around his neck)* Look: see this?

Anna: Your amulet?

Edgar: It was your mother's. She wore it for good luck.

Isis: Doesn't seem to have done her much good.

Edgar: If you must know, Isis, she got it *after* she fell ill. But she always felt better when she was wearing it, and I've been wearing it in her honor, ever since she died. I was going to wear it into battle, but now I suspect that Anna will feel better if *she* has it. Here, Anna, I want you to have this.

Anna: Oh, no, Daddy; that's for you to wear. I could never accept it. What if something should happen to you? I could never forgive myself.

Edgar: Nothing is going to happen to me; I told you that. Please take the amulet.

Anna: I'd love to, Father. But why don't you give it to me right after your return from the war?

Edgar: I'd feel much happier going into battle, knowing you had it.

Anna: And I'd feel much happier staying at home, knowing it was protecting *you.*

Edgar: You don't want me to command you as King, do you?

Anna: I'd prefer you postpone the gift till you get home safe.

Edgar: I want the gift to be now, and I want you to accept it now.

> *Silence*

Anna: Are you commanding me as my King?

Edgar: I'm asking you as your father. While I'm off fighting the enemies of this country, I'd feel a lot better if the Heir Apparent were safe.

Anna: Heir Apparent...

Edgar: That's you, you know. Here, let me put the amulet on you.

> *He does.*

How does it feel?

Anna: Nice. It feels good.

Edgar: It's yours. And never, *never* let anyone else have it, no matter what they say to you. Do you understand?

Anna: Yes, Sire.

Edgar: You *can* call me, "Daddy," you know.

Anna: Thanks for the amulet, Daddy. I do seem to feel different with it on.

Edgar: Wear it in health, my darling.

> *He kisses her brow tenderly*

Jane: I want an amulet, too!

Isis: If you're handing out amulets, my lord, why not one for me?

> *Edgar gives Isis an exasperated look, then turns to Jane.*

Edgar: Janey dear, if your mother had two amulets, you'd have the other. But she had only the one, and Anna, as eldest, must wear it. If you keep close to her, it will protect you, too.

The Amulet

Jane: I don't see why *she's* so special.

Edgar: You're both special, Jane, each in your own way. I love you both the same. But I have only one amulet to give, and so Anna gets it.

Jane: Will you bring me one back from the war?

Edgar: Wonderful idea! I'll try to.

Jane: You promise?

Edgar: I'll do my best.

> *EDGAR kisses her, after which TURCO lopes in, followed by a strapping soldier.*

Turco: *(announcing)* Captain Leon Steele!

Steele: *(stepping forward and saluting)* Your Majesty.

Edgar: Good morning, Captain. Is the Guard ready?

Steele: We're saddled up, and your horse is prepared, Sire.

Edgar: Ajax?

Steele: Champing at the bit and eager to go—just like the rest of us.

Edgar: Wonderful. Tell the men I'll be down in a moment.

Steele: Yes, Sire.

> *He salutes, then leaves briskly*

Edgar: Now look, children, I really have to be going. Who will see me off? Who will blow me kisses?

Jane: I will! I will!

Anna: Of course we will, Father.

Edgar: And you, Isis, will you also see me off?

Isis: My lord, goodbyes depress me. I've said farewells to scores of people, it seems, and have never seen them again alive. But I see their ghosts all over the place, and when you get on your horse they'll be crowding around so thick I won't be able even to *throw* you a kiss. So let's have a goodbye kiss here—a quick kiss. Then off you go with the children.

Edgar: Very well.

> *Very formally, she proffers her hand to be kissed, and equally formally, he kisses it.*

Isis: Farewell, my liege.

Edgar: That's the second time you've called me your liege. Are you then my vassal?

Isis: Am I not?

Edgar: You are not. Does it please you to think you *are*?

Isis: Not particularly.

Edgar: Then enough of this foolishness.

Isis: Very well, my lord. Rest easy: your children are in good hands.

> *EDGAR turns to go; ANNA & JANE, taking his hands, prepare to go with him; TURCO & PRUDENCE prepare to follow them off.*

My lord, do you mind if Prudence remains behind? I would have some conference with her.

Edgar: Of course, if you wish it.

Isis: You don't mind, Prudence?

Prudence: *(to Isis)* I'm at your service as always, Your Grace.

The Amulet

Edgar: Then farewell, my Queen. And fear nothing; we shall meet again.

> *Exeunt KING, ANNA, JANE, & TURCO.*

Isis: Prudence, you may approach.

> *PRUDENCE does so, and curtsies deeply.*

Prudence: Your Grace.

Isis: We are the only ones not seeing His Majesty off. You and I are quite alone.

Prudence: Yes, Ma'am.

Isis: We may speak frankly.

Prudence: Yes, Ma'am.

Isis: Prudence, have you ever wondered why Turco outranks you at court?

Prudence: Does he?

Isis: Well, he's the one always chosen for the honor of introducing guests, making toasts, presenting gifts—all that sort of thing. Not only that, his recompense is one and one half that of yours.

Prudence: I never thought much about these things.

Isis: Oh please. You mean to tell me that you *never* compare his good fortune to yours, and that you *never* eat your heart out in envy? Eating one's heart out is the universal human condition. If *you* don't do it, that makes you a saint, and I would be distinctly uncomfortable having a saint in my employ. I wouldn't know what to do with you.

Prudence: I assure you, I'm no saint.

Isis: Heavens be praised! This means that you *have* compared your status with his.

Prudence: Only in a general way. I mean, it's obvious that while Turco attends His Majesty, I attend you.

Isis: You poor dear. While Turco gets Edgar, you're stuck with me.

Prudence: It pleases you, Ma'am, to play with me.

Isis: No such thing. Everyone is stuck with me. I'm stuck with myself, obviously, and I don't like it one bit, so I presume that any sensible person must feel the same way.

Prudence: Well I don't, and I hope I'm a sensible person. As far as I'm concerned, attending either King or Queen is honor enough for anyone. As for Turco, whatever good fortune comes his way, I congratulate him. Life is too short for envy.

Isis: I knew it, I knew it; you *are* a saint, just as I feared. You put me to shame. Unlike you, I'm susceptible to every temptation that comes along, especially envy and revenge. But you—angelic creature that you are—you just plant that saintly smirk upon your face, and sail serene above it all, untouched by even one unworthy thought. I'm becoming extremely annoyed.

Prudence: Please, Ma'am. With all due respect, I'm no saint. I'm as susceptible to temptation as the next person. I just don't envy Turco.

Isis: But doesn't it gall you to see everything going to that witless fool?

Prudence: I grant you that Turco is a trifle...boyish.

The Amulet

Isis: Just a little!

Prudence: But give him a few more years—ten at the most—and he'll grow into his full promise as a man.

Isis: But you don't want to wait that long, surely.

Prudence: For Turco? He hasn't intimated the slightest interest in me, ma'am. It would be inappropriate, unfair to us both, for me to wait for him—or for anyone else, for that matter.

Isis: So you are free to seize your own fortune—such as it is.

Prudence: Such as it is, indeed. Your taking me on as maidservant has been my only good fortune. Your bringing me with you when you married His Majesty has brought me more happiness than I could have dreamed of.

Isis: I thank you for the compliments. But your aspirations—flattering as they are to me—are scarcely worthy of what *could* be yours, if you dared only lift your eyes higher.

Prudence: I cannot think of anything higher than waiting on Your Grace.

Isis: You lack imagination. Think of a brilliant marriage—to a man of great wealth—or if not a wealthy man, then a man with looks and prospects.

Prudence: Surely you don't mean...?

Isis: At last you understand me. No, my dear girl, of course I don't mean Turco.

Prudence: My head is spinning. Are you saying that you have somebody specific in mind?

Isis: That's exactly what I *am* saying—actually I have *many* specific men in mind—men who could be very attracted to a woman with your looks and your great wealth.

Pause

Prudence: With all respect, Ma'am, I think you've been too much in the sun. My looks are debatable, but my poverty is not. Were it not for my service to you, I wouldn't have a penny to my name.

Isis: I'm not talking about now. I'm talking about...afterwards.

Prudence: After *what?*

Isis: After my project goes into action.

Prudence: Project?

Isis: My dear, if I tell you the project, then you are bound to be a co-worker in it.

Prudence: You're saying that once I hear it, I must take part in it?

Isis: Correct. Because if you knew it and rejected it, you would become a threat that would have to be...dealt with.

Silence

Prudence: This sounds like a conspiracy.

Isis: Such an uncomfortable word. I dislike it. I prefer to use the word *project.* Shall I reveal more?

Silence

Prudence: By confiding to me as much as you have, you've already bound me. For even if I refuse to know more, I already *suspect* enough to make me a threat: you're fomenting something...not very good.

40

The Amulet

Isis: Fomenting? Another uncomfortable word.

Prudence: What word would you have? You're in the kitchen, as it were, cooking up something. If I choose not to join you in the kitchen, I choose something else that's...even more uncomfortable.

Isis: *Distinctly* uncomfortable.

Prudence: The Man-Eating Moat?

Isis: A peculiar hobby of mine, but now quite apt for my purpose, don't you think?

Prudence: If you say so.

Isis: To be sure, it's an expensive hobby to maintain, what with all the livestock we have to throw in there, to feed the flesh-eating fish—every day or so, two or three sheep or a small cow—it does add up. But as a means of getting rid of traitors, it tends to be useful. And as a *threat,* it is supreme. That's why I've made sure that all the animals thrown in there are thrown in *alive.* Their screams can be heard half a mile away.

Prudence: *(shuddering)* It's horrible. I wonder why His Majesty ever agreed to it.

Isis: He hasn't. Not really. But while he was away on one of his campaigns, I just *did* it, so that when he returned, he found it a *fait accompli.* He didn't like it much, but whenever he got around to countermanding my order, I found ways to— shall we say—distract him. And after a while, he just got used to it. It's amazing what one can get used to.

Prudence: I don't think I'll ever get used to it.

Isis: I don't blame you. I can think of easier deaths than the Moat.

Prudence: So I...*must* join you, mustn't I?

Isis: It's your choice.

Prudence: It's a choice that's no choice.

Isis: Whatever you say.

Prudence: I give up. What do you want from me?

Isis: You disappoint me, Prudence. I had thought you'd ask where we'll find the money that will make you a rich woman.

Prudence: I suppose that's my cue. All right, where *will* you find the money?

Isis: Edgar has hidden millions in gold and jewels somewhere—either in the castle, or very near it.

Prudence: How do you know?

Isis: He said so. He told me that when Marianne died, he put all her treasure—together with much of his own—into a large oaken chest and, in his words, "sequestered it in a spot so secret that no scoundrel or skulldugger could ever find it." All those sibilances—singular, aren't they?

Prudence: He told you this?

Isis: Sibilances and all. But unfortunately, that's *all* he told me. He never even alluded to the treasure again. Apparently, he lumped *me* together with the scoundrels and skullduggers. *ME!* Can you imagine?

Prudence: No! But as you say, I lack imagination.

The Amulet

Isis: Of course, he never gave any of the treasure to me. Heaven forbid! Not even earrings. It was all for Anna and Jane. All for his darlings. Nothing for me except cold courtesy. *(pause)* But I'm going to find that treasure, take it, and with my share of it, disappear and live the way I want.

Prudence: What is your share?

Isis: Half.

Prudence: What happens to the other half?

Isis: You get it. And half of those millions is a huge sum.

Prudence: Which will put me pretty deep into these doings.

Isis: You're already in pretty deep. You might as well take your reward.

Prudence: I'm afraid to ask what I have to do to earn this reward… Don't tell me kill His Majesty!

Isis: Unnecessary. The way Edgar exposes himself to danger, the war will kill him off before either of us gets a chance to. If he should make it home in one piece, and you are stupid enough not to have fled with your new riches to another country, you could always push him into the Moat if you've a mind to. But I don't require it. Regicide will not be one of your duties.

Prudence: I'm relieved to hear it. But what *will* my duties be?

Isis: Simply to locate the treasure.

Prudence: Simply?! Ha! Surely you jest, Ma'am. You need a wizard, not me. I have no such talent. I cannot dowse for water, let alone gold.

Isis: Again unnecessary. Now that the King is away, you have a talent that's very rare in this castle, and it's just what we need.

Prudence: And what would that talent be?

Isis: You have gained Anna's confidence.

Pause

Prudence: You've lost me.

Isis: I'll find you if you'll just listen: When Marianne died, the King became even closer to Anna, and confided to her almost everything.

Prudence: Including the location of the gold and jewels?

Isis: I feel sure of it.

Prudence: What makes you so sure?

Isis: Once, when Anna was eight, I gave her a gold coin. A week later I asked her what she had done with it, and she said, in her little voice, "I sequestered it in a spot so secret that no scoundrel or skulldugger could ever find it." Word for word.

Prudence: What does that prove? Only that His Majesty used those words in her hearing. It doesn't mean he told her where he hid the treasure.

Isis: Just listen: Not long ago, when you were out walking with the children, I went through her belongings—I do that routinely—and I found, in a little keepsake box, a solid gold bracelet that Edgar had given Marianne a few years earlier.

Prudence: How do you know where it came from?

The Amulet

Isis: I picked it up and saw the dated inscription on the inside of it. I replaced it exactly as I found it, and checked the box a week later. The bracelet was gone.

Prudence: Maybe she sold it?

Isis: A treasure that had been her beloved mother's? That would be so very unlike Anna. No. She simply put it back in its secret location.

Prudence: You *suppose* she did. You have no real proof.

Isis: *(raising her voice)* I'm telling you, Prudence: Anna and Edgar have been in league against me from the beginning, and I'm positive he has told her the treasure's location. I'm positive! Do you hear?

> *Beat*

Which brings me to the point of all this: Your mission, dear girl, will be first to get that amulet away from Anna, and then to get her to share with you the location of the spot so secret that no scoundrel or skulldugger—other than me, that is—could ever find it.

> *Pause*

Prudence: How long do I have?

Isis: Thirty days.

Prudence: Too little time! I'll need a year, at the very least.

Isis: Sixty days.

Prudence: You may as well push me into the Moat right now; sixty days is too little time.

Isis: I'll give you four months, not one day longer. This is my final word on the matter.

Pause

Prudence: And if I fail after four months?

Isis: You become useless to me—and a threat which I will have to...eliminate.

Prudence: How do I know that—once you get your hands on the treasure—you won't turn around and...eliminate me anyway—together with their Royal Highnesses?

Isis: How do *I* know that you won't betray *me,* by telling Anna my purpose? Or worse, betray me by getting the treasure yourself and escaping with it and the children?

Prudence: Each of us suspects the other of treachery.

Isis: Of course we do. What else is life about? But I am surprised that you, my dear saintly Prudence, would have the idea of betrayal so fixed in your mind.

Prudence: I learn from the best.

Isis: From me, you mean? Because I choose this way of repaying the King for his indifference to me? For making me into a glorified nanny? For quitting my bedroom and leaving me longing—for him, to start with, and then for my former lovers, who by that time were all dead and gone...

Prudence: *All* of them—dead and gone?

Isis: An amazing coincidence. They all died young. Which left me pacing the floor late at night, wishing I could see them again. What was even more amazing, I did see one or another of them; they appeared before me with such reality that I felt I could touch them—and often felt I *did* touch them. Sometimes it is useful to have a vivid imagination.

The Amulet

Prudence: I wouldn't know. I'm having a hard time getting my mind around what you've just told me. I presume His Majesty knows none of it.

Isis: Of course not; I've made sure he doesn't. Nobody knows—except you. So I'm sure I can rely on your discretion, Prudence. Because if word of this gets to the King—or to *anyone*—I'll know where it came from.

Prudence: *(quietly)* You can rely on me.

Isis: I thought so. Oo-oo, this is so gratifying! I'm glad I didn't give way to my first impulse, which was to make you and Turco disappear, then imprison Jane and torture Anna until I got the truth out of her. Once the treasure was in my hands, I wouldn't leave until I had destroyed what Edgar values most of all—his two children. Only after killing them both would I quit this place. That was my first impulse, but I thought better of it.

Prudence: I'm glad of that! What made you change your mind?

Isis: I asked myself: what do I really want in all this? The treasure! And I figured I could get it more conveniently by employing *you.* What do you say to that?

Prudence curtsies low.

Prudence: I am your most obedient servant.

BLACKOUT

Act Two

Scene 1

Before the lights come up, we become aware of a ghostly music, which continues as the lights come up to reveal the same room as the first act, but lit in a ghostly, penumbral light. QUEEN MARIANNE'S picture is draped in a black cloth. Standing in front of it is QUEEN MARIANNE herself. She is wearing a voluminous cape. She opens the cape wide to reveal ANNA & JANE, clinging to her.

Jane: Mommy!

Anna: Dear Mommy! We thought we'd never see you again.

Marianne: My darlings!

> *MARIANNE falls to her knees and embraces the children. Her face is smiling, but her eyes are full of tears.*

At last I can hold you again; I can kiss you at last.

Anna: Oh, Mommy!

Jane: Where have you been so long, Mommy?

Anna: Never leave us again.

Marianne: Oh, I don't want to...I don't want to...

Jane: We'll keep you right here, we won't let you go.

Marianne: Don't ever let me go.

Anna: We'll hold you and hold you...

Marianne: And I'll hold *you*. Have you been good children?

Jane: I've been good!

The Amulet

Anna: I've been *trying* to be good, Mommy, but since Daddy went off to war, this castle has become a prison. Isis won't let us go anywhere...

Jane: She's mean!

Anna: And there are eyes everywhere, watching us, watching us...

Marianne: Oh, I know, I know. Come, let's take a little walk together, just the way we used to. Would you like that?

Jane: Oh, yes!

Anna: I must be dreaming!

Marianne: Just take my hands—you remember the way...

The children take her hands

We'll walk, children, we'll take it so slow...

They begin walking off, but in slow motion.

And we'll enjoy every minute, every second, and make our short time with each other seem... like a life time...our few seconds, a lifetime...a lifetime...a lifetime...a lifetime...

Lights dim to black

Scene 2

Regular lights come up on the same room in the Castle. Portraits of royal ancestors adorn the back wall, as before, and the portrait of QUEEN MARIANNE is draped in black cloth, as before. Enter ISIS.

Isis: Where's Prudence? Where *is* that goody two-shoes? Lately she's been making me wait so long, you'd think she's trying to avoid me! Not that I blame her. If *I* had to meet me

49

I'd put it off for as long as possible. I mean, who needs the abuse? Of course, being Queen, I've a right to avoid confronting me. But Prudence has no such privilege, and as soon as she shows up—if she ever does—I'll remind her that I'm the abuser, and she the abusee. It's only right. Well, even if it *isn't* right, it's going to *be. Period!*

She yawns

I'm exhausted. Got very little sleep last night—or any night in the past three months, for that matter. Which is a royal shame: I need *more* sleep than most people—not less. I mean, scheming is hard work! For each of my schemes, there is always so much that can go wrong. So I have to spin out *more* schemes to cope with the possible failure of the original ones, but these new schemes could also go wrong, so to cope with that I have to spin out yet even more schemes which could also go wrong. And so on. And so on! The contingencies are endless; I think I'm spun out—I'm too old for this! Of course, everyone *else* in this place sleeps soundly as a bear in winter. With lovely ursine dreams, I'm sure. The children, doubtless, are dreaming that Queen Marianne has returned to life and has thrown me into the Moat. Wonderful! For *them*, that is. And Prudence dreams of getting Turco into her clutches, while Turco dreams of escaping them. Or maybe it's the other way around; you never can tell with these young people. Not that it matters. In a month or two, if all my schemes work out, they'll both be dead. They'll *all* be dead. Delicious! For *me*, that is.

Beat

The Amulet

Where is that woman?! If she isn't here in a few seconds, I'll find someone else to do my work, and as for Prudence I'll just march that young thing down to the Moat, and then *push!!!* I still know how to push—I haven't lost it *that* much. But here she comes—at last.

Enter PRUDENCE

Prudence: *(out of breath)* I'm so sorry for being late.

Isis: If you don't have a good excuse for it, I daresay you'll be even sorrier.

Prudence: I'm groggy from lack of sleep.

Isis: You too couldn't sleep—from scheming, probably?

Prudence: Something like that.

Isis: You're a woman after my own heart.

Prudence: *(aside)* I hate to hear it.

Isis: I don't hear so well as I used to. What did you say?

Prudence: I said it's great to hear it. Great to hear I'm becoming like you.

Aside

Like hell it is.

Isis: What did you say?

Prudence: I said how swell it is that we're getting on so well together.

Isis: Well, *I* think so. Unfortunately, your lateness gives us less time to talk before the children arrive. You said you were meeting them here?

Prudence: In a few minutes. We're to decide where to walk, today.

Isis: The three of you?

Prudence: The four of us. Turco is coming along.

Isis: Turco?! Then he knows about—

Prudence: *(interrupting)* He knows nothing, the poor dear. He's as innocent as ever.

Isis: Nobody's innocent.

Prudence: What are you talking about? He knows nothing; he's done nothing.

Isis: So you say. All the same, he has to be guilty of *some*thing or another. Everyone is. Even your precious Anna. She *appears* modest and self-effacing, but who knows what ambitions are festering in that brilliant mind of hers? She says she adores her father, but for all we know, she may be scheming to replace him.

Prudence: So you're saying that everyone is born like you?

Isis: Yes—potentially. But unlike me, most people never reach their full potential.

Prudence: Whereas you are fully realized?

Isis: Look at me. Have you ever seen anyone more capable of cruelty?

Prudence: I can't say that I have. But occasionally, I do see you perform—well, if not an act of kindness—at least something harmless. From time to time.

Isis: Nobody's perfect.

Prudence: *I* certainly am not.

The Amulet

Isis: What did you say?

Prudence: *(raising her voice)* I SAID I'M NOT PERFECT!!!

Isis: *(shouting)* GOOD! *(in a more normal voice)* But there's no need to shout!

Prudence: Sorry, ma'am.

Isis: Don't let it happen again.

Prudence: I'll try not to.

Isis: Good. Have you been making progress with Anna?

Prudence: She's a tough nut to crack; I'm afraid there's been little progress.

Isis: Really! Not in three months?

Prudence: No.

Isis: Why not?

Prudence: I'm not sure—that's the worst of it. When I ask to see the amulet, she takes it out and holds it with both hands, as if it would save her from drowning. She doesn't say much, just looks at me with those wide eyes and clings to that thing—and my heart melts.

Isis: Your heart melts? Let me remind you, Prudence: I'm not paying you for your heart to melt.

Prudence: So far, actually, you're not paying me anything at all.

Isis: Because I'm waiting to see what *coin* to pay you in. If you deserve gold, I'll pay you in that. If you don't deserve gold, I'll pay you in…another coin, if you get my meaning.

Prudence: It couldn't be clearer.

Isis: Good. Because to move against Anna, first I need to get my hands on that amulet. Can't you just take it away from her?

Prudence: I'd have to club her unconscious.

Isis: Let's hope it doesn't come to that. I'd hate to be tormented by the ghost of her tyrannical father.

Prudence: The ghost?! You don't mean he's dead, then?

Isis: Right now? I'm not sure. But I have a feeling that he won't survive this war.

Prudence: I hope you haven't said that to Her Royal Highness. Oh my God, they're coming. Please get out of here, Ma'am. If Anna sees me with you, there goes whatever trust in me she may have left.

Isis: Trust she may have left? You're losing her trust?

Prudence: *Please* Ma'am, please leave at once!

Isis: No—*you come with me.* I want to count out to you the thirty days you have left.

> *Exeunt ISIS & PRUDENCE, with ISIS steering PRUDENCE by her elbow. As soon as they are out of sight, enter ANNA, JANE, & TURCO*

Anna: *(to Turco)* Wasn't Prudence supposed to meet us here?

Turco: It's not like her to be late. Shall I look for her, Your Highness?

Anna: If you wouldn't mind.

Turco: Not at all, Ma'am. I'll go at once.

> *He bows, and lopes away.*

The Amulet

Jane: I hope he comes back soon. Queen Isis says we can't walk without someone to escort us. Our real mommy never said that, did she? She was never mean to us, was she? Our real mommy? Do you remember what she looked like?

Anna: I'll never forget her. And do you know what, Janey?

Jane: What?

Anna: Last night I dreamt of her.

Jane: Me, too!

Anna: Really! Was she wearing her great cape?

Jane: Uh huh.

Anna: And did she kneel on the floor, and hug us and kiss us? And did we hold hands with her to go for a walk outside?

Jane: Yes, but when we started walking, I woke up.

Anna: So did I. I wanted to go back to sleep and keep on dreaming, keep on walking, but I couldn't. I was wide awake. And already the dream was fading. I tried to remember every detail, but it was hard...

Jane: I want to go for a walk.

Anna: We'll go, we'll go. As soon as Turco gets back. But listen, Jane, don't you think it's strange that we both should have the exact same dream?

Jane: I guess so.

Anna: It's very strange. Maybe Mommy was really here. But why now?

Jane: So we'll remember?

Anna: I'll remember. I'll never forget her.

Jane: I won't either...*now.*

> *Enter TURCO and PRUDENCE. As they enter, TURCO is gleeful:*

Turco: I found her, Your Highnesses, I found her! She was talking with Her Grace, and I boldly went up and said that unless Her Grace released Prudence, Your Highnesses could not go for a walk. Wasn't that brave of me? I asserted myself, said what was right, and Her Grace—well, first she gave me a nasty look, which I did not appreciate. But I stood my ground; I was firm and forthright and I looked right back at her—not nastily, but firmly, as I said, and forthrightly, too. And finally, after a few tense moments, she did release Prudence. Phew! All of which goes to show that there's something better than talking, and that's *doing!* Don't you agree?

Anna: It would be hard to disagree with that, Turco.

Turco: So you can see that while you were waiting for us, Prudence and I were involved in a scene that was positively fraught—*fraught,* I tell you!

> *PRUDENCE curtsies deeply*

Prudence: *(to Anna)* I am deeply sorry for being late, Your Highness. I know how you hate to waste people's time, and there I was wasting yours.

Anna: But while we were waiting, Jane and I found something so interesting that our time wasn't wasted at all.

Prudence: You are as generous as you are wise, Your Highness.

The Amulet

Anna: I don't know about all that; no more on it, please. And now, where shall we walk—as if it made any difference.

Turco: No difference, Your Highness?

Anna: Well, we are confined, aren't we, within these walls, as if they were a prison?

Turco: How so are they a prison?

Anna: They limit us. We cannot go wherever we want, but only where Her Grace allows us—for our safety, she says.

Turco: But that need not make you *feel* imprisoned.

Jane: *(loudly)* **Can we start walking?**

Anna: Wait a minute, Jane, I want to hear his explanation. Go ahead, Turco.

Turco: Well, Your Highness, if we wanted to walk to the outer wall, we'd first have to go half way, wouldn't we?

Anna: We would.

Turco: And having reached the half way point, if we wanted to walk the distance remaining, we'd first have to walk half way of *that*, yes? And once at the *new* half way point, we could complete the remaining distance only by first walking half way of **that**, right?

Anna: I see your point. Using this logic, we'd never be able to reach the wall.

Turco: Precisely. Then how can you feel imprisoned by walls so distant that you are unable to reach them?

Anna: You could say the same for a six by six foot cell; if we were in one of those, your logic would prevent us from reaching those walls also.

Turco: True.

Anna: Yet given the choice, I should much prefer these castle walls to a six by six foot cell.

Turco: My point exactly. If you compare the castle to the cell, you must rejoice in your relative freedom and enjoy the castle. Because someday you *will* be much greater, and your living space—indeed, your very *realm*—will be much greater, too.

Anna: No doubt. But if I now feel such prison-like constraints as heir apparent, won't the constraints grow greater along with my station? So that as Queen, might I sometimes have so little room for maneuver that I'd feel as if I were living indeed within a six by six foot cell?

Turco: I surely hope not.

Anna: Dear Turco, you mean well, and I've enjoyed our little debate. But to tell the truth, I've lost my desire for walking.

Jane: Aw, I knew we were not going to walk!

Anna: You can still go, Janey, even though I don't want to. You can walk with Turco, who'll be glad to point out many details that the rest of us would never think to notice.

Turco: It will be my honor.

Jane: Then let's go, let's go; we've been wasting time!

    Exeunt JANE & TURCO.

Anna: *(to Prudence)* I fear I myself have been wasting time these past few minutes.

Prudence: How so, Your Highness?

Anna: For a while I forgot to listen to the clock ticking.

The Amulet

Prudence: That means you're enjoying yourself.

Anna: Of course I am; I must be. Look, it's a wonderful day, the sun is shining, the birds are singing, and the brook out back continues to make music. And if the Queen restricts my movements, it's all for my own safety, isn't that right? Isn't that the official version of things?

Prudence: If you say so, Your Highness.

Anna: Well, is there another explanation? Something not quite so official, something which explains why my every move is followed by every eye in this castle, including yours?

Prudence: Your Highness, I grieve that something has driven a wedge between us. You used to be very open with me, and share with me all that was on your mind. But now—you're very private. What's happened?

Anna: You tell me. We used to be able to talk freely with each other—without constraint of any kind.

Prudence: We still can.

Anna: I'm not so sure. For the past few weeks, you've been very guarded, very circumspect on what you say to me, as if the very birds in the trees were reporting our conversations to Queen Isis.

Prudence: *(nervously)* What a...what an amusing thought!

Anna: I'm glad *somebody's* amused around here.

Prudence: Is it disloyal to be amused?

Anna: Only if it's loyal to be sober.

Prudence: You are fencing with me, Your Highness.

Anna: I would have said that it is you who are fencing with *me*.

Prudence: Heavens! All I was trying to say was that obviously you know that the birds in the trees are not tweeting to Queen Isis.

Anna: Obviously. But somebody else *might* be.

Prudence: Who?

Anna: That is for you tell me.

> *Long pause, while ANNA looks at PRUDENCE full in the face*

Prudence: I hope you don't think that *I* would do such a thing!

Anna: I don't know. Would you?

Prudence: If I betrayed you that way, then I should be reviled as a traitor. And I should hate myself.

Anna: And I should mourn the loss of one of my few real friends in this place.

Prudence: Then let's not let it happen. Let's try to be as before—telling each other *everything.* We can do that, can't we?

Anna: I'm not sure. How would we?

Prudence: To start, we could go to a place without eavesdroppers of any kind—avian or otherwise.

> *She gestures that they should walk out, ANNA nods agreement, and they both begin to exit*

Anna: Does such a place exist around here?

Prudence: Let's try to find one.

As they walk out, the lights dim to black

Scene 3

Scene: A penumbral light rises on QUEEN ISIS, sitting at her vanity table, brushing her hair. The ghostly music we heard earlier starts to play. ISIS looks into her mirror, and sees something disquieting. She whirls around in her chair, and faces someone unseen by us.

Isis: What are you doing here? You can't keep coming back like this. I keep telling you, it's over; I'm married now—*very well* married, thank you very much—and my husband must never know of you. It was nice while it lasted, more than nice. But now I'm a married woman, and it's over, you hear? *Do you hear?! Don't you remember?* I slit your throat to make *sure* it was over! *(pause)* It *is* over—isn't it?

BLACKOUT

Scene 4

Scene: An indeterminate space. Enter TURCO and JANE

Jane: Where are we?

Turco: Between here and there.

Jane: That's no help.

Turco: Why not?

Jane: You're not telling me where we are.

Turco: I'm not smart enough. It's not obvious.

Jane: It's obvious to *me.*

Turco: Then where are we?

Jane: Inside the castle walls.

Turco: How do you know that?

Jane: Because I haven't gone through any gates.

Turco: How do you know you haven't?

Jane: Because I didn't *see* any.

Turco: Are all gates visible?

Jane: Of course they are.

Turco: Are you sure you're right about this?

Jane: Of course I am.

Turco: Too bad. If you're right, then you're still inside the castle.

Jane: I just told you that, silly! For an adult, you can be really stupid. *(crestfallen)* I knew I was right.

Turco: Does that make you happy?

Jane: No.

Turco: Why not?

Jane: Because I don't *want* to be right. I don't *want* to be inside the castle.

Turco: Well, suppose some gates were invisible? What then?

Jane: What good would they do? They couldn't keep anyone out. They couldn't hold anyone in.

The Amulet

Turco: Don't be so sure. There are lots of invisible gates that keep plenty of enemies at bay, or hordes of people imprisoned. There's such a gate right here.

Jane: What gate?

Turco: This one. Right here. Right in front of you. If you walk through it, you could be anywhere you wanted.

Jane: That's the silliest thing I ever heard.

Turco: Isn't there somewhere else you would rather be?

Jane: Of course! I'd rather be anywhere else, so long as I didn't have to be afraid of Queen Isis.

Turco: Then walk through this gate, and you won't be afraid of her.

Jane: I don't see any gate.

Turco: That doesn't mean it's not there. Just go through it, and you'll know what I mean.

Jane: How can you go through a gate you cannot see?

Turco: I know it's hard, but you can do it. Look: I'm afraid of Queen Isis, too. But I'll just walk through this gate, to see what happens.

He walks through the imaginary gate.

Aha!

Jane: What?

Turco: I think I'm no longer afraid of Queen Isis!

Jane: Really?

Turco: Really. Try it.

JANE—very dubiously—walks through the gate

63

Good! Now, are you still afraid of Queen Isis?

Jane: Yes.

Turco: Then you didn't really walk through it.

Jane: This is stupid!

Turco: If you say so.

JANE starts to walk in the opposite direction

Jane: I'm going *this way.* Come on.

Turco: No. I'm staying right here, where I'm not afraid of Queen Isis. If I followed you, I'd have to walk back through the gate and be scared all over again.

Jane: You're really not scared of Queen Isis?

Turco: Not any more. You don't have to be, either. Just walk through the gate.

Jane: But I did go through it, and it didn't work.

Turco: That's because you didn't really *see* it. How tall is this gate? How wide? How thick are its iron bars? Don't tell me. Just go back over there—go ahead...

She does

Now look at it, see it, *feel it.* When you *really* sense it, then walk through it. Are you ready?

Jane: Wait a minute...now I'm ready.

Turco: Then go ahead—walk through the gate.

She does

Now, how do you feel?

A pause

The Amulet

Jane: I...I think I'm not afraid.

Turco: Wonderful! It's much better on this side of the gate, isn't it?

Jane: I can breathe!

Turco: Lovely, isn't it?

Jane: I don't want to go back.

Turco: Neither do I.

Blackout

Scene 5

Scene: Lights up on the same room in the Castle with all the portraits of ancestors, and that of QUEEN MARIANNE shrouded in black as before) Enter ANNA & PRUDENCE, coming back from their walk. They are in the middle of conversation.

Anna: It's never over! Tyrants never get tired of it.

Prudence: Ssh! We're back where she can hear you!

Anna: I don't care if she hears me! If she wants to kill me, let her try!

Prudence: I wish I had your confidence.

Anna: There *is* something of mine you want, but it isn't just my confidence, now is it? You want more.

Prudence: What more?

Anna: You wish you had my *amulet*. Isn't that it?

Prudence: No, no! I've never said so. What makes you think so?

Anna: You've been hinting about it these past weeks—wanting to see it, to touch it, to see how it feels to wear it. Come on, confess: you wish you had it.

Prudence: Well—one would have to be crazy not to want such a thing. I mean—whether it actually works or not—it seems to give you such confidence.

Anna: Or hope, maybe. I do hope my amulet will protect me. And—call me a superstitious fool, if you like—but I feel that as long as I am wearing it, I'm safe. I only wish Daddy—I mean His Majesty—were wearing it. He needs it more than I do—much more. I fear for his life...I wonder if Isis is keeping something from me. Maybe she knows that something has happened to him, and *that's* the reason that she dares be so mean to me. Maybe she knows that Daddy's not coming home! Oh God...that must be it: he's not coming home!

Her eyes fill with tears

Prudence: I feel sure that nothing like that has happened to him. If it had, she would have told me.

ANNA recovers, then eyes PRUDENCE closely

Anna: You are that close to Her Grace?

Long pause while PRUDENCE considers her reply

Prudence: *That* close? How close is *that* close?

Anna: Your sword is up. You're fencing again.

Prudence: I don't mean to be.

Anna: Then answer me: Is she close enough to confide in you?

The Amulet

Prudence Well...you might say so...up to a point...I mean, she doesn't tell me everything...

Anna: If she were plotting something against me, would she tell you?

Prudence: I don't know how to answer that.

Anna: One word will do it: yes, or no.

    Silence

Prudence, I'm asking you: if Isis were plotting something against me, would she tell you?

    Silence

Prudence: *(quietly)* I cannot stand this charade any longer.

Anna: You've lowered your sword...

Prudence: *(drawing Anna over to the side)* Come over here, where she's less likely to hear it.

Anna: To hear what?

Prudence: *(sotto voce)* To hear me confess that I've been lying to you, Anna, pretending to be your friend.

Anna: *(in a normal voice)* I feared as much.

Prudence: Shhhh! *(sotto voce, as before)* I *used* to be your friend, and I wish I still were.

    Until specified otherwise, the dialogue between Prudence & Anna is in hushed tones.

Anna: Why can't you be?

Prudence: I'm being paid *not* to be. Queen Isis is convinced that you know the location of the King's cache of gold and jewels. I've been given four months to get that location

67

from you. Three months have already elapsed, which leaves me thirty days.

ANNA regards PRUDENCE with sorrow.

Anna: Oh Prudence.

PRUDENCE shrugs helplessly

What if I don't tell you?

Prudence: I get killed, and you probably will be tortured until you tell them where the treasure is.

Anna: But if I do tell you, what do you get then?

Prudence: To hear Isis tell it, I get half the treasure. But I think she's lying, and that what I'm really going to get is the booby prize. As soon as she gets her hands on the treasure, I think she'll throw me into the Man-Eating Moat, along with you and Janey. And then she'll disappear for good.

Anna: Oh, my God.

Pause

What has possessed her to try such a thing?

Prudence: Revenge, Anna. According to her, when the King married her, he was dizzy in love with her.

Anna: Yes, she made sure of that.

Prudence: But his infatuation didn't last long. He grew cold to her, while you and he began to share confidences...and she was shut out. And, as you can well imagine, Isis is not a woman to take rejection easily.

Anna: No, she is not to be crossed.

Beat

The Amulet

Which means, Prudence, that you have put yourself in my power. One word to Isis from me, one raised eyebrow, and your life is over.

Prudence: It's already over. As soon as I agreed to betray you, my life ended. But if I can help you while I still breathe, I'd like to try.

Anna: How can you help me?

Prudence: By telling you never to give up that amulet. It's your best chance to be safe from Isis. She's very superstitious, and so wrought up, she sees visions of people who are not there! You can imagine how afraid she is to move against you while you're still wearing that thing. I was supposed to get it from you, but I stalled for time, hoping that His Majesty would return before I'd have to do anything. But even if I had wanted to take the amulet, I don't think I could have. When you produced it, and held onto it for dear life, I couldn't go further. I just didn't have the heart.

Anna: Yes heart—if one only had that. I've been sensing that royal crown getting closer and closer, and the closer it gets the more I see it is made not of gold but of lead. It's as if I've become Queen already, with none of the benefits of power—only the burdens.

Prudence: I am sorry for my part in it.

Beat

Anna: What will you do, Prudence?

Prudence: I'm not sure. The prospect of being devoured alive by flesh eating fish—I can't say I love it any more it than the next person.

Anna: It doesn't much appeal to me, either.

Prudence: Since the King went off, this castle has been locked down tighter than a fist about to punch! There's really no place to hide—her cronies are everywhere. But I'll try to evade them as long as I can, and hope that the King will return before Isis finds me. And she'll be out to get *you* even more than me. You can come with me if you like.

Anna: I'd be an albatross around your neck. Everyone knows me. I'd make it harder for you to hide. You're less well known; you've a better chance without me.

Prudence: She wants to kill you, Your Highness.

Anna: I know it.

Prudence: Your amulet may not protect you this time.

Anna: If not, then not. There are no guarantees; there weren't any for my mother. Still, I have a chance.

Prudence: But your sister has no chance if she's separated from you. Where is she?

Isis: *(entering)* Wouldn't you both like to know!

Prudence: *(curtseying deeply)* Your Grace!

Isis: You may go now, Prudence; I've done with you for a while. When you're needed again, you'll hear from me soon enough. In the meantime, stay close. If you try to escape, then all the sooner will dinner be served...

Prudence: Dinner?

The Amulet

Isis: In the Moat. Now go.

Prudence: *(in a croak)* Your Grace.

> *She curtseys, then backs out of the hall, eyes ever fixed on Isis*

Anna: Isis, where is Jane?

Isis: Where she is perfectly safe—for now. And if you hand over the amulet, she'll stay safe—for a little while. If not, then she'll prove an admirable appetizer—for right now.

Anna: If you touch one hair on her head, you'll never find the treasure. I don't care what you do to me.

Isis: You will care—when I start doing it...Oh, I do have to tell you, Anna, that I've been spending a lot of time dreaming of what I will do with the treasure. But I may be placing too much importance on mere material things, don't you think? I mean, at the end of the day they're so...trivial, aren't they really? And...oh God! I'm going to have an epiphany—yes, a real one, it's coming, it's coming to me of all people—a genuine epiphany—it's here! It's revealed to me! And the revelation is that non-material things can mean so much more than material ones. Because, after all, riches *can* be taken away from a person—I'm taking yours. But a memory—like my memory of your first moments in the Moat—can never be taken away.

> *ANNA reaches into her blouse, and pulls out the amulet, which she holds with both hands*

You think that trinket will influence me now? I've just got word that the King your father died in battle. He can no longer send his power into the amulet; he is dead.

71

Anna: You're trying to scare me, but it won't work; I don't believe you. Daddy said I would see him again, and I believe *him.*

Isis: You are such a gallant spirit; I feel sorry for you. It's too bad the Kingdom has to lose you.

> *With both hands, ANNA holds the amulet high, and calls out*

Anna: Father...Daddy! Please help me! I know you're alive somewhere. I know it! Please help me and Janey! Save us!

> *The ghostly music starts to play, the penumbral light casts its shadows, and ISIS, sensing something is behind her, turns slowly around so that her back is to ANNA, who stares amazed as ISIS plays the following scene with a figure seen neither by ANNA nor by the audience.*

Isis: Oh my God...Edgar! I thought you were...they told me you were...

> *Without turning, she speaks to ANNA:*

Anna: Is there anyone else in the room besides us? Do you see King Edgar?

> *She whirls around to face ANNA*

Speak up!

> *But ANNA backs away, her wide eyes fixed on ISIS, and her hand covering her mouth.*

Of course you don't see him, you simpleton; I always said you lack imagination. And that's what it is—imagination. When I turn around, he'll be gone.

72

The Amulet

She turns around.

Still there? Hah. I know what you are. You're an ill-digested particle of what they served me for breakfast—that crème brûlée over tomato sauce. Prudence warned me against it, but oh, no—I had to have the latest thing from Paris. Serves me right!

She smothers a burp

Oh! My stomach's turning over just to think of it, so of course *you* have to appear. It's only fitting. There were times when my stomach turned over every time I thought of *you,* dear Edgar, but what could I say—that every time you kissed me, I wanted a bowl to barf in? Oh no, that wouldn't have gone over very well. I wouldn't have remained Queen for very long, would I? I might not have remained *alive* for very long, either—you were always so awfully thin skinned, poor dear. So I pretended to love you, and I pretended to believe you when you lied and said you loved me—and what is my reward for this elaborate pretense? To be cut off before I can reach the climax of my art—my villainy—to have to suffer the pangs of *villainous interruptus,* as it were—is that fair? I feel so...so incomplete!

She senses EDGAR lunging at her, so she backs away, and, with a laugh, very daintily spins out of his reach, effectively trading places with him.

Oo-oo-oo! Making a pass at me after all these years? Oo-oo-oo! Going to chase me, are you? Going to run after me until I snare you? That would be thrilling! But you'll have to catch me first—that is, if I *let* you catch me! Come on...come on...catch me if you can...I know you want me...

And with girlish giggles, she backs away, dodging his advances, until with a final "oo-oo-oo", she turns and runs away, laughing merrily until we hear a splash and a brief, throttled scream as the Moat takes her. By this time, ANNA has fallen to her knees, head in her hands. A beat, during which regular lighting is restored, and the ghostly music fades. CAPTAIN STEELE runs in.

Steele: Your Majesty!

He takes ANNA'S hands and lifts her to her feet, while she gazes at him, all dazed and uncomprehending.

Anna: What...? What...? Who...? Is it you, Captain Steele?

Steele: Your Majesty, there's very bad news: The King, your father, is dead, killed in battle.

Anna: *Oh no!*

ANNA speaks the following very quietly *as she summons all her strength to fight back tears, and to keep from collapsing*

My fault. All my fault. The amulet...he needed it...but I let him give it to me. God help me, but I wanted it...I wanted it...Oh God...

She feels herself growing faint; STEELE sees this and grabs her shoulders.

The Amulet

Steele: Steady yourself, Your Majesty; there's good news, too: The enemy is in full flight. The day is ours! Your father the King gave his life to make it possible.

Anna: *(finally beginning to understand)* Oh...oh!

ANNA sobs quietly. STEELE starts to put his hand on her shoulder, but thinks better of it, and refrains from touching her.

Steele: Yes, Your Majesty. The King is dead.

STEELE kneels before ANNA

Long live the Queen!

Pause

Anna: What did you say?

Steele: I said, long live the Queen!

A pause while ANNA stares at him. Then STEELE says, quietly:

That is you, Your Majesty.

He kisses her hand. ANNA takes all this in, and finally says

Anna: No longer will you be Captain Steele. Rise, Colonel.

He does.

Steele: Thank you ma'am.

Anna: Colonel Steele, please stay by me.

STEELE salutes, then says:

Steele: I shall, for as long as you need me, ma'am.

JANE rushes in, followed by TURCO and PRUDENCE, who are walking more slowly.

Jane: Anna, Anna! Everybody is cheering 'cause Queen Isis threw herself into the moat! And I wanted to see, but Turco and Prudence wouldn't let me!

Turco: There's nothing to see.

Prudence: *Almost nothing.* There's a bit left.

Anna: Horrible.

Turco: After Her Royal Highness ran on ahead, someone told us the sad news, Your Majesty.

TURCO kneels, and PRUDENCE follows his lead.

Prudence: Your Majesty.

Turco: *(to Jane)* Your Royal Highness, your sister is now Her Majesty Queen Anna. You should kneel.

Jane: You mean...Daddy is not coming home?

Anna: I fear not, Janey.

Jane: But he said we'd see him again!

Anna: He wasn't able to keep his promise, Janey. He tried, but he couldn't.

Pause while it dawns on JANE that now both parents are dead

Jane: When Mommy died, Daddy was there to hug me. But now there's nobody.

Anna: There's me, Janey. I'll be here to hug you.

Anna kneels and puts her arms around Jane, kissing her repeatedly.

76

From now on, I'll be both mother and father to you, Janey.

Steele: And so you shall, ma'am, for everyone in the nation.

JANE looks at ANNA, then kneels.

Jane: I guess you really *are* special, now.

Anna: I love you, Janey.

ANNA rises, but everyone else remains kneeling

And you can get up. Everyone, please: do rise.

TURCO, PRUDENCE & JANE rise. ANNA turns to PRUDENCE.

Prudence, would you remove the cover from my mother's picture?

Prudence: Yes, ma'am.

PRUDENCE removes the cover, revealing the smiling portrait of MARIANNE

Turco: And now, ma'am, what are your plans?

Anna: There will be a full month of mourning for King Edgar.

Turco: Yes, of course.

Anna: And that month will also be the time to mourn Queen Isis.

Prudence: What?!

Anna: She was a human being like all of us. She had a chance to do a great deal of good in the world, but she failed to do it. That is what we shall mourn.

Prudence: I suppose so, Ma'am.

Anna: You don't sound very enthusiastic.

Prudence: Begging your pardon, Ma'am, I don't like it much at all. Isis was a witch—causing harm to thousands. But instead of getting away with murder like many tyrants, this one gets her just deserts, suffers the same fate as her victims, thus sparing the lives of many more innocents, including you, Your Majesty, and Her Royal Highness. This is nothing to mourn, ma'am—we should be dancing in the streets!

Anna: While our windows are draped in black because of the death of my father the King? This is no time for dancing.

Turco: Begging your pardon, Ma'am, may I suggest a middle course? In public we definitely should not dance in glee, lest the mourners say, "I'm glad *somebody's* happy." Nor should we sob convulsively, lest the unfeeling say, "why are you crying? The witch is dead!" No no. Instead, we should affect a faint, philosophic smile, yet meld it with a wan world-weariness—like this...

He demonstrates

...so that when someone greets us and says, "how do you do?" we smile faintly, philosophically, *world wearily,* and say, "oh...I'm doing as well as can be expected, *under the circumstances."* And if someone comes up and says, with more enthusiasm than tact, "isn't this a wonderful day!" we simply sigh with our wisest world-weariness...

He emits a profound sigh

...and say, "I suppose." In this way, by waiting for *privacy* before we express our paroxysms of pain or joy, we edify everyone and offend no one.

Anna: We'll take it under advisement.

The Amulet

Turco: Thank you ma'am.

Anna: In the meantime: Colonel Steele, I want a chance to review the troops and thank them personally—as soon as most of them are home from the front. Can that be arranged?

Steele: I'll see to it, Ma'am.

Anna: One other thing: The late King, my father, said he had organized what he called a regiment of statesmen to advise me. I want to begin discussions with them—starting tomorrow, if possible. Can that be done?

Steele: If it can be done, it *shall* be done, ma'am.

Jane: Anna—I mean your Majesty—can we have a walk?

Anna: I'd love one. Turco and Prudence, will you join us?

Turco & Prudence: *(in unison)* With pleasure, ma'am.

Anna: Colonel Steele, can you arrange for the Guard to accompany us?

Steele: *Yes, Ma'am!!*

> *STEELE salutes, then exits*

Anna: Turco, you were right about how much you can find even in a limited space. Within these walls I saw a world of greed and treachery, but I also saw loyalty and love. I saw just about everything.

Turco: Begging your pardon, Ma'am, but unfortunately, there is one thing you did not see—your father's return.

Anna: Dear Turco, there you may be mistaken.

Turco: Really!

Anna: Yes. In a way, I think I did see him. In fact...I *know* I did.

Blackout

Unbelievable

Scene: a small parlor in a large apartment in New York City. One can hear the sounds of a big party going on in an adjoining room. Discovered is JONATHAN, sitting alone on a couch and reading his Kindle. Next to him on the couch is a clipboard with some papers clipped to it. To the side of the couch is a little table on which is a tumbler of whiskey, resting on a coaster.

Enter MELANIE, carrying a tote bag. She sees Jonathan and pauses.

Melanie: Oh! Excuse me—I didn't know there was anyone in here.

Jonathan: It's just me. I can vacate, if you want to be alone.

Melanie: No, no—the last thing I want to be is alone. I just don't want to disturb you.

Jonathan: You're not disturbing me. Would you like to come in?

Melanie: If you don't mind.

Jonathan: Not at all.

He moves the clipboard to make room for her, and, keeping the tote bag near her, she sits next to him on the couch.

81

Melanie: Thanks. It's a relief to talk to someone without having to raise your voice.

Jonathan: I know what you mean.

Melanie: Are you here alone?

Jonathan: *(smiling)* No—I'm here with you.

Melanie: I meant, did you come here by yourself?

Jonathan: All by myself—unless you count my Kindle and my clipboard. That would make three of us.

Melanie: Always with you, are they?

Jonathan: More or less. The clipboard has been with me since college. But the Kindle is more recent. My ex-wife gave it to me.

Melanie: That was a thoughtful gift.

Jonathan: More like a bribe—to coax me to take her to parties like this. "You don't have to talk to anyone," she would say, "all you have to do is find yourself a nice, inconspicuous corner, and, when nobody's looking, take out your Kindle and read." If this party had been thrown two years ago, Betty would have been in the other room having a marvelous time, while I'd be here, catching up on my reading.

Melanie: A couple of years ago?

Jonathan: Last year was when we split. And since then, of course, I've been getting fewer invitations to parties, so when I do get one, I feel should appear to prove that I still *can*.

Unbelievable

Melanie: Then once you appear, you *dis*appear into another room.

Jonathan: Something like that.

Melanie: I'm having a good time.

Jonathan: I'm glad someone is.

Melanie: Oh! I shouldn't have bothered you.

Jonathan: No. You're not bothering me. On the contrary, you draw me out quite nicely. Perhaps you're studying to go into journalism?

Melanie: No. I'm an actress.

Jonathan: Ah! Would I have seen you on any of our stages hereabouts?

Melanie: No. I'm afraid that nobody's ever heard of me.

Jonathan: Well—you're just getting started. You're very young. There's still time for you to get on the stage.

Melanie: If I wanted it.

Jonathan: You don't?

Melanie: Not really. I want to act in films.

Jonathan: Then you're near the wrong coast. You should be on the West Coast, where the action is.

Melanie: There's none on the East Coast?

Jonathan: Well, I do know of a few local productions—very low-budget.

Melanie: Perhaps you know any of the people involved? Since you're a writer and all?

Jonathan: How do you know I'm a writer?

Melanie: That's what they said you were.

Jonathan: Who said?

Melanie: Everyone—I mean, everyone here at the party.

She gestures to where the sounds are coming from.

In there.

Jonathan: Ah! Then you must be a very good actress indeed. You had me convinced that all you wanted was a place to escape from all the noise in there. When in fact, you had an ulterior motive—an action, as they call it in acting school.

Melanie: *(a little stiffly)* I know what an action is.

Jonathan: I'm sure you do. Yours tonight is to troll for connections to help you become a film actress. Am I right?

Melanie: No, actually. I mean, for your sake it would be great if you knew anyone in the film business—but for me it's a little too late for that.

Jonathan: For someone as young as you? What do you mean, too late?

Melanie: To use my connections, if I had any. The way I see it, the only way I'll ever be in a movie is for someone to write one for me. And as soon as possible. That's where you come in. You could write me one.

Jonathan: Who says so?

Melanie: *(gesturing to the adjoining room)* The crowd in there.

Jonathan: Did any of them say I could write screen plays?

Melanie: I asked, but nobody could say for certain.

Unbelievable

Jonathan: That's because I cannot. That is, I never *have* written one. I write stage plays—well, I used to. Nowadays, I'm not doing too much writing of any kind—dramatic or otherwise.

Melanie: You must be writing *something*. I see that clipboard of yours. What do you put on that?

Jonathan: Ideas. I bring it with me just in case I should have one.

> *He picks it up and shows it to her. It is blank.*

As you can see, I haven't had too many ideas, lately.

Melanie: That's too bad. Your scripts could be useful.

Jonathan: *(smiling)* To wrap fish in, right?

Melanie: No, no—for me to star in.

Jonathan: This is marvelous. You come in out of nowhere and tell me I should write something for you—a film script, no less—a starring vehicle! And meanwhile, to hear you tell it, nobody's ever heard of you.

Melanie: That's true enough.

Jonathan: Don't worry about it. Nobody's ever heard of me, either.

Melanie: What about all those dudes in there? *They've* heard of you.

Jonathan: But nobody's heard of *them*. They're not famous, either.

Melanie: So we're both unknowns. Though I'm far less known than you. My High School Year Book forgot to put in my name and picture, and it was downhill from then on.

Jonathan: You can't have hit bottom yet, because if you had, you wouldn't have been invited to the party.

Melanie: I wasn't.

Jonathan: What did you do—crash it?

Melanie: Didn't have to. The invitation wasn't for me, it was for my ex-boyfriend. The invitations were always for him. He was my social contact; I just came along for the ride.

Jonathan: I know the feeling; I'm here on Betty's invitation.

Melanie: Two gate crashers closeted in the same room—unbelievable!

Jonathan: Not so unbelievable—it's a fact. The word "unbelievable" is overused nowadays.

Melanie: What are you—a schoolteacher?

Jonathan: That, unfortunately, is how I make my living.

Melanie: A playwright like you? Unbelievable! Oops—I better watch my step with you.

Jonathan: Don't worry. I don't bite. At a party like this, I try to drop my schoolteacher persona, find an inconspicuous corner, and read.

Melanie: If that's all you do, why bother coming at all?

Jonathan: I like the sounds of people talking to each other. To me it's as soothing as the sounds of a woodland brook. A *babbling* brook. I like to hear the babble—but not get into it.

Melanie: I like to do both. But just now, the hostess had me give her my ex-boyfriend's address, and I got the feeling that from now on, her invitations will go to *him*, not me. So you could say I'm close to hitting bottom.

Jonathan: And now, to demonstrate this, you're asking me to write you a screen play, despite the fact that I've never written one, and that nobody's ever heard of either of us. Are you crazy—or just desperate?

Melanie: Both. But I have artistically redeeming value. I've got a good visual sense, and a great imagination. And if we work together, it shouldn't be too hard to do up a screen play.

Jonathan: I wouldn't know how to begin.

Melanie: The beginning is the simple part.

Jonathan: Oh really? How would you do it?

Melanie: Easy: while the titles flash, a high camera is angling down at a young woman with a tote bag. She's in a large, crowded room, and the camera follows her as she goes from person to person, talking to each briefly, still carrying her tote bag as if she's afraid to set it down. The camera follows her to an adjoining room where she sees a guy with his Kindle. He's morose and full of self pity, but all the same she--

Jonathan: *(interrupting)* I am not morose! I am not full of self pity!

Melanie: This is a screenplay, silly—any resemblance to persons living or dead is purely coincidental. This is not about you, and not about me. It's about art—it's about *life.*

Jonathan: All the same, I object to your characterization. I am not morose—I am sober and realistic.

Melanie: *Boring!* Better your character should be soured on life, because then you'd need someone to sweeten you up, namely me—I mean my character. Don't you see—for the sake of the screen play? For the sake of art?

Jonathan: *(starting to smile)* All right. Art for art's sake.

Melanie: You should say *Ars Gratia Artis*. That's what you see around the MGM Lion—which is much more appropriate since we're making a movie.

Jonathan: All right! For the sake of the MGM lion, my character will be soured on life. Go ahead.

Melanie: Okay: my character sees that your character is down in the dumps, but she likes him anyway, and decides to cheer him up by proposing that they do a screen play together.

Jonathan: A play within a play—is that how you see it?

Melanie: What's wrong with that?

Jonathan: It can get awfully recursive.

Melanie: Recursive?

Jonathan: Like this: In your screenplay, the leading lady suggests a screenplay be written, whose leading lady suggests a screenplay be written, whose leading lady suggests a screenplay be written, whose leading--

Melanie: *(interrupting)* Stop, I get it already. But if she wants to cheer him up, and he's a writer, what else could she suggest?

Jonathan: They could leave the party.

Melanie: You want to leave the party?

Unbelievable

Jonathan: Not necessarily. But in our screen play, *my character* might want to leave the party.

Melanie: I see. We could have a shot of us opening the front door and another of us coming down the long brick stairway.

Jonathan: This brownstone has only one step in front of it, and it's made of concrete.

Melanie: Concrete? Boring! Anything else would be better.

Jonathan: How about cast iron?

Melanie: That will do. So we're coming down the cast iron stairs, and it's ten p.m. already.

Jonathan: Though it's three in the afternoon now.

Melanie: Where's your imagination?! I'm telling you that it's ten at night, and our faces are lit by street lamps and the occasional passing taxi, and we're holding hands...

Jonathan: Holding hands? We've got to that point, have we?

Melanie: Oh, sure. And the camera is far enough back to show us holding hands, and as it slowly zooms in, we see my hair blown in a gust of wind...you're to my right...your character, that is...and my accent light is off to my left, so you won't block it. We put our arms around each other's waists, as the camera continues to zoom in so that the screen is filled with our happy faces, lit with the promise of an evening together—our first date.

Jonathan: Impressive. But does anybody say anything?

Melanie: Nobody *has* to. That's the beauty of cinema—you can have those moments where words can't add anything—they can only subtract. All you need are actors whose faces—whose entire bodies—are magnetic.

Jonathan: That must be where you come in.

Melanie: Not only me; don't put yourself down. You seem pretty magnetic, yourself.

Jonathan: That's because it's getting dark.

Melanie: I won't hear a word against my leading man.

Jonathan: Your leading man, am I? You don't even know my name.

Melanie: Actually, I do. It's Jonathan Cantwell.

Jonathan: They must have told you. But I don't know yours.

Melanie: Melanie. Melanie Miller.

Jonathan: A very euphonious name.

Melanie: Thank you. I chose it myself. It's my *nom de cinema*.

Jonathan: Well then, Melanie Miller, you've gotten us down the stairs, and our faces fill the screen as we savor the prospect of our first date.

Melanie: Not quite.

Jonathan: But that's what you said.

Melanie: I know that's what I said. I left the story on a temporary peak of pleasure.

Jonathan: Temporary?

Melanie: I'm afraid so. For already, my character's face is clouding over with worry. She glances nervously to the left and to the right.

Jonathan: What's the matter?

Unbelievable

Melanie: It's a secret.

Jonathan: Oh?

Melanie: She wants to keep it from him as long as possible. So she smiles bravely up at him, and suggests they go for a walk.

Jonathan: Where to?

Melanie: "We'll see," she says mysteriously, and the scene jump-cuts to the pedestrian walkway of the Williamsburgh Bridge.

Jonathan: That's quite a jump.

Melanie: It's quite a scene. All that heavy, oppressive steel work, and a cold full-moon high behind them, and a bit to the side. Our characters are standing next to each other, gazing at the dark river, below. They are not holding hands. They are somewhat silhouetted by the moon, but all the same you can see her widened eyes as she tells him how glad she is that they are together, so she can enjoy whatever time she has left.

Jonathan: Time she has left?!

Melanie: Yes, he's startled by this, and turns to her, reaching for her shoulders so he can turn her to face him. Now his is the face with a glint of moonlight on it, but hers is all in shadow as she tells him that every moment is precious.

Jonathan: Of course it is, he says, that's true all the time, but is it more true now than usual? That's what my character wants to know!

Paul R. Cooper

Melanie: And that's what I don't know how to tell you, she says, but you'll learn it soon enough, and the camera zooms in on her clasped hands shaking against her shivering body.

JONATHAN gazes at her, not sure of what to make of all this.

Jonathan: Let's find a place out of the cold, he says, I could use a scotch.

JONATHAN reaches for the tumbler of whiskey and

takes a swig.

I had been on the wagon, he says, his face filling the screen; but I sure feel like falling off it now. The camera backs away showing him flagging a cab on Second Avenue—they're off the bridge by this time. Is that all right?

Melanie: Perfect! You're catching on just fine!

Jonathan: Do we jump-cut to the table inside the cafe?

Melanie: Better to show them approaching the front door. That way we get the name of the place painted on the sign above the door: "Joe's Drinks and Eats." Shows the kind of dive he's taking her to. Close up of her face shows she's game for anything.

Jonathan: Then we cut to the table?

Melanie: Better cut to the other side of the door, to show it opening, and to see my character's face as she takes in the scene: It's definitely a neighborhood joint—overcrowded with casually dressed folks all raising their voices and gesticulating madly so they can be heard in the hubbub. Close up of her widened eyes taking it all in.

Unbelievable

Jonathan: That's the second time you've referred to your widened eyes.

Melanie: Well, I've seen some pretty wild stuff.

Jonathan: Like what?

Melanie: Let's sit down, first.

Jonathan: Okay—we jump-cut to the waiter showing us our table. We sit down. Now you can tell me some of that wild stuff you've seen.

Melanie: Wait: the waiter wants to know if we'll have anything to drink. I say ginger ale will be fine.

Jonathan: And I say double scotch, no rocks.

Melanie: *That'll* warm you up.

He takes another swig from the tumbler of whiskey.

Jonathan: It *is* warming me up—quite nicely. And now what about those wild sights you've been seeing?

Melanie: What about your falling off the wagon?

Jonathan: I asked first.

Melanie: I know you did. But since I'm a woman, you should be gracious, and humor me.

Jonathan: Is that right?

Melanie: I think so.

A long pause

Jonathan: Okay. I started drinking after Betty walked out.

Melanie: I'm sure that must have been traumatic. What did she tell you?

Jonathan: Nothing much—except that I was so boring she could hardly wait to get out of my house.

Melanie: Unbelievable!

Jonathan: You really can't believe she called me boring?

Melanie: Well—if you say so, then it must have happened. But to think that she would say such a thing! It's hard to believe that one could be so deliberately cruel.

Jonathan: Thousands are deliberately cruel every day, and she had better reason than some. I'm sure she was disappointed in me. She thought she was getting a glamorous intellectual, only to find out that what she had landed was a stay-at-home stick-in-the-mud.

Melanie: May I ask why you married her?

Jonathan: Because this dazzlingly beautiful woman, the life of every party, batted her eyes at me and told me that she loved me, and I believed her. I'm not the first man to be stupid in these matters. The story's an old one.

Melanie: And it's so—I'm not going to say "unbelievable" any more. It's not so unbelievable—it's just sad.

Jonathan: You're right about that. But we had no children to hold her back. She wanted to trade up: I was a schoolteacher, the new guy was a Bank President; she saw a chance to do better, so she split. It happens all the time. No big deal.

Melanie: It's a very big deal—to me. I need you sober enough to write up my story—our story—and make it into a movie. I need you to stay well enough so that even if nobody sees our movie you'll keep telling our story long after I'm gone.

Unbelievable

Jonathan: Gone where?

Melanie: Away. Where do you think?

Jonathan: I don't know what to think. You're so damned mysterious about what is frightening you—frightening your character—and I don't know how much is real.

Melanie: This is art, isn't it? It's *all* real.

She reaches for his tumbler of whiskey.

Do you mind if I have some of that?

Jonathan: Sure, go ahead.

He hands the glass to her.

Melanie: Thanks.

She takes a sip.

Jonathan: Is this in the movie?

Melanie: Sure, if you like.

Jonathan: It's you who have to like it. It's your story.

Melanie: It's *our* story. Later, we'll get back to your apartment...

Jonathan: Really?

Melanie: It has to be yours. They know where I live. They're probably casing the place right now, waiting for me to come back.

Jonathan: You're being followed?

Melanie: I hope not, she says. The screen fills with images of her immediate past as we hear her say that she left the house with a change of clothing in her backpack, and ducked into a hotel restroom, changed her clothes, and put what she had been wearing, along with the backpack, in a tote bag that she had also brought in the backpack. Then she ducked out the backdoor of the restaurant, and did her best to shake them.

Jonathan: Shake whom? Who is following you?

Melanie: I was going to leave the tote bag in the foyer behind the front door, she said, but I thought it was safer to bring it with me.

> *She reaches for the tote bag, and draws it to her*

Jonathan: Are you going to tell me what's going on, or am I going to have to end the movie?

Melanie: The camera is behind him as he speaks, so we see her face grow taut, and the fingers of both hands grip on her now empty tumbler.

Jonathan: Speak, Melanie; talk to me.

Melanie: I so wish I had ordered scotch, she says, like you.

Jonathan: Look: why don't you have some more of mine?

> *He reaches into his vest pocket and produces a flask, from which he adds an additional shot of whiskey into the tumbler. He hands it to her, and waits till she has had a couple of sips of it.*

Now then, who are you running from? And why?

Melanie: Give me the camera shot.

Jonathan: Oh God...!

> *With some irritation*

Okay: the camera is far enough away from them so as to motivate hearing the sounds of background conversations, but close enough to hear him say, "now then, who are you running from, and why?" As she begins to speak, the camera moves in to focus on her every word and the background noises fade away.

Melanie: I was in a joint sorta like this, except the TV was bigger, and there were photos of sports heroes on the walls. It was in New Jersey, wouldn't you know? This was Danny's favorite hangout.

Jonathan: Danny?

Melanie: My ex-boyfriend. He loved coming there because he was a sports nut and occasionally he'd see some of his heroes in the place and get them to autograph his napkin, or whatever he had with him. Now I didn't care much about sports, but Danny was so crazy about them that I went along; it was good to see him happy. So he was a regular there, and I was, too. Everyone knew our names, where we lived—our life stories, in fact. So when Danny dumped me, the last place I wanted to go was that sports bar; I didn't want to answer everyone's questions about where was Danny, and what was I doing out by myself? But then I started thinking, was this the bitter end—simply because Danny dumped me? Just because I didn't have a boyfriend, was I going to stay holed up in my apartment forever? No—I could go out by myself; I'd just stay away from that sports bar. And then I thought that sports bar was the one place I *had* to go to—nobody was going to tell me where I couldn't go. Which all sounds ridiculous, but as soon as I decided I was over Danny, I went straight to that bar, just to see if I could.

Pause

It felt weird walking in there alone, and I ordered a drink so I'd have something to hold on to. And then I noticed a young couple in a small corner table. His back was to me, but I could see her face; she was beautiful, with fiery red hair that fell to her shoulders. He was taking both her hands in his, and he was kissing her hands. Her eyes were dark with love, and I just knew they could hardly wait till they were home together. Oh, Jonathan! That's a scene that we've got to have in our movie: not them, but us—I mean our characters. I see a close up of you removing my blouse—but all one can see is my head and shoulders, that's it. But it's enough. If we do it right, it will be very sexy.

Jonathan: So our encounter will be scripted, will it?

Melanie: In the movie it will have to be—the outlines, anyway. But in real life of course, the less scripting the better.

Jonathan: We could do the real life first—sort of as a warm up.

Melanie: That would be something to look forward to.

Jonathan: You have me interested.

Melanie: I'm glad!

Jonathan: But I'm still wondering: who are you running from? And why? Did you think you would distract me from that?

Melanie: It was worth a try.

Jonathan: Didn't work. So just tell me.

> There is a long pause. Finally MELANIE speaks.

Unbelievable

Melanie: In this dive I was telling you about—the one with the loving couple in the corner—I saw something that will stay with me as long as I live—however long that is.

Jonathan: Go ahead...

Melanie: I was by myself, sitting at a table near the front door. There was a stiff breeze outside, so every time the door opened, a few dead leaves blew inside the restaurant, and I felt the chill. And that's what happened when a big guy wearing a black raincoat opened the door, but didn't bother closing it. A bunch of leaves were blowing around inside like crazy, and it got really chilly as this man, calm as you please, walked a few yards to a table across from me, took out a huge pistol and shot a guy in the head.

Jonathan: Good god!

Melanie: There was blood all over the wall—brains too, I think. I heard shrieking, and saw that people were looking away...but I kept staring at the guy with the gun, and—this is weird—all I could think of: his pistol was as black as his raincoat! The killer noticed me staring at him. He started moving towards me, but I got up and ran out the door, then up the street so fast—I thought my heart was going to burst from my chest! Ever since then I've been a marked woman. I'm stressed out of my mind.

Jonathan: I don't blame you. But take a breath—don't let your imagination run away with you. In all likelihood, nobody is gunning for you. And even if someone were: this is a big city. How could the killer find you, even if he wanted to?

Melanie: All he'd have to do would be to send a...a colleague of his to the sports bar to inquire about me. You forget, they know my name over there; they know the block where I live.

Jonathan: You're making too much of this.

Melanie: Am I? A few days after, I got a phone call, but when I picked up the receiver, someone on the other end hung up.

Jonathan: That can happen any time. Wrong number or something. Any time.

Melanie: Repeatedly? And I've been noticing the same car—a black Lincoln driving slowly up the street. I'm telling you, Jonathan, I'm afraid to go home!

Jonathan: I don't blame you. Come home with me. They don't know where *I* live.

Melanie: If they followed me home with you, they'd find out, soon enough. I can't go home with you, Jonathan. I'd never forgive myself if something happened to you. Whatever happens, better it's just me. The only thing I ask you is write a screen play about this—or, if you feel you can't do the screen play, then write a regular play script—just as long as you tell my story. Try to get it produced, and if you can't, then try to get it read. And if you can't even do that, just tell my story any way you can, to whomever you meet. Will you promise?

There is a long pause in which JONATHAN studies her.

Jonathan: Has there been a casting call for a movie with this theme?

Melanie: Not that I know of.

Unbelievable

Jonathan: Nothing with an innocent heroine pursued by the mob?

Melanie: If there were I'd audition for it.

Jonathan: Do you know what, Melanie? That's what I believe you're doing now—auditioning—or more likely, *rehearsing* an audition to come, before an audience that will be more important than I.

Melanie: You think that?

Jonathan: I feel sure of it. I've heard how some of these auditions go—the actor shows up in costume, *in character*, and says everything—scripted and unscripted—as if he were being filmed.

Melanie: That's a wonderful idea—I love it! You do have imagination after all! And you can go on believing that story if it helps you.

Jonathan: Come on, Melanie, if there were a shooting in a sports bar, don't you think it would be in all the New York papers—even if it happened in New Jersey? I don't remember seeing any such story.

Melanie: *(gently)* It's all right, Jonathan. You remember what you like—just as long as you remember to write the story. You gotta write it—*please!* I don't want...my light snuffed out like some...odd candle in the corner, with nobody noticing.

Jonathan: You know, Melanie, you're very good at this; you're totally believable.

Melanie: I've earned it, trust me—or don't; it doesn't matter anymore. All that matters is that you promise you'll write it. I gotta go. Promise me—please?

Jonathan: I promise—but the whole thing seems so fantastic; I can scarcely believe I'm not dreaming. When you've gone, how will I know I didn't hallucinate the whole thing? Give me something to remember you by—to remind me that *you* at least are real—whatever your story—and that I haven't dreamed you up.

Melanie: *(reaching into her tote bag)* I'm very real.

   She produces a pair of red nylon panties.

Here—this oughta remind you. My mother always used to say that you should always wear good panties, so that if they find you dead somewhere, you won't be embarrassed.

   She laughs nervously. Then she turns to go, but at the doorway, she turns to look at him.

Please don't make me seem too crazy.

Jonathan: I'll do my best.

Melanie: I know it. Bye-bye.

   MELANIE exits.

Jonathan: *(talking to himself)* That was something else! Did it really happen? Was a mysterious girl who calls herself Melanie right here in this room, sitting beside me, talking to me, drawing me out, pulling me in? O my god—she's got me talking to myself! Too much scotch. I gotta get back on the wagon. I gotta forget the whole thing. But can I? Oh no. Besides—a promise is a promise. I better get at it.

   He picks up the clipboard, and begins writing:

Unbelievable

Scene: a small parlor in a large apartment. One can hear the sounds of a big party going on in an adjoining room. Discovered is Jonathan, sitting alone on a couch, and reading his Kindle.

MELANIE rushes in.

Melanie: I shouldn't have given you those panties, I may need them later.

Jonathan: No problem. I'm really glad you're back.

He rises and hands the panties to her.

Melanie: Thanks. Did you miss me?

He gestures to the clipboard; she sees there is writing on it.

You've started already? Oh! I love you!

She throws her arms around him and kisses him passionately, and at length. When they come up for air, he says:

Jonathan: I sure will remember *that*. Will I see you again?

Melanie: I love you, Jonathan. Goodbye.

And off she goes.

Jonathan: Unbelievable.

BLACKOUT

Being Authentic
ACT ONE

(Year: 2011. Where: In a suburb of New York. Scene: living room of a middle class family. Enter, from the dining room, EGON BRICKER, his wife, ANGELA, and their daughter, ELIZABETH. EGON, in his late forties, is powerfully built, and towers over ANGELA. ELIZABETH, in her mid-twenties, is wearing a colorful blouse, which she allows to hang loosely over her blue jeans.)

Egon: That was a great meal.

Elizabeth: I was starved. I hope I didn't eat like a pig.

Angela: No such thing. I'm glad that seven years away from us hasn't lessened your appetite.

Egon: It looked hearty to me; I'm amazed, Liz! I mean, you rode forty-four hours on that bus. A trip like that might have killed my appetite, but not my little one's.

Elizabeth: Your little one, am I?

Egon: Well, aren't you?

Elizabeth considers her reply

Elizabeth: (looking away) I won't be anyone's little one, if I keep eating at this rate.

Angela: Darling, I hope you never lose your appetite.

Elizabeth: I nearly did lose it after twenty-one hours having to sit next to that guy.

Egon: What guy?

Elizabeth: Do you really want to know, Father?

Egon: If I didn't, would I have asked? And what is this "Father" business? Why are we so formal, now?

Elizabeth: I'm sorry. What I was trying to say is that he got on at Atlanta, last night at around eight. I'd been on that bus for almost thirteen hours, and I was tired. I really didn't want to sit next to anyone, so I put on an angry look to discourage people. But as the bus filled up, I realized that I was going to have to sit next to someone. So I let my face get softer. I hoped that maybe a little old lady might want to sit next to me, and I wouldn't have to spend all that time with some man or other.

Egon: Good thinking.

Elizabeth: For a change, you mean?

Egon: Don't put words into my mouth, Liz. All I said was that was good thinking.

Elizabeth: Well, my good thinking didn't work. Because the last people on the bus were three men, two of whom looked as if they hadn't bathed in a couple of weeks. The other guy seemed relatively clean; in fact he was actually handsome in an oddball kind of way. So as he got closer, I scooched over toward the window, as if to make room for him.

Angela: Good move.

Elizabeth: Yeah, you'd think so.

Egon: What happened?

Elizabeth: Nothing happened, Dad. Except that he took the hint, said, "may I sit here?" And I said, "why not?" and he said "thank you" and sat down.

Egon: What's so bad about that?

Elizabeth: He started telling me the story of his life, and his parents' lives. Most of all, he told me about Michelle, his girlfriend – his ex-girlfriend, that is – he had just broken up with her. Before they broke up, they must have had eight or ten dates – and he went through every one of them, conversation by conversation, kiss by kiss, and on the later dates, when they started going to bed, he regaled me with every—

Egon: (interrupting) You're not saying—

Elizabeth: (interrupting) I *am* saying.

Egon: Disgusting.

Elizabeth: I don't know about disgusting. He was just self-absorbed. He went on and on about Michelle, and about his life – except for a couple of times when he asked me about mine.

Egon: I hope you didn't tell him anything important.

Elizabeth: What are you afraid of, Dad? All I mentioned was one or two trivial details. I didn't have time for anything more, because he kept interrupting me with this doomed relationship – every smile, every frown, every move – and he kept saying, "Where did I go wrong? What did I do wrong?" I didn't know what to tell him. I mean, what the hell do I know about boyfriends – they keep running through my fingers like water. So I mumbled something, and he kept talking and talking until, mercifully, he talked himself out, and finally, at one in the morning, he fell asleep – on my shoulder! I thought of waking him up, and then thought better of it. He was kinda cute when he wasn't talking.

Egon: He was using you for a pillow?

Elizabeth: Yeah. When he sat down he needed my shoulder for crying on, then he needed it for sleeping on. But it was so long since a guy needed my shoulder that way that I let him lie there and snore. Of course, I couldn't sleep with him on me, and it became uncomfortable, but I tried not to move; I didn't want to wake him. I spent seven hours with that guy sleeping on my shoulder.

Angela: It shows the sweetness of your nature.

Egon: Your motherly side.

Elizabeth: Or my masochistic side, I'm not sure which. Anyway, he finally woke up, and he seemed refreshed and pleased with himself. "That was wonderful," he said. "Was it good for you, too?"

Egon: Disgusting.

Elizabeth: He was just joking.

Egon: You don't talk that way to a lady.

Elizabeth: Father, lighten up! This is the twenty-first century. Things have changed.

Egon: Not that much. If you're talking to a woman you don't even know, you don't joke that way – unless she's a whore.

Being Authentic

Elizabeth: (uncomfortably) That's just...you're impossible, Dad.

Angela: Don't talk to your father that way, Lizzie. Maybe in some ways he's a little behind the times, but he's entirely possible. And he happens to be your father, so be respectful.

Elizabeth: I'm sorry, Dad. I came in on edge. I'll try to do better.

Egon: Don't worry about it.

Elizabeth: Chalk it up to the long bus ride. I didn't get much sleep.

Egon: In spite of that you still look pretty good – healthy and strong. If you like, we can start up with those ballet classes again, if you still want 'em.

Elizabeth: Not right now, Dad, thank you. I'd have to lose a little weight before I'd care to show up in tights.

Egon: Been getting plenty to eat down south, have you?

Elizabeth: I manage. But it isn't easy. In the South, you have to be determined just to find a salad.

Egon: Well, if there was ever a woman with determination, it's you, Elizabeth.

Angela: Listen to that, Lizzie! Coming from Daddy, it's praise from Caesar.

Egon: Caesar, am I? Not bad! If you mean that I built my business with strength and willpower, sure, I guess you can call me Caesar. I'll bet I'm not the only contractor who feels this way. Sure – call me Caesar, if you like! But

109

you, Lizzie, you can call me Daddy, 'cause I'd like to think you get your determination from me.

Elizabeth: Why not, Dad, if it pleases you to think so.

Angela: It is so.

Egon: I mean, look Liz: You're really special to us...

Elizabeth: (a little patronizingly) Yes, I know the story – I'm your little miracle, 'cause until I came along, the doctors said you guys would never be able to have children, which all goes to show that doctors don't know everything – right?

Egon: Exactly. Doctors may know a lot, but God knows more. And after He gave you to us, it's natural for me to hope you'll take after me in some way or other.

Angela: Of course she does, Egon – she takes after you in many ways.

Egon: That's all I'm saying.

Elizabeth: I hear you, Dad. And even if I like salads better than you, it doesn't mean I don't take after you.

Egon: I like a good salad from time to time. But some of them can get pricey.

Elizabeth: They can and they certainly did!

Egon: But you had that job, you said – at an architecture office, right?

Elizabeth: Right – I was the Office Manager for a team of architects – and that kept me in salads, and a whole lot else...

Egon: That's my girl.

Being Authentic

Elizabeth: Yeah, it was good – until the recession hit, and the firm went belly-up, 'cause nothing was being built anymore – except prisons, maybe. Meanwhile I was out of a job.

Elizabeth: I looked for work, like everyone else. I did what I could – odd jobs, when I could find them. A little of this and a little of that. Whatever paid.

Egon: Sounds practical to me.

Angela: Listen to that! According to Daddy, you're not only determined, but practical.

Egon: Fair is fair. I call 'em as I see 'em.

Elizabeth: It sounds like you're surprised.

Egon: Not surprised, really – just interested. I mean, since you've been more of less out of touch for the past six years...

Elizabeth: I called you from time to time.

Egon: Not a hell of a lot, Liz. There were times we didn't know whether you were still breathing.

Elizabeth: I'm really sorry I didn't call more often. It must have worried the hell out of you both.

Egon: Well now, you're here, so don't fret about it. Now I can catch up with you and make up for lost time.

Elizabeth: Too bad you couldn't have started seven years ago.

Egon: What's that supposed to mean?

Elizabeth: Nothing, Dad. Forget about it.

Egon: Well, maybe I can ask you a question, Liz.

Angela: Be careful Egon. Don't start anything.

Egon: It's just an innocent question.

Elizabeth: Really?

Egon: I mean, we're glad to have you home, and all that. But why *did* you come home?

> *Silence*

I mean, to hear you talk, you've been doing great, whatever it is you've been doing. Why break it up to spend time with us?

Angela: Maybe she's homesick or something; who cares? She's here, isn't she?

Egon: You've been homesick, Elizabeth? Is that it?

Elizabeth: If I said yes, would you believe me?

Egon: Not really. As I remember it, homesickness is why you left here.

Angela: What?!

Egon: She wasn't sick *for* home, Angie, she was sick *of* it.

Angela: Egon! What a thing to say!

Egon: I may have a ton of faults, Angie, but lying's not one of them. As I say, I call 'em as I see 'em.

Elizabeth: You're right about that, Dad. Whatever else can be said about you, you're certainly authentic. What we see is what we get.

Egon: I'm not sure if that's a compliment or not.

Being Authentic

Elizabeth: It means you don't pretend to be something you're not. You're true to yourself – regardless of the consequences.

Egon: So is that a compliment?

Elizabeth: If you'd like it to be.

Angela: I'm sure it is a compliment.

Egon: Well then, I'm grateful.

Elizabeth: I'd like to be authentic, too – as much as I can be under the circumstances. So I need to tell you that if I had anywhere else to go, I would have gone there instead of here.

Angela: Oh, Lizzie...

Elizabeth: Home is where they have to take you in, isn't that what they say? We'll see if it's true.

Angela: Darling! Why on earth wouldn't we want to take you in?

Elizabeth: Maybe Dad will come up with something.

Angela: That's silly, dear.

Egon: What's the matter? Have you done something wrong?

Silence

Elizabeth: I managed to pay for the rent and the groceries. If that was wrong, then I did wrong.

Egon: How did you get the money – after the office manager job, I mean?

Elizabeth: I told you.

Egon: Not really. All you said was, "a little of this and a little of that."

Elizabeth: Well…that's what it was.

Egon: Could you maybe give us an idea of "a little of this", or maybe even a sample of "a little of that"?

Elizabeth: No.

Egon: What d'ya mean, no?

Elizabeth: What I mean is – with all due respect – that it's none of your business.

Egon: None of my…?!

He looks at her incredulously

Elizabeth: You heard me. If I'm to be subjected to the third degree…

She stands up, her voice rising

If I'm to be cross-examined like a goddam criminal—

Egon: (interrupting) Don't use that language.

Elizabeth: I'll use the language I want.

Egon: Not while I'm sitting at the head of the table.

Elizabeth: I don't care where the fuck you are sitting, it's my language and I'll use it.

Egon: That will be enough! I will not have you dirty my home with that sort of talk.

Elizabeth: So I dirty your home, do I? It was a mistake for me to come here.

Egon: Perhaps it was.

Elizabeth: I'm leaving.

Being Authentic

Egon: (producing his wallet) Here's some money for a cab.

Elizabeth: You can keep your money, and stuff it where the sun doesn't shine!

She storms out of the room.

Angela: Now you've done it.

Egon: *I've* done it?

Angela: You kept provoking her, asking questions she clearly didn't want to answer. You went over the line – way over it.

Egon: Well, she came in with an attitude!

Angela: Really? Well let me tell you something, Mr. Egon Bricker: If our daughter walks out that door because of you, I won't be far behind.

Egon: What are you saying?

Angela: I will leave you. Is that clear enough?

Egon: You'd do that?

Angela: In a heartbeat.

Egon: Am I allowed to say that little miss high-and-mighty aggravates the hell out of me?

Angela: If she does, it's because she reminds you of *you,* my dear, and you can't stand it. And I don't blame you. If I were you, I couldn't stand myself either.

A fraught silence

Egon: I'm sorry, Angela.

Angela: I'm not the one you have to apologize to.

Egon: You want me to apologize to that...*whatsis*?

Angela: That...*whatsis* happens to be your daughter, whom I love. Yes, you have to apologize to her – more than that: you have to beg her forgiveness.

Egon: Whoa – beg her forgiveness, now?!

Angela: If you don't want to lose me.

Egon: You've been threatening to leave me for years. How do you know I still care?

Angela: I *don't* know.

> *Enter ELIZABETH with a suitcase in each hand. She strides to the door and places the suitcases down so she can open the door.*

Elizabeth: Goodbye you two. Have a nice life.

Egon: Wait a minute, Lizzie – I want to say something.

> *ELIZABETH pauses*

Elizabeth: Say it.

Egon: I'm sorry for what happened. I was outta line. Hey – you gotta forgive me.

Elizabeth: Wow. Did Mom put those words into your mouth?

Egon: Well...

Angela: I told him he'd better say something very much like it.

Elizabeth: Oh, Mommy...

Angela: I don't want to live in a house where my only child's not welcome. This is your home too, Lizzie, but you've been here only ninety minutes. Please don't leave. Don't break my heart.

Elizabeth: I don't want to be where I'm not wanted.

Angela: Well, I want you.

Elizabeth: Dad doesn't.

Angela: Sure he does. He loves you, believe it or not, and he'd tell you himself, if he weren't so damn pig-headed. Come on, dear. You need a hug – and I do, too.

They embrace

Elizabeth: (quietly) Thank you.

Egon: I'll just take these things back upstairs.

EGON exits with the bags

Angela: Come, Lizzie. Sit down next to me.

ELIZABETH sits

There, darling, isn't this much better?

Elizabeth: Dad will be down soon.

Angela: I doubt it. He's too humiliated.

Elizabeth: For having to apologize to me?

Angela: Yes, among other things.

Elizabeth: Such as...?

Angela: Having to admit he needs someone. For Daddy, needing anyone is a weakness. He wants to be above all that.

Elizabeth: Nobody's above all that. I know I'm not.

Angela: Oh, darling, I'm so glad you've come home. As long as I draw breath, this is your home. Seven years ago, when you left, this place went dark like a mausoleum. But when you walked in that door an hour and a half ago, the light came back. Did you notice at supper I lit the candles?

Elizabeth: They seemed more beautiful than ever.

Angela: They were lit for the first time in seven years. When you were gone, I didn't have the heart to light them, but I kept polishing those silver candlesticks anyway, once a month, religiously. I just knew that someday you would return, and when you did I wanted them ready and shining. I knew how you loved them.

Elizabeth: (quietly) I'm glad you still love me – despite everything.

Angela: I don't know what "everything" is, but it doesn't matter. I'll never stop loving you – no matter what – nor will Daddy, if the truth be known.

Elizabeth: The truth?! The truth is Dad has never told me he loves me – not once.

Angela: Of course not, silly; he's a man – what do you expect? It's not easy for men to express emotions. The most I ever got from *my* father was, "You're a good girl, and I like you." But I knew what that meant, and I treasured it.

Beat

Elizabeth: Mom, I need to tell you something, and I need you to promise me you won't tell Dad.

Angela: Your father and I have never kept secrets from each other.

Elizabeth: Please, just this once, until I'm ready to tell him?

Angela: But what if you're never ready to tell him?

Elizabeth: He'll figure it out for himself. In not too long, it'll be obvious.

Angela: (after a pause) Oh god.

Being Authentic

Elizabeth: That's right. I'm pregnant.

Silence

Angela: Oh god.

Elizabeth: You've said that.

Angela: (quietly) I should never have let you go.

Elizabeth: There was nothing you could have done about it – short of locking me up.

Angela: This is my punishment.

Elizabeth: For what? Having me as your daughter?

Angela: No – of course not.

Elizabeth: It sounded that way to me.

Angela: You took it the wrong way. I meant something else.

Elizabeth: What?

Silence

Why are you being punished?

Angela: I suppose Hank is the father?

Elizabeth: I'm not getting an answer.

Angela: Nor will you – for now, anyway. But tell me, Lizzie: Is Hank the father?

Elizabeth: No. After we split I never saw him again. Which in some ways was a relief. Especially after I wished him luck, and he said what a mistake he had made and what could he have been thinking of?

Angela: You poor kid. I never had to suffer a rejection like that.

Elizabeth: You were never rejected?

Angela: I never wanted anyone 'til I met your father. And when I knew he wanted me, that was it. My world was made.

Elizabeth: Lucky you.

Angela: In some ways. I've never had to worry about his leaving me. Oh no—not old faithful. All his devotion, his pig-headed stubbornness—they're all mine so long as I can stand him.

Elizabeth: You no longer love Daddy?

Angela: Well, I can still stand him—I suppose. Which means I must still love him—don't you think?

Elizabeth: How long has it been like this?

Angela: At least fifteen years.

Elizabeth: How have you managed?

Angela: You pick your battles—like I did with your father just now. If you had walked out of here, I would have, too—and he knew it. As for the less important stuff, you just seem to acquiesce, like a docile, submissive little mouse, and let the man think he's the big thing.

Elizabeth: Not an ideal partnership!

Angela: No. But it works.

Elizabeth: I had hoped that Hank and I would do so much better. I was crazy about him, but apparently the feeling wasn't mutual.

Angela: That must have been a very lonely feeling.

Elizabeth: It was. But I got over it.

Being Authentic

Angela: After all that.

Elizabeth: Yeah, after all that. I never saw him again, so it couldn't have been him.

Angela: Well then, who?

Elizabeth: (forcing a smile) I can't say for sure.

Angela: What do you mean, you can't say for sure?

Elizabeth: Just what I said. What part of "I can't say for sure" don't you understand?

Angela: I see.

Elizabeth: What d'ya see, Mommy? That your daughter's a...a tramp – and you're ashamed of me?

Angela: Not a bit. I love you, period. But I see...that you're in more trouble than I thought. If you don't know who the father is, you can't count on his support when the time comes. Maybe you could try to establish paternity with DNA, or something?

Elizabeth: Oh, come on, Mom! Even if I could locate these guys, even if I could force the DNA test on 'em, it wouldn't be worth the effort. No matter who the father turned out to be, I couldn't count on his support for shit. Not the kind of men I've been seeing.

Angela: I'm glad your father isn't hearing all this.

Elizabeth: But it's okay for *you* to hear?

Angela: Absolutely. I may not like what I hear, but I need to know it. As for Daddy...he's going to *have* to know, some time. We can't keep it from him forever; he's going to have to learn...*all* of it. But not right away. We don't have to rush to tell him. We'll start to let him know when the time is right.

Elizabeth: And when will that be?

Angela: I'll know. I always know. In the meantime, we've got to decide what to do about that baby inside you. I imagine you've been thinking a lot about it.

Elizabeth: I think of nothing else.

Angela: And...?

Elizabeth: I've got to get rid of it.

Angela: Oh, no.

Elizabeth: I don't want it.

Angela: I do.

Elizabeth: What? Are you going to bring it up?

Angela: I'll sure help! You're going to need to finish High School, go to College, and—

Elizabeth: *(interrupting)* College, huh? And who's going to pay for that?

Angela: Your father and I will. Along with any child care expenses that might come up. We'll do it gladly.

Elizabeth: Gladly?! I don't see Daddy being glad about it.

Angela: Believe me: He'll be a lot happier than if you get an abortion. You know how he is about things like that.

Elizabeth: Yeah—I sure do. And how do you think he'll react when he sees me pregnant, but not sure who the father is?

Angela: Leave Daddy's reaction to me.

Elizabeth: Why can't I just have an abortion and leave to you Daddy's reaction to *that?*

Angela: You really don't want this child, do you?

Elizabeth: I'd just as soon not let it see the light of day. Its name is *Disgrace*.

Angela: Wrong name. Its name should be *Hope*—for the future, and what he or she might bring to it.

Elizabeth: Very pretty.

Angela: Look, Elizabeth: did you think you could come home, tell me this news, and somehow have me spirit you away, and pay for your secret abortion while your father thinks you're visiting friends or something? It won't work.

Elizabeth: Why not?

Angela: Because I have never lied to your father for long, never hid anything from him for long, and I don't propose to start now. Our marriage isn't perfect, but I have never faked a thing, nor has your father. I won't risk that for anything.

Elizabeth: Not even for your daughter?

Angela: Why should I have any more concern for *my* child than she has for *hers*?

Elizabeth: So that if I had an abortion, you'd let me starve?

Angela: Of course not. I'd love you anyway. I was exaggerating to make a point.

Elizabeth: Well, you've made it.

Angela: I hope you understand me, Elizabeth: If you were starving, with no realistic hope for support, then to bring a child into that world might be...a problem. But here you have parents who love you, and who would cherish a grandchild, and who have the means to support it as long as required. For you to punish yourself for past mistakes is unwise. But to punish your child is immoral, and I will not be a party to it.

Elizabeth: I can't be pushed on this thing. I need time to think it out.

Angela: How far along are you?

Elizabeth: Two months, I think.

Angela: Then you better figure it out quickly—you don't have much time.

Elizabeth: I've come to the wrong place.

Angela: You've come to exactly the right place.

Elizabeth: You have over me the power of the purse, but you cannot make me do anything—or *not* do anything—against my will. Nobody can. I'll make up my own mind on it.

Angela: Oh god—stubborn as ever—just like your father.

Enter EGON

Egon: Well then, I suppose you two have been talking about Roger?

Elizabeth: Roger?! No, we haven't. What about him?

Egon: Uh oh. I guess I let the cat out of the bag. But I figured, Angela, you'd have mentioned Roger since he'll be arriving any minute.

Elizabeth: Oh, my god! With me looking like this?

ELIZABETH rushes out, as ANGELA calls to her:

Angela: You look fine, dear!

Being Authentic

Egon: Well at least she wants to look her best for Roger. That's a good sign. But you could have mentioned the subject a little earlier.

Angela: So could you.

Egon: But you were the one who did all the arranging. The news would come more naturally from you.

Angela: The time didn't seem right.

Egon: But you would have thought that the ideal time would be when you two were alone.

Angela: (with exaggerated patience) Yes Egon, you would have thought. But it didn't work out that way.

Egon: So what *did* you talk about?

Angela: Nothing much. Except I said to her that in all our married life you and I have never hid anything from each other.

Egon: True enough. But what brought that on?

She considers her answer

Angela: It couldn't have been more trivial. She told me she's on a diet, but she didn't want you to know, lest you take it as her admitting that she has gained weight. She's very sensitive about it. So do us all a favor and don't mention that she has filled out, regardless of how she looks.

Egon: Women! I meant it as a compliment. I think she looks great.

Angela: She does. Just don't mention the weight thing for a while.

Egon: You got it.

Beat

So you were telling her that you never hide anything from me, is that right?

Angela: That's right.

Egon: That means a lot to me. I'm very proud that you trust me, and that you tell me everything.

Angela: Yes. Sooner or later I tell you the whole truth.

Egon: Sooner or later?

Angela: Oh sure. Remember that traffic ticket?

Egon: Oh, right.

Angela: I knew I was going to have to tell you sooner or later—I just had to wait for the right time.

Egon: Yeah. Like after I landed the Boleslavsky contract—for the first time, a whole house to build—a McMansion! I was on cloud nine for a week!

Angela: The perfect time to spring the ticket on you. You barely gave it a thought.

Egon: True enough. We do all right together.

Angela: We've done pretty well.

Egon: Not so well when it comes to Liz, I'm afraid. If I had been more flexible with her, gone with the flow a little, she might not have run off.

Angela: Perhaps.

Beat

But look: now she's home. Maybe the jury's still out on whether we've done a good job there.

Being Authentic

Enter ELIZABETH. She has done up her hair, put on a little make up, and exchanged her blue jeans for a blue denim skirt, over which her blouse still hangs loosely, as before.

Egon: Wow – what a change! And in record time.

Elizabeth: I take it that Roger isn't here yet.

Egon: Not yet. But he should be here any moment.

Elizabeth: So you said. I've been away from this place for almost seven years, yet less than two hours after I return, Roger is expected! What a coincidence! Or is it?

Angela: It's no coincidence, Lizzie. As soon as I heard that you were coming home, I phoned him.

Elizabeth: For heaven's sake, why?

Angela: Because he asked me to. Not long after you ran off, he called and wanted to speak to you. Of course I told him that you had left with Hank—

Elizabeth: (interrupting) Oh god!

Angela: (patiently) And that you were heading south where Hank had a job waiting for him. Roger seemed taken aback, but then he asked us to keep him informed about you. And after each of the few times you called us, I sent him an email letting him know what you were up to...

Egon: What little we knew of it...

Angela: And when you stopped calling us, I stopped emailing him. But we would see him every so often around town, or at the mall, and he'd ask how you were doing. And we'd have to say that we had no idea. And he would say, "if you ever hear from her, let me know." So when we learned that you were coming home, I took it upon myself to give him a call, and I said you'd be home from Galveston today on the 4:45 bus.

Elizabeth: All that? Why didn't you tell him the story of my life while you were at it?

Egon: Be nice to your mother.

Angela: I don't see anything wrong in what I said.

Elizabeth: There wouldn't have been – if Roger didn't know me, and was never likely to see me again. But he does know me, and I'm seeing him in a minute or two!

Angela: I meant no harm.

Elizabeth: Oh god. Don't worry about it, Mom: I tend to make mountains out of molehills.

Angela: It's in the past. We love you.

Elizabeth: So you told Roger when I was coming in...

Angela: I did, I said so.

Elizabeth: And what did he say?

Angela: He said would we mind if he showed up at the house early this evening, and I said of course we wouldn't mind.

Elizabeth: No, of course you wouldn't.

Egon: Be *nice*.

Elizabeth: I'm sorry for breathing!

Angela: Take it easy, Liz. What did I know? Roger had seemed to be very persistent all these years. I had no idea you had a thing going with him.

128

Elizabeth: I didn't. I don't.

Angela: No?

Elizabeth: Mother, there's nothing between Roger and me. Never was. He's a very nice guy, and all that – he was talking about going to seminary right after High School. He was thinking of the priesthood.

Angela: I didn't know he was Catholic.

Elizabeth: He's not – he's Episcopal. Not that it mattered much to me. I couldn't understand half of what he was saying anyway; he bored the crap out of me.

The doorbell rings

Angela: Well, apparently you didn't bore him, because here he is.

Elizabeth: Oh god – after a forty-four hour bus trip I now have to put up with Roger?

Angela: Shall I send him away?

Elizabeth: No! Since he's come all this way, I might as well see him.

Egon: Don't do us any favors.

Elizabeth: No – I'd like to.

The doorbell rings again

Egon: Will someone answer the door?

Angela: (to Elizabeth) Why don't you, darling?

Elizabeth: (as she rises and goes to the door) No rest for the weary.

She opens the door.

Roger Whitehead! It's been a long time!

Pause

Roger: May I come in?

Elizabeth: Of course! Sorry! Come right in.

He does

Roger, of course you know my mother and father.

Roger: (to Egon and Angela) You're the perfect parents. Whenever I came over to help Liz with calculus, you said something polite and disappeared.

Angela: (to Roger) It's been a long while since those calculus days, and you haven't changed a bit.

Roger: Sorry to hear it.

Angela: I meant you're still as good looking and athletic as you were then. But you know what? Egon and I have something to cook up in the kitchen.

Egon: The kitchen?

Angela: Yes, Egon. Where else would we cook up something?

Egon: Ah, the kitchen! Of course.

He rises

Excuse us.

Angela: Bye.

EGON and ANGELA disappear into the kitchen, after which ROGER laughs

Roger: They haven't changed a bit either.

ELIZABETH and ROGER laugh together

Elizabeth: One thing has changed: you're not here to help me with calculus – or are you?

Roger: I hope not.

Elizabeth: Good. Then to what do I owe the honor? No, wait – let me guess: you're here to convert me.

Roger: To what?

Elizabeth: Episcopalianism?

Roger: Certainly not. I'm not in the Episcopal business anymore.

Elizabeth: Not at all?

Roger: Not one bit. I've dropped out of seminary.

Elizabeth: Really? Why? Wasn't it important to you?

Roger: I suppose it was...once upon a time. But when my mother took a turn for the worse...

Elizabeth: Oh, I'm sorry to hear that...

Roger: Thanks. Well, when that happened, I took a leave of absence; Mother needed me more than the Church...

He shakes his head

I was holding her hand when she passed.

Elizabeth: Oh, Roger, I'm so sorry!

Roger: Thank you.

Elizabeth: You were so devoted to her.

Roger: Yeah. Well, nothing is forever.

Elizabeth: Your faith must have been a big help to you.

Roger: Not really. Nowadays, the only time I go to church is when my friends get married in one.

Elizabeth: Oh my god.

Roger: As it were.

Elizabeth: So…you gave up on Heaven.

Roger: True.

Elizabeth: And you figured you'd go looking in the opposite direction?

Roger: Towards Hell, you mean?

Elizabeth: Exactly. And you've come to visit me.

Roger: You're living in Hell?

Elizabeth: Have been for years.

Roger: Interesting.

Elizabeth: Very. Have you come to show me a way out of Hell? Is that your purpose?

Roger: I hadn't thought of that. No, I've come simply to see you. No other purpose.

Elizabeth: Were you always so irrational? In High School you seemed like such a sensible guy.

Roger: You weren't paying attention.

Elizabeth: It wouldn't have been the first time. But if I had been paying attention, what would I have seen?

Roger: My forlorn self, mumbling in my milk, "This girl is so attractive, so exciting, what does one have to do to get a date with her?"

Elizabeth: Well, for starters, one could ask. That's always helpful.

Roger: Too easy – and too hard. I was floored by the existential ramifications of the act.

Elizabeth: The act of asking?

Roger: The act of asking *you.*

Elizabeth: Existential?

Roger: You don't want to know. But I've worked through them all. So – here goes:

He clears his throat

Elizabeth, would you like to go to the movies with me?

Elizabeth: You say goodbye to god and hello to *me* – is that it?

Roger: That's putting the worst face on it.

Elizabeth: Is there a better face for it?

Roger: I've gotten up the courage to do what I ought to have done seven years ago – if it's not too late. I could use some company – and I thought of you.

Elizabeth: Why me? There are plenty of others who'd show you a better time.

Roger: I haven't been able to think of any.

Elizabeth: You lack imagination.

Roger: Among other things. You might not want anyone like me.

Elizabeth: More to the point: you might not want anyone like *me.*

Roger : How do you know what I want?

Elizabeth: I know what most men want.

Roger: I'm not like most men. I just want to go to the movies.

Elizabeth: What? You come here, behold my glamorous self, and all you want is to go to the movies?

Roger: That's all I'll admit to.

Elizabeth: Aha – I thought so.

Roger: What will you admit to?

Elizabeth: Wanting to know a little more about you. You said you were running from god—

Roger: (interrupting) No way. How can I run from something that doesn't exist?

Elizabeth: *Touché.* You weren't running from god – you just stopped looking.

Roger: Much better.

Elizabeth: So you stopped looking. Which meant that suddenly you had a whole lot of time on your hands.

Roger: True.

Elizabeth: So how did you fill the time?

Roger: Looking for something to look for.

Elizabeth: It would have been better to pretend god existed. It would have been easier.

Roger: Too easy – and too hard.

Elizabeth: With you, is everything too easy – and too hard?

Roger: I told you that you might not want anyone like me.

Elizabeth: Ah – so you think you've won the title, have you?

Roger: What title?

Elizabeth: The most boring person in the world?

Roger: I'm used to it.

Elizabeth: Well don't be. That title belongs to me; I've achieved nothing. Whereas you – you're not going to tell me that you've been twiddling your thumbs all this time, are you?

Roger: Far from it. I found a group of young men who needed a basketball coach.

Elizabeth: Do you know anything about basketball?

Roger: As it happens, that's one of my sports.

Elizabeth : You have others?

Roger: I also do a bit of wrestling. But don't tell anyone about either. I don't want to spoil my image as an intellectual.

Elizabeth: You've already spoiled it. Doesn't the team know the truth about you?

Roger: They know I'm passionate about basketball. They have no idea about the rest.

Elizabeth: So long as they win, they probably don't care.

Roger: You may be right. Because when my team started winning, a lot of young men became interested. And one thing led to another...

Elizabeth: It usually does...

Roger: And what we've ended up with is a community center, with not only sports, but arts. In fact, as we speak, the theatre wing is preparing a staging of O'Neill's The Emperor Jones.

Elizabeth: Well that settles that.

Roger: Now you know I'm not the one you want?

Elizabeth: On the contrary: I know that I'm not the one *you* want.

Roger: What's the matter – you've something against basketball?

Elizabeth: No – I like it a lot.

Roger: Maybe you hate the arts?

Elizabeth : I love them!

Roger: What's the problem, then?

A moment while she formulates her answer

Elizabeth: It must have been hard work shaping up these boys into a team.

Roger: Yes it was. So what?

Elizabeth: Hear me out. Some of these kids must have been failing in school, and yet somehow you got them to focus.

Roger: Well, I made it a condition that they had to improve in school in order to play on the team. And they did both. So what?

Elizabeth: You fuckin' saved their lives.

Roger: They saved themselves. All I did was settle for nothing but their best.

Elizabeth: Oh – is that all? A mere nothing like that?

Roger: All right – it was a wrestling match, I admit it. But I'm stubborn; I like wrestling matches, and I don't give up.

Elizabeth: Oh god. I'm definitely not the one you want.

Roger: For Christ's sake! What is the problem?

Being Authentic

Elizabeth: You. You're way out of my league, buster. You may stay away from churches, but you've made a god-spot of your own – the community center.

Roger: Don't make too much of it. You've seen only the face I show to newsmen and donors. You haven't seen my office. My desk is piled high with a mess of papers – it's worse than disorganized – it's chaos in there!

Elizabeth: So how can you get through the day?

Roger: I wonder myself. And then – there are the warts.

Elizabeth: You have warts?

Roger: Figuratively speaking – plenty of them.

Elizabeth: Tell me a few.

Roger: Now wait a minute. I've been telling you all sorts of things about myself, and you haven't said one word about you.

Elizabeth: You've noticed that, have you?

Roger: I'd have to be comatose not to. I tell you what: I'll mention something not so pretty about me, on condition that you follow with something not so pretty about you. Are you game?

Elizabeth: Shoot.

Roger: Okay – here's something not so pretty: Every morning, after breakfast, I floss my teeth in the kitchen.

Elizabeth: Ewww!

Roger: I told you it wasn't pretty.

Elizabeth: That you did.

Roger: Now it's your turn.

Elizabeth: You want unpretty? How about this: Every so often I clip my toe nails, but instead of throwing them out, I put them in a bottle, and when I've saved twenty or thirty of the things, then I go and—

Roger: (interrupting) Too much information, too much information!

Elizabeth: Are you grossed out?

Roger: Totally.

Elizabeth: Good!

Roger: Why good?

Elizabeth: Because I'm not wholesome, and I want you to know it. I want to try to be as authentic as possible – even if it means grossing you out.

Roger: Oh, come on. I'm not as grossed out as all that. Did you think you'd repel me with this? Even the most fastidious people have a gross-out factor; their partners just learn to put up with it.

Elizabeth: But the toenails, Roger!

Roger: Well yes: Saving and using one's clipped toe-nails is – shall we say – a bit unusual. But in the larger scheme of things it doesn't mean much.

Elizabeth: Good of you. And I have to say the same about flossing in the kitchen. There are worse things. I hesitate to think what they are, but I'm sure that there have to be worse things. Somewhere...

She shudders

there have to be.

138

Being Authentic

Roger: Well of course there are: character flaws.

Elizabeth: Are you about to tell me one of yours? I hope so. I don't want you pretending to be perfect. I want you authentic.

Roger: Do you still think I'm out of your league?

Elizabeth: I fear that you are very much out of my league – in spite of the dental floss.

Roger: Then I must disabuse you by telling you one of my character flaws – provided of course, that you tell me one of yours. If I'm going to be authentic, then you must be authentic, too.

ELIZABETH laughs

Elizabeth: This is like a game we used to play as children – I'll show you mine if you'll show me yours. Did you play that game?

Roger: I was too bashful. Which brings me to my character flaw: I'm morbidly shy. I can't get up the courage to ask a girl out on a date.

Elizabeth: You just did with me.

Roger: But look how long it took me – seven years!

Elizabeth: You must not get around very much.

Roger: Sexually? Not at all. I'm twenty-four years old, and I can guarantee that everyone else my age has more experience than I do – they would have to.

Elizabeth: That must feel lonely.

Roger: It does.

She looks at him

Elizabeth: Forgive me for suggesting this, but maybe you've chosen the wrong gender to be interested in?

Roger: I've thought of that. But I've learned that I am definitely not interested in men. No way. Women are what interest me – or would, if I could get up the nerve. I was always backward in that department. In junior high, my mother told me I better start dating right away, lest I marry the first girl who was nice to me – and she added that she would hate the girl no matter who she was, since in her opinion no girl was good enough for me.

He thinks about it.

Poor Mom. Through her illness I spent every spare moment with her, since to me, it was unthinkable to date while my mother was in so much pain. And even after her passing I've waited, because I've had the idea – it's crazy I know – that to link up with a woman too soon after Mom's death would be...disrespectful. And the trouble is, the longer I wait, the bigger deal it becomes, and the harder it is to...make progress, if you know what I mean.

Elizabeth: I happen to know exactly what you mean.

Roger: You do?

Elizabeth: Of course. It was the same for me getting up the nerve to come home. At first, the difficulty seemed a relatively minor bump in the road, but seven years later it had grown as big as a mountain.

Roger: When you finally did get home, was it as bad as you'd feared?

Being Authentic

Elizabeth: Actually, no it wasn't...now that I think of it. Not nearly. And Roger, when you find the one who's right for you, you'll feel that your hill of difficulties has become—

Roger: (interrupting) A smooth and level plain, is that it?

Elizabeth: More likely, your hill of difficulties will become...a mountain of delight.

ROGER takes this in

Roger: You're a lovely person.

Elizabeth: Hardly. I'm at least as bad as everyone else. Probably worse.

Roger: Ah – you're about to tell me one of your character flaws?

Elizabeth: I have to go through that?

Roger: I thought so.

Elizabeth: I never promised you I would.

Roger: It never occurred to me that you wouldn't. That would be unfair, and I could never imagine you like that.

Elizabeth: Well, since you put it that way, I must tell you...do I really have to go through with this?

Roger: Well, you said that you wanted to be authentic.

Elizabeth: Yes, I did say that.

Roger: I want to hold you to it.

She summons the nerve

Elizabeth: Okay: I have a character flaw which is the opposite of yours.

Roger: Opposite of flossing?

Elizabeth: No – opposite of not getting around. You say you get around too little. But I've been around too much.

Roger: You've plenty of experience?

Elizabeth: Enough for us both – more than enough.

Roger: I'm glad, actually. At least one of us should know what we're doing.

Elizabeth: I don't think you understand what I'm getting at.

Roger: I don't?

Elizabeth: I'm afraid not.

> *She pats her womb*

I have a baby in here. And I have no idea who the father is. Not even a clue.

> *a brief pause, while he swallows that. Then he takes a breath.*

Roger: (matter of factly) All right.

Elizabeth: You don't seem upset.

Roger: Well – things happen.

Elizabeth: Yeah, they happen.

Roger: So, do you have any plans?

Elizabeth: What's it to you?

Roger: I'm interested.

Elizabeth: And that entitles you? Do you have a need to know?

> *ROGER rises*

Roger: I see I've upset you. I'm sorry. My timing is off.

> *He turns to go*

Being Authentic

Elizabeth: No, don't go. I'm the one who was rude. I'm sorry.

Roger: No apology needed. This is rough.

Elizabeth: Tell me about it.

Roger: No. You tell me about it.

Elizabeth: I'll ask you a question: Should I abort this pregnancy?

Roger: I can't tell you what I would do, because I'll never get pregnant.

Elizabeth: Fair enough. But as my friend...?

Roger: As your friend I'd support you whatever you chose.

Elizabeth: Yes, that's what I'd expect my friends to say – if I had any.

Roger: I hope you have me.

Elizabeth: Thanks.

Roger: So – about the abortion: How are you leaning?

Elizabeth: Towards the abortion. If I didn't, then every time I looked at my baby's face I'd remember how he was conceived. The whole scene.

Roger: But you said that you had no idea who the father is.

Elizabeth: I don't, but no matter who the father might have been, the scene with all of them was the same.

Roger: Then why did you ask if you should have an abortion? Isn't your mind already made up?

Elizabeth: I'm torn, obviously – who wouldn't be? Ending a life – no matter how undeveloped – isn't easy to think about, much less to do! But the truth is that I resent this baby. Isn't that horrible? I resent it. And if I should carry it to term, do you think I'd cease resenting it once it was born?

Roger: That has happened to others. They even grow to love it.

Elizabeth: I can't imagine it happening to me. I'd be too dependent on my parents – dependent for everything. How could I love anyone if I didn't love myself?

Roger: Dependency is that bad?

Elizabeth: On the surface, no. My mother has promised that they'd support us, help look after the baby, pay for my education until I could get my feet under me. She wants this baby. Unlike me.

Roger: What about your father? Does he want it?

Elizabeth: He doesn't even know I'm pregnant - yeah, that's right – and it must be kept from him as long as possible.

Roger: Oh boy.

Elizabeth: Yeah, some situation. You can see why I'm tempted to get it over with and bury my shame along with the baby.

Roger: Do you really think that if the baby died, your shame would die with it?

Elizabeth: No, of course not. I'd still feel it – perhaps worse than ever. I'd know. But nobody else would know – except my parents, of course...oh god! Whatever choice I make is going to be wrong in somebody's eyes – my own, especially.

Being Authentic

Roger: Look, here's what I think: it's your body, and your life. I'd like to be involved in both, of course, but what you do is your choice. Whatever choice you make, I'll support it.

Elizabeth: You *say* all the right things...

Roger: Well, I don't want to say the wrong thing.

Elizabeth: Yet it's obvious you'd have me go through with the pregnancy.

Roger: (carefully) What makes you say so?

Elizabeth: Questions like isn't my mind already made up, and am I sure my shame would die along with the baby. Come on. My judgment may be flawed, but I'm not stupid.

Roger: Quite the reverse: You're very sharp, and you're quite right. I do favor your going through with the pregnancy, though it's not my place to say so.

Elizabeth: You've already said so.

Roger: You forced me to say it. I would rather have not.

Elizabeth: Instead you'd rather ask clever questions which will gently maneuver me away from an abortion.

Roger: What's so bad about that?

Elizabeth: It's dishonest. Instead of encountering me authentically, person to person, you process me as if I were a client in a therapy session.

Roger: That's not fair!

Elizabeth: So now I'm unfair?

Roger: Yes! I wanted to be careful. I didn't want to drive you away!

Elizabeth: Well that's what you're doing. It would have been better if you were less slimy, and more authentic.

Roger: You want authentic? Try this: I think you feel you haven't punished yourself enough for getting pregnant, and for whatever else you did before I got here. You haven't dug a deep enough hole for yourself, and you won't be satisfied until the hole is so deep you can never climb out. Then you can complain to the world, pity poor me, for there's nothing I can do! Pity me, please!

Elizabeth: Are you finished?

Roger: Damn right I'm finished.

> *ROGER rises, goes to the door, and exits, slamming the door behind him. ELIZABETH does her best to keep her face impassive. A beat. Then we hear loud pounding on the door. At the same time, EGON and ANGELA enter. The pounding continues through the following dialogue, in which each line tumbles out before its predecessor is finished.*

Egon: What's going on here...?

Angela: Are you all right, Lizzie...?

Egon: We heard the door slam...

Angela: Who's at the door now...?

Egon: Will someone open it? Okay, I'll open the damned door...

Elizabeth: (rising and going to the door) No, no! It's for me – I'll get it!

> *ELIZABETH opens the door.*

Elizabeth: Roger.

Angela: Roger?

Egon: Roger?

Roger: You got it; that's my name.

Elizabeth: Roger, what are you—

Egon: (interrupting) What's going on here, Roger?

ROGER enters

Roger: You may well ask.

Egon: I did ask.

Roger: It's easy to explain…very easy…

Egon: Well, then, explain.

Roger: Okay, here it is: Elizabeth had agreed to go out on a date with me to the movies, when I realized that I had left my cell phone in the car. So I ran out to get it.

Egon: I'm almost afraid to ask this, but why do you need a cell phone to make a date?

Roger: Because I keep my social calendar on that phone. It's a smart phone. Smarter than I am, apparently, because when I got back I discovered that I had locked myself out. So I banged on the door.

Angela: But you seemed to be leaving in a huff. I mean, we heard the door slam.

Roger: You're right, I was angry.

Elizabeth: (warning) Roger…

Roger: I was angry at myself, for having left the cell phone in the car. I had come over for the express purpose of making a date with Elizabeth, but when I reached for the phone to find a good day and time for us both, the phone wasn't there, and I thought to myself, you stupid fool, you leave the phone in the car just when you need it most! I was furious with myself.

Egon: It's just a cell phone. Weren't you over-reacting?

Elizabeth: (with exaggerated patience) Not nowadays, Dad. Our generation lives or dies by our cell phones.

Angela: (soothingly) Well, now that you have yours, you can arrange whatever you like.

Elizabeth: Thanks, Mom.

Angela: But first, wouldn't it be soothing to have a bit of tea?

Elizabeth: Well, I don't know…

Roger: I'm not so sure…

Angela: But it will be lovely! Won't it, Egon?

Egon: Oh yes. Lovely.

Angela: And we can have Chamomile Tea – it's so soothing. Isn't that right, Egon?

Egon: Yes. Very soothing.

Angela: You see? I'll just duck into the kitchen, and get up some Chamomile Tea, and set out some – what? Fig Newtons?

Egon: Well, *I* like 'em.

Angela: That settles it then. Chamomile Tea and Fig Newtons – coming right up. It shouldn't take too long – I have some water already heated.

She disappears into the kitchen

Being Authentic

Egon: I have to apologize for my wife: She's so enthusiastic about Chamomile Tea and Fig Newtons. Once she sees an opportunity to bring 'em out, there's no stopping her.

Roger: No need to apologize. I haven't had either in years – I'm sure it will be fine.

Elizabeth: Absolutely.

Egon: (to Roger) I want to tell you: We're not in the habit of interrupting Liz and her gentlemen callers.

Elizabeth: How could you be? I've been away for seven years. But it won't take you long to get the habit. This is the first caller I've had since I've got home, so you're getting off to a good start.

Egon: I'm really sorry about it. I'm sure you two have a lot to talk about, and the last thing you need is for old fogeys like us to break up the party.

Elizabeth: You never can tell. Maybe this interruption was exactly what we needed.

Roger: She has a point.

Egon: Couldn't agree about the movie to see, am I right?

Roger: Something like that.

Egon: Well, if you don't mind my giving advice, Roger, it's best to choose whatever your lady wants.

Roger: I'll remember that.

Egon: So, what was it, Liz? What was the movie you chose?

Elizabeth: Chose? Well I...I'm really embarrassed...I can't remember.

Egon: But that's just the point! It's not really important what you chose. You may not even remember it. But what you will remember is that whatever it was, Roger said yes.

Roger: Very good!

Egon: But the advantages don't stop there. If the movie turns out to be great, then your lady gets all the credit – which you'll be sure to give her, Roger.

Roger: Gotcha. But what happens if the movie turns out to be a stinker?

Egon: That's the best part. If the movie is a stinker, then it's all her fault!

Roger: Aha!

Egon: But you don't blame her, of course. You just let her know how forgiving you are. You say things like, anybody can make a mistake. And critics are so unreliable, nowadays – you get the picture.

Roger: I certainly do. You know, Elizabeth, your father is a fount of marital wisdom!

Elizabeth: Isn't he, though? It's really remarkable.

Egon: Not so remarkable when you consider we've been married thirty years. That should count for something.

Roger: Oh, it does, it does. It's wonderful – almost inspirational.

Egon: Inspirational? Don't overdo it. Marriage is a lot of work – a big job, like anything else.

He calls out to ANGELA

Angie! Where's the tea? I want my Fig Newtons!

Being Authentic

Voice of Angela: Coming right up, Egon – don't you worry about a thing!

Roger: (to Elizabeth) Sounds like your mother has some marital wisdom of her own.

Enter ANGELA with a tray of tea things

Egon: Ah! Looks beautiful.

Angela: Thank you, dear. (as she serves Roger) Here you go, Roger, I hope you enjoy it.

Roger: It looks wonderful. Thanks for your hospitality.

Angela: It's our pleasure.

She serves EGON

This is for you, Egon...

Egon: It looks great!

Without waiting for ANGELA to serve herself, EGON, unlike ROGER, begins sipping his tea immediately. Meanwhile, ANGELA serves ELIZABETH

Angela: This is for you, Lizzie dear...

Elizabeth: Thanks, Mom.

Taking her cue from ROGER, ELIZABETH refrains from lifting the cup to her lips, waiting until her mother does. ANGELA finally serves herself, and notices that ROGER and ELIZABETH have been waiting for her.

Angela: Oh, you two needn't have waited for me. You just make yourself at home, Roger. You too, Lizzie.

151

ROGER takes a polite bite out of a Fig Newton.

Roger: These Fig Newtons are delicious, Mrs. Bricker. No wonder your husband likes them so much.

Elizabeth: It's all so wonderful, Mom. What's even more wonderful is the time you've taken out of your busy schedule to be with us. You both have so much to do!

Egon: Not really.

Elizabeth: Oh, but Dad, don't you remember that you and Mom were going to go over the plans for the new addition?

Egon: What?

Angela: Elizabeth is quite right. We do have a lot of work to do – stupid of us to let it slip our minds – symptom of aging, I guess. Come along, Egon; take your cup and cookies, and we'll go into the kitchen.

Egon: The kitchen?

Angela: The kitchen, Egon. We'll discuss the new plans over tea. Much better that way – Roger and Elizabeth deserve their time alone together.

EGON and ANGELA go into the Kitchen

Roger: (*sotto voce*) Elizabeth, you are amazing! I was wondering how you were going to get rid of them.

Elizabeth: I take my cue from my mom. My father's a bit on the unconscious side, but my mother's very conscious. You know that act she puts on – the submissive little mousie? It's all for Dad's benefit.

Roger: I wondered. And does it work?

Elizabeth: Like a charm. It lets her plant all sorts of notions into his head which he then thinks are his own. By this time, she has probably convinced him that it was his idea to go into the kitchen and leave us alone.

Roger: Well it worked: We're alone.

Elizabeth: Yeah, we're alone

> *Beat*

Roger and Elizabeth: (in unison) Now what?

> *Surprised at this coincidence, they stare at each other.*
>
> ***BLACKOUT***

ACT TWO

The next day. Early Afternoon. Same living room. ELIZABETH is reading. Enter ANGELA

Angela: Elizabeth, I want to tell you something—

Elizabeth: (interrupting) Where's Dad?

Angela: In the upstairs office, paying bills. If he stirs, we'll hear him. But you're right: we should keep it down anyway. I just want to tell you something before you finally make up your mind about the—

Elizabeth: (interrupting) I have made up my mind, so it won't do you any good.

Angela: If it does you *some* good I'll be satisfied. May I tell you? Will you listen?

Elizabeth: I can't stop you from talking.

Angela: It has to do with your father and me. We had found out from the doctors that we could never have children together – we've told you that.

Elizabeth: Many times.

Angela: What you don't know is that the problem was with your father.

Elizabeth: I wondered.

Angela: He is infertile.

Elizabeth: I see.

Angela: He took it hard. Became very depressed – a shell of himself. I felt I was living with a ghost. There seemed to

155

be nothing I could do for him. And then one day, his good friend Andy stopped by on his way to shipping out with the Navy. He asked if he could sleep over one night, and of course we said yes.

Elizabeth: I hope I don't know where this is going.

Angela: Let me continue...while I still can. We set up the guest room for Andy, and then, in the wee hours of the morning, when your father was sound asleep, I crept out of bed and went to Andy's room. I told Andy the situation. I said that if he could get me pregnant, Egon would think the baby was his. That's what I wanted – nothing romantic, just the baby. Now Andy wasn't eager to betray his friend that way, but I assured him he'd be doing us a favor, and that it would be a secret between him and me. I finally got him to agree. So we did it, and in the morning he drove away to Baltimore where his unit was shipping out to Panama. And I got pregnant.

Elizabeth: Oh my god. You're telling me—

Angela: (interrupting) Let me finish. I began feeling guilty. The thing was – that night with Andy – I enjoyed it. I hadn't gone there to enjoy myself, but there it was: I had a good time, and another man's baby was growing inside me, and I felt miserable. I had betrayed your father, betrayed my vows...and yes, I felt I had to get rid of it.

   Silence

So I made an appointment with a clinic out of town, made up some sort of excuse to your father, and I went there. The clinic was in the City, and I took the train there. Walked in the door. There was a certain...smell. Not only of antiseptic – I knew what that was. It was

156

something else. I couldn't quite place it. It was something...well, maybe it was my imagination, but all I could think of was a butcher shop. That's what it smelled like, to me.

Silence

The nurses and orderlies all looked...hard and grim, with faces clenched like fists. But worse than that were the faces of the...the clients. They seemed to be in their own private hell. I had to look away; I had to get out of there. I went home, and told your father I was pregnant. That was enough: He was jubilant. He said that god had granted an exception for our sake – a miracle! I wasn't going to disabuse him. My reward has been you, darling, and if Daddy wants to think of you as god's gift to us, I'll never say no. He may be right.

Elizabeth: You said you never keep secrets from Egon. But you were lying. Our whole life in this house has been one great big lie.

Angela: Yes, there's been a lot of lying. But when I gave you to Egon for him to hold, my love for him was no lie. And our love for you now is no lie. I love you so much I'd like to spare you what I sensed was going on in that clinic.

Elizabeth: And spare yourself the expense of paying for my abortion?

Angela: Liz, that is so unworthy of you, and I don't deserve it. I will pay for the abortion if you still insist on it. And I will cook up more lies to cover our tracks. All I ask is that you consider what I've said before you decide. And that you never breathe a word of this to your father.

157

Elizabeth: (tremulously) Please don't call him that. He's not my father.

Angela: Yes he certainly is – he raised you and he loves you. He took it upon himself to hire a detective to search for you. When the detective found you looking okay, your father paid him off and did nothing more about it. He didn't want you to know he was spying on you. Your biological father is dead – killed in the invasion of Panama. Life isn't black and white, Liz. Give us a break. And while you're at it, give yourself a break, too. You deserve it.

> *The doorbell rings*

Elizabeth: That's Roger.

Angela: You don't need me.

> *ANGELA exits. ELIZABETH goes to the door and opens it.*

Elizabeth: (quavering) Roger! I'm so glad...

> *He enters, closes the door behind him, then puts his hand on her shoulder.*

Roger: You're shaking!

Elizabeth: I need you to hold me...

Roger: (putting his arms around her) What's the matter?

Elizabeth: Just hold me...

Roger: Did something happen?

Elizabeth: I'm not sure who I am any more, or where I am...all I know is I want to be...as true as I can. With no lying. No pretending. I want to be authentic. I want to be real.

Roger: (still holding her) You seem real to me.

Being Authentic

Elizabeth: (disengaging herself from him) You don't know...you don't know what happened.

Roger: Do you want to tell me?

Elizabeth: I wouldn't know where to start.

Roger: The beginning's a good place.

Elizabeth: You want the beginning? How about Egon's trying to interfere in my life?

Roger: Your father?

Elizabeth: Whatever you want to call him. The truth was I couldn't hack my home life, so I took off. But unlike you, it took me seven years to come back—and that only under duress.

Roger: What was going on?

Elizabeth: The typical trouble—I can't claim to be original even in that. My father disapproved of my boy friend, thought he was unreliable, said he didn't want me to see him anymore, the usual shit. And of course, I rebelled, ran off with the boy friend—what did my father know?

Roger: What *did* he know?

Elizabeth: More than I did, apparently. My thing with the boyfriend lasted two weeks, then he dumped me. I was in Alabama, a long way from here. I know I should have called Egon collect, and asked for the fare to come home.

Roger: Why didn't you?

Elizabeth: Pride. I didn't want to give him the satisfaction.

Roger: Very understandable.

Elizabeth: You're not being authentic.

Roger: What am I being?

Elizabeth: Polite. I don't want you in polite mode. I want you in authentic mode.

Roger: Last time I was in that mode, you didn't like it much.

Elizabeth: I gotta learn to deal with it.

Roger: You mean it?

Elizabeth: More than you know.

Roger: Okay, I'll be as real as I can.

Elizabeth: Thanks.

Roger: Er, tell me again: What was I supposed to be real about?

Elizabeth: My being too proud to call Egon.

Roger: Oh, right. Well, being real, I'd say that your attitude was dumb-ass stupid, and that I hope that you've grown up since then.

Elizabeth: (applauding) Bravo! That was wonderful! The truth – a breath of fresh air!

Roger: You enjoyed that? I could slap you around a little, if you'd like—maybe with a palm strike or something?

Elizabeth: Palm strike?

Roger: It's a wrestling move – looks like this.

He demonstrates against an imaginary opponent.

If you'd like, I could show you how it feels.

Elizabeth: Not right now, though it may come to that. What made you think of it?

Roger: Well, you want me to be authentic, and in your book, authentic means hurtful, apparently.

Being Authentic

Elizabeth: Oh, is that so?

Roger: Sure. When I'm nice to you, you think I'm insincere, but when I say something mean, then you think I'm telling you the truth and you believe me completely. So to please you, I might as well hit you and get it over with.

Pause

I'm being real here, you know; I'm not being nice.

Elizabeth: Tell me something I don't know.

Roger: Oh, I see I've hurt your feelings.

Elizabeth: You were being authentic. I can take it. Perhaps I can be authentic with you?

Roger: Uh-oh. Go ahead. Hit me.

Elizabeth: Of all the people who ever asked me on a date, you are the wimpiest. Compared to you, Mr. Rogers is a gangster.

Roger: Probably true – but it's you who are not being real now.

Elizabeth: What do you mean? I gave you the stiffest punch I knew how.

Roger: And I felt it! But what I'm saying is that being a bitch is not your true self.

Elizabeth: Bullshit. Nobody's more unpleasant than I am. And anybody who deals with me is going to see the unvarnished, ugly truth.

Roger: Oh, it's ugly, all right. You got that down to a science. There's only one problem.

Elizabeth: What's that?

Roger: It isn't real.

Elizabeth: Get outta town. Bitchiness is the realest thing about me.

Roger: If it were, I wouldn't have put up with you even for five minutes. But I'm sure you've got another side that you're trying desperately to conceal.

Elizabeth: And what would that side be, pray tell?

Roger: Your nurturing, caring side.

Pause

Elizabeth: How the hell would you know?

Roger: I have it on good authority.

Elizabeth: Does this authority have a name?

Roger: Norman.

Elizabeth: Norman who?

Roger: Why should it matter to you?

Elizabeth: It should matter to *you*, Roger. If Norman had a last name, it would lend credibility to this fictional character.

Roger: He's not fictional, and he does have a last name. For your information, his last name is—

Elizabeth: (interrupting) Whoa! You think quickly, don't you?

Roger: Whitehead. His last name is Whitehead.

Elizabeth: Same as yours. What a coincidence!

Roger: He's a cousin.

Elizabeth: But of course! A distant cousin, is he? Recently emigrated from Lower Slobbovia?

Being Authentic

Roger: No, he's a first cousin. Lives in Atlanta. Ever been to Atlanta?

Elizabeth: Yesterday, in fact. For a 10-minute layover on the Greyhound bus.

Roger: That's where he got on. A wonderful woman let him sit next to her, and listened to him with the patience of a saint, and when he had talked himself out, she was good enough to let him sleep on her shoulder for a long time, being careful not to wake him up until he woke by himself seven or eight hours later. He was very impressed by this woman. Said he never would have had the generosity or the patience to do the same for her, even though he found her very good looking.

Pause

He talked endlessly about this wonderful person, said he wished he had her name and address, and since your mother was good enough to tell me when you were coming in from Galveston, I put two and two together and figured out it was you. But I didn't tell him, of course. After he had detailed all your kindness, I wanted you for myself.

A considerable silence

Elizabeth: Holy shit.

Roger: Your language is improving.

Elizabeth: Give me a break.

Roger: No, I'm serious. Since god doesn't exist, it's good to know that at least certain shit can be holy.

Elizabeth: Will you stop this?

Roger: Sorry. I've stopped.

Elizabeth: Thank god.

Roger: There you go again.

Elizabeth: WILL YOU CUT THAT OUT? Just tell me if you picked up this...this cousin when he got off the bus.

Roger: I picked him up at a prearranged street corner – not in the terminal.

Elizabeth: That must have been why I didn't see you.

Roger: I had wondered whether I should try to pick you up, too – but it's a good thing I didn't. All the way to my place he kept singing the praises of the "mysterious angel" who had befriended him on the bus. You would have been very embarrassed.

Elizabeth: I'm embarrassed now. I assure you, Roger: What happened on the bus was an aberration. I'm normally not like that at all. I'm a hard-boiled egg who doesn't give a flying fuck about anything or anybody.

Roger: You'll forgive me if I don't believe you. I seem to remember there was somebody in the theatre – Ibsen or somebody – who said that a character fully reveals himself by what he does when there's nobody looking.

Elizabeth: But there were plenty of others on that bus – it was full.

Roger: But nobody knew you or cared enough to pay attention to you. And Norman didn't know you from a hole in the wall. So you let your guard down and revealed a softer side of you that you normally keep hidden, probably because you've been hurt too much to let people see it.

Being Authentic

Elizabeth: You're making too much of this.

Roger: Oh, I don't know about you, Elizabeth Bricker. You gotta be more careful about doing a kindness in public. The word might get out, and your whole reputation could be ruined!

He laughs

Elizabeth: Oh yes – very funny! Almost as funny as the fact that you're a full grown man – twenty-four years old – and still a virgin!

A silence full of her shock and his dismay

Oh! Oh! I'm so sorry – I shouldn't have said that! Forgive me – I'm so sorry!

She seizes his hand and kisses it

Roger: Please don't do that.

Elizabeth: Oh, I'm bad – don't listen to me – I'm bad!

Roger enfolds her in his arms

Roger: No, no – you're not bad, you're not bad.

She disengages herself from him

Elizabeth: But I *am* bad – you don't understand.

Roger: What don't I understand?

Elizabeth: I'm a prostitute.

Roger: A what?

Elizabeth: A PROSTITUTE! – a whore! Do you get it now?

Roger: (quietly) Prostitute.

During the next speech, she looks away from him

Elizabeth: Well, I *was* one. Down South, that's what I ended up having to do. Not at first – for a while I was okay; I managed to find work as an office manager – for architects, no less. Did pretty well at it, too – held onto that job for five years.

Silence

That was good...except...I felt exiled in a foreign country. It was my fault, of course – I was the one who had run off; I had exiled myself. But I couldn't face that – so I blamed my folks – Egon especially. I wanted to come home, but I wouldn't give him the satisfaction. I began to be angry at him for keeping me away, can you believe it? And the more I was angry, the more I hated him and the more I hated myself for it. I called them less and less. In fact, for the last six years I barely communicated with them at all. I was boxed in a coffin of my own making. It felt...so stupid...so stupid...

Roger: Poor Liz.

Elizabeth: But still I had the job as Office Manager, so I fed my ego with that. Then my boss's business failed, along with a whole lot of others in this damn recession, and for the next year and a half I simply couldn't find anything else that would both pay the rent and put food on the table. Oh, I got a few gigs as a waitress, dishwasher – that sort of thing. But they didn't pay enough to live. Of course I could have called home for money, but I was too proud...too proud... So, in my final six months, I turned tricks. And they paid a lot more, let me tell you! But after each one I'd go into the shower and scrub the slime off my body and kept telling myself, this wasn't me; it wasn't me; I was forced into it! And I kept scrubbing and scrubbing the filth off until my body felt raw. My showers took a long time, and I wasn't very productive. My pimp thought it was because I was new to the trade, but the real reason was I dreaded what my next...customer...might make me do.

Roger: Awful.

Elizabeth: Yes. And almost as bad were the lonely ones. They had nobody. They didn't need to get off so much as they needed someone to listen to them, be with them. A few stank so bad you could understand why they were alone. These poor guys had to pay money just to have someone hold them! But after I heard their stories, my heart *broke*... and I would have held them for nothing.

Roger: I believe it.

Elizabeth: So you can see that as a worker in the sex trade, I was a washout. After a while my pimp told me that if I held out on him anymore, he'd hurt me.

Roger: Terrible. What did you do?

Elizabeth: I quit. Left town. And spent almost my last dollar moving into a rat hole where I nearly gagged on the stench of urine mixing with the reek of mold. And finally, after the electricity was cut off for non-payment, at long last, I gave up. I called Egon...

  Pause

  My father.

Roger: I'm so glad.

Elizabeth: All the way home on the bus, I kept thinking, how will I be able to face anyone?

167

Roger: You can start by facing me. Look at me.

> *Gently, he turns her to face him. But she avoids looking at him, looking at the floor instead. Gently, he lifts her head so that she has to look at him.*

Look at me. Look at me. Now tell me, do I look horrified?

Elizabeth: I don't think so.

Roger: Because I heard nothing horrifying. Saddening, yes. Horrifying, no.

Elizabeth: Didn't you hear anything I said?

Roger: Oh, I heard it all. And one thing you said did stick in my mind.

Elizabeth: What was that?

Roger: You worked as an office manager.

Elizabeth: That's it? After everything I said, all you got out of it was that I worked as an office manager?

Roger: Well, much of it was a story I've heard many times before – some in versions even worse than what you told me.

Elizabeth: What could be worse?

Roger: The victims were destroyed – not physically killed, though they might just as well have been. Their souls were shattered; they had no self left.

Elizabeth: My god. I haven't sunk that low. At least not yet.

Roger: Of course you haven't; you've still got yourself, and that's to your credit.

Elizabeth: You mean, after all this, I still have something to my credit?

Being Authentic

Roger: Of course you do. You're too strong to let anyone shatter you. You got in a jam, and to get out of it you did what you had to, which is remarkable. Not everyone could.

Elizabeth: You make me sound like a heroine.

Roger: In my book, you are.

Elizabeth: Well, I'm not, though it's very kind of you to say so.

Roger: I'm not being very kind; I'm being very selfish.

Elizabeth: Aha. You have an ulterior motive?

Roger: I confess I do. There's something about your experience that deeply fascinates me.

Elizabeth: Here it comes.

Roger: I've already told you what it is. You've worked as an office manager. Now that interests me.

Elizabeth: Why? Are you going to do a study about what happens to office managers thrown out of work in a recession?

Roger: No. I'm going to ask one of them to come work for me. I told you what a mess my desk is. I need an office manager to clean it up and keep it clean. The starting pay is minimum wage, but if you work out, I'll double it at the very least. If you continue to work out I'll give you more raises. How about it?

Elizabeth: No.

Roger: No?

Elizabeth: No. I won't take charity from anyone.

Roger: Charity? You'd be doing me a favor. I can't find anybody I'd trust not to rob me blind. But you I would trust.

Elizabeth: Nothing doing.

Roger: If it's the baby you're worried about, don't worry – I'll give you plenty of maternity leave.

Elizabeth: That does it. Please leave.

Roger: What did I say?

Elizabeth: I won't be pressured to continue this pregnancy!

Roger: (beginning to lose it) You know what, Lizzie – you're crazy. CRAZY!!! There's no reasoning with you! I make you an offer you can't refuse, and you refuse it anyway!

Elizabeth: So what are you, the Godfather? Are you going to pull out your machine gun and mow me down?

Roger: You'd like that, wouldn't you! You and the baby, dead in one fell swoop, and with your last breath you scream, "I told you so, there was no saving me!" Not that I'd want to save you – you're impossible! You're driving me nuts!

Elizabeth: You get out of here or I'll scream!

Roger: (screaming himself) Go ahead, nutcase! Scream your bloody head off!

EGON and ANGELA rush in

Egon: What's going on?

Angela: Why are you shouting?

Elizabeth: I told him to leave, and he won't!

Angela & Egon: (to Roger) YOU WON'T?!

Being Authentic

Roger: I'm offering her a job, and she won't take it!

Egon: She won't?!

Elizabeth: That's my right.

Egon: (to Roger) What sort of job?

> *ROGER is still beside himself*

Roger: Office Mannequin – sorry – Office *Manager* – for my community center, which is going to wrack and ruin for lack of one.

Egon: What's the job description?

Roger: Maintaining Accounts Payable and Receivable, tracking physical assets, keeping my appointment schedule – that sort of thing.

Angela: (suspicious) Would those be *all* her duties?

Roger: Absolutely. You have my word as an ex-Episcopalian. At five o'clock, she'd be free to go home, having made a few bucks and done a world of good.

Angela: And would the hours be flexible enough so she could continue her education?

Roger: Of course. They would allow for that, and any other non-work priority...such as, for example...

Elizabeth: (warning) Roger...

Roger: Sick days.

Egon: (suspicious) Why are you offering all this?

Roger: Because I feel like it. The better question is, why is she refusing it?

Egon: Well, why is she?

Roger: You'd better ask *her.*

Egon: (to Elizabeth) Why are you refusing it?

Elizabeth: He flosses his teeth in the kitchen.

Egon: What?

Elizabeth: He told me.

Egon: What is this nonsense?

Elizabeth: Do I have to tell you everything?

Egon: No, but while I'm supporting you in this house, it would help if you told me a little.

Long silence

Elizabeth: I see I'm coerced into this thing.

Angela: Nobody's forcing you.

Elizabeth: There's no help for it. (to Roger) I accept your offer.

Egon: Now you're talking.

Angela: Wonderful.

Elizabeth: (to her parents) Now if you two could make yourselves scarce, I'd appreciate it.

Angela: Egon, we are *de trop.*

Egon: What does that mean?

ANGELA gives him a significant inclination of the head.

I get it. The kitchen?

Angela: The kitchen.

ANGELA and EGON go into the kitchen.

Elizabeth: Do you know what you're getting into, Roger?

Being Authentic

Roger: I hope so.

Elizabeth: You know you'll probably rue the day you offered me this job? I'll probably do my best to make you rue it.

Roger: That I know.

Elizabeth: Then why are you pressing on with this?

Roger: I'm a stubborn man, maybe more stubborn even than you, Elizabeth Bricker. You want to wriggle out of it, but you can't with me: You've met your match.

Elizabeth: Have I?

Roger: You'll see. I'll pin you, that's my job – to pin you to the mat, and make you see that you are not unlovable.

Elizabeth: Pin me to the mat, will you? With your body pressing me down?

Roger: That's how it's done. But I was speaking figuratively, of course – not literally.

Elizabeth: I betcha you'd love it to be literal.

Roger: Maybe I would.

Elizabeth: You're no saint.

Roger: Never said I was.

Elizabeth: You could have fooled me.

Roger: Then maybe I can persuade you that you're worth loving.

Elizabeth: Bullshit. And you want me to swallow it?

Roger: Not if you don't want to. You can go on doing your bitch act until you get tired of it.

Elizabeth: I can?

Roger: You can try.

Elizabeth: Then I want you to know, Roger, that I'm doing this under duress.

Roger: Understood.

Elizabeth: And I will get no satisfaction from this, much less pleasure.

Roger: Understood.

Elizabeth: And that whatever task you'd have me do, I'll do it because I'm forced to.

Roger: In that case, I have a special request to make.

She gives him a sharp look.

Elizabeth: A special request? Aha. Now it comes.

Roger: I'd like to go to the movies.

She takes this in.

Elizabeth: Understood.

BLACKOUT

The Choice

Time: Now

Scene: A hospital room with two beds. Each of the beds is occupied by an elderly lady. One of them—JANE, the lady on stage right—is reading a newspaper, the other, AGNES, on stage left, is half asleep, her eyes closed, and her mouth slightly open. Stage right of JANE'S bed is a bed table, with a telephone on it. Stage left of AGNES' bed is another bed table, with another telephone. This rings. AGNES opens her eyes, tries to reach for the phone with her left hand, but remembers, to her dismay, that she cannot. The phone continues to ring. JANE gets out of bed, goes to AGNES' bed, picks up the phone, and puts the receiver into the right hand of AGNES.

Agnes: *(quietly, to Jane)* Thank you.

Jane: You're welcome.

Agnes: *(into the phone)* Hello? *(pause)* Eddie! I'm so glad you called! *(pause)* I'm okay—sort of. I'm out of the Stroke Center, and they've just put me into a semi-private room. The doc says my left side might recover—I might even regain full use of it. This could have been a lot worse. *(after a pause, she says, gravely:)* I know. *(recovering:)* But don't you worry about a thing, darling; everything's going to be all right. *(pause, while she hears some good news)* You are?

175

Oh, Eddie, that's wonderful! When? *(more good news)* Today!? But how...*(she listens to the explanation)* Oh my god! But why didn't you call me? *(pause)* Well you could have called me after you got on the plane. Never mind—I'm thrilled, just thrilled. I can hardly wait. *(pause)* And I love you too, darling. See you soon. I love you, Eddie.

> *She kisses the microphone of the handset, and listens to the person at the other end hanging up. Holding the handset, she looks at the JANE, who gets up, takes the handset from her hand, and replaces it in its cradle.*

Agnes: Thanks again.

Jane: Don't mention it; no problem at all.

Agnes: My name is Agnes.

Jane: Mine is Jane. Jane Sharpe.

> *AGNES extends her right hand to JANE, who shakes it*

Agnes: Thank god I can still shake hands.

Jane: Hi Agnes.

Agnes: Hi Jane. Is that Sharpe with an "E" at the end of it?

Jane: It used to be.

Agnes: Not now?

Jane: Well, since I've been on dialysis I've lost a lot of weight.

Agnes: So?

Jane: Well, since my body has dropped some pounds, I'm thinking of dropping a letter from my last name. If I keep on at this rate, I may have to drop my last name entirely. And if the dialysis kills me, as well it may, then you can drop in the garbage can what's left of my name, along with the rest of me.

Agnes: That's quite an introduction! Well, with or without the E, it's great to meet you, Jane.

Jane: Even in a place like this?

Agnes: Especially in a place like this. Here, you take nothing for granted.

Jane: (returning to her bed) I've been learning that.

Agnes: Been here a while?

Jane: My dialysis connection is temperamental—sometimes it works, sometimes not.

Agnes: Oh dear. I imagine that's one thing that you need to work all the time.

Jane: It would be nice! Three times a week, if it's not too much to ask.

Agnes: Oh, I'm sure they'll figure it out.

Jane: I'm glad *someone's* sure.

    Beat

Was that family who just called?

Agnes: My son, Eddie. He's coming! He's just landed in La Guardia, he'll be here very soon!

Jane: Very nice.

Agnes: It's wonderful! He lives in San Francisco, so I don't see him anywhere near as often as I would like. I wish we lived closer to each other.

Jane: Maybe you should move out there.

Agnes: Ed says he would love it. Ever since my husband died, Ed and his wife have been trying to get me out there to live with them. But I'm not so sure I'd like that.

Jane: You're uncomfortable with them?

Agnes: No, no, they're lovely people. They've offered to make a special three-room apartment for me. With my own bathroom and separate kitchen.

Jane: Very nice.

Agnes: More than that: it's a very handsome offer, very generous. But I want to live in my own house. I want my independence.

Jane: I know the feeling.

Agnes: But now with this stroke, I don't know how much longer I can hold out. I guess when you get to a certain age, you know how lucky you are to have family.

Jane: You can say that again.

AGNES gives her a speculative look.

Agnes: Do you have family, Jane?

Jane: Nope. No husband, no children. No siblings or cousins, either—not alive, anyway.

She thinks

I think there might be a few people left that I used to call friends, but I'm not sure—they've made themselves scarce. So there's no one to visit me—if that's what you're getting at.

Agnes: It *is* what I'm getting at. You must be lonely.

Jane: Not that lonely. I've got plenty of hobgoblins to keep me company.

Agnes: I meant people.

The Choice

Jane: Oh! People? Well, if these screw-up doctors ever get my dialysis connection working—then back I go to the County Home, where there'll be—if not people—at least plenty of warm bodies to look at. Barely warm bodies. Endlessly fascinating.

Agnes: Oh dear.

Jane: You get used to it. But enough about me. I bet you have grandchildren to brag about.

Agnes: Six! And there's a great grandchild on the way.

Jane: *Very* nice! And when the family gets together, you can beam at all the beautiful babies, and be proud. You can be honored as the beloved matriarch who got it all going. That's the payoff for your life's work.

Agnes: *Our* life's work. It was Max and I.

Jane: Of course. And on family occasions, you all can imagine that Max is up in heaven beaming down at you and blessing you.

Agnes: (a little stiffly) I don't have to imagine it; I know it.

Jane: Did I offend you?

Agnes: Well...not exactly...but it sounded like you were making fun of me.

Jane: That would be wrong of me. After all, you got married and had children who had children of their own, who now are begetting another generation...you were fruitful and you multiplied. That's not only admirable—by god, it's positively biblical.

Agnes: (quietly) You *were* making fun of me.

Jane: Making fun of myself, really.

Agnes: How so?

Jane: I chose another path. I'm an artist—a painter. At least I was.

Agnes: You've stopped painting?

Jane: My work is very large, and there's no room inside the Home to set up my easel, even if I still owned one.

Agnes: That's too bad. I'm sorry.

Jane: Are you?

Agnes: But of course.

>   *Beat*

Did you used to paint landscapes?

Jane: No, not really.

Agnes: You did portraits?

Jane: Nope. I didn't paint people, or haystacks, or fruit in a bowl...

Agnes: So what did you paint?

Jane: Nothing.

Agnes: Nothing?!

Jane: Nothing you'd recognize. I painted pictures of how I felt at the time.

Agnes: You were an abstract expressionist?

Jane: *(surprised)* That's it! That's exactly what I am...what I was. You got it!

Agnes: I never get it. When I see these things in museums—

Jane: *(interrupting)* So you go to museums?

Agnes: Of course I go to museums. Always have. Do you think I stayed home all day, breeding? Do you realize how insulting that sounds?

The Choice

Jane: I'm sorry.

Agnes: Are you?

Jane: But of course.

Agnes: Of course.

Jane: I *said* of course. I'm glad you're a museum-goer. At home you probably have one or two Monet reproductions on the wall.

Agnes: I do happen to have a Monet reproduction at home; is that a crime?

Jane: Of course not.

Agnes: I've made it well past Monet, thank you very much. I have reproductions of a Wyeth, and a Hopper.

Jane: Do you have anything in your house that is real? I mean original—not a reproduction.

Agnes: I certainly do. I like to patronize artists I know personally. There's a local landscapist who does lovely work, and I have one of his. And I have a pastel of flowers in a vase—absolutely beautiful, and done by a lovely woman who lives down the street. Art is important to me, and I try to be broad minded.

Jane: Glad to hear it.

Agnes: But, to be perfectly honest, I just don't get Abstract Expressionism.

Jane: Don't let it bother you. Neither does anyone else, nowadays. These days, if you're a painter, your work had better show people something they recognize, or present an idea that can be put into so many words. Abstraction is old hat.

Agnes: Well, all I know is that for me, it's easier to appreciate a painting if I know what it's about. But abstract works seem mainly about themselves.

Jane: And that's not enough for you?

Agnes: Not enough for me to remember them, as a rule. Would I have seen your paintings anywhere?

Jane: You're asking was I big time.

Agnes: I'm asking no such thing.

Jane: Be honest. You want to know if I was important. You want to know if my work was reviewed, if the reviewer was well known, and if the review was positive. Then you'd know how to relate to me—depending on whether I'm a "has been," or a "never was."

Silence

Agnes: If the subject is painful to you, we don't need to discuss it.

Jane: Well, there was a time my work was shown at the Corcoran—once even at Moma.

Agnes: The Museum of Modern Art? Wow!

Jane: I was 27.

Agnes: Your parents must have been thrilled.

Jane: Were they ever! Standing in front of my painting, they proclaimed to the crowd that I was god's gift to the paint brush! It was the one thing they could agree on. Over everything else they screamed like banshees.

Agnes: Oh dear.

Jane: Yeah. Not long afterwards, they divorced. I was crushed. For years I had felt that it was my talent that held them together; I wanted to shine for their sake. But not even my talent could save that marriage.

Agnes: Did anyone else know how distressed you were?

Jane: I kept it to myself. My private life was nobody else's business.

Agnes: Of course. Though it must have been hard to hold onto your privacy. You were a rising star.

Jane: Not to everyone. I was unknown to the vast majority— to people like you, Agnes.

Agnes: *(ironically)* Thank you very much.

Jane: Well, I was scarcely a household name! But some curators knew my name, my work. And some editors of art magazines and of course some collectors also knew me. And to my students, naturally, I was very important. Some of them wanted to paint just like me. Well of course I did my best to discourage them from this. I wanted them to paint not just like me, but like *themselves*. But some of them aped me anyway.

Agnes: Flattering.

Jane: I thought so at the time. But on looking back, I realize I failed to show some of them how to find their own authentic voice.

Agnes: How do you do that—find your own authentic voice?

Jane: You really want to know?

Agnes: How condescending! You speak as if raising a family disqualifies me even from asking the question, let alone understanding the answer!

Jane: I'm to distill a lifetime of experience so you can drink it in a tea cup?

Agnes: Forget it.

Silence

Jane: You start by recognizing something important. You point your body toward it, you open up every pore of your being, and connect it to everything in the space. You...let everything in the space pervade you, you let it connect with everything that *is* you. If that happens, truly happens, you'll have an epiphany, and you'll speak with your own voice, and nobody else's.

Pause

I can speak like that to art students, for many of them have had the experience, or want to, but when I describe it to others I feel self-conscious.

Agnes: No need to feel self-conscious with me. I think I know what you're talking about.

Jane: Really? Have you experienced this?

Agnes: The night we conceived Eddie. We'd been trying to conceive a child for months, with no luck. We'd been to doctors and undergone tests, but they couldn't find anything and we began talking about adopting. Then one day Max read an article about the timing method.

Jane: Timing method?

Agnes: You've never heard of it? Of course you haven't.

Jane: I may have. Refresh me.

Agnes: I'll give you an oversimplified version.

Jane: Kind of you.

Agnes: Not kind, just trying to be polite. But if you'd rather not hear, I'll keep quiet.

Jane: No, go on.

The Choice

Silence

Please.

Agnes: You take the wife's temperature when she wakes up, and you plot the results on a chart. You keep doing that until you learn when in her cycle is the optimum day for her to conceive. In our case, when the designated night rolled around, Max and I came together full of purpose, and full of love. As you say, every pore of me was open—open to *him*. I drank him in. And I knew that for Max, only I could give him what he needed.

Jane: Very nice.

Agnes: It was more than that—much more than that. The bed we were on had belonged to my mother; it was the bed where *I* was conceived. I felt part of something much bigger than me—the cycle of life. It was flowing through me, and I gave myself...lost myself...but in return I was given everything. That was epiphany enough for me.

Jane: So that when you gave birth, you were finally speaking in your own authentic voice.

Agnes: More authentic, you mean, than if I had written an essay or short story? That's rather demeaning. Maybe even insulting.

Jane: Hang in; it's early yet. You may hear worse.

Agnes: That was bad enough. You seemed to be saying that, as a woman, the most significant thing I could do was bear a child.

Jane: But it was you who were talking that way. You said that when you conceived you had an epiphany. What you had,

185

dear Agnes, was a baby. Doubtless others in the suburban herd were having similar epiphanies, with similar results.

Agnes: Herd?! I'm a member of a herd? You're right: this insult *is* worse than before. I'm no cow in a herd! And my son is no cookie-cutter copy of other sons.

Jane: Spoken like a devoted mother—like *all* the devoted mothers—in the herd.

Agnes: *(with some heat)* But they are right; all the devoted mothers are right: each child *is* unique, just as each fingerprint, each snowflake, is unique. Nobody is exactly like my son, just as nobody is exactly like *you*, Jane—*thank god!*

Jane: Calm down, Agnes. There's little chance of another like me: I'm childless, after all. That's because, unlike you, I couldn't attract a male whom I loved so much that I felt I had to have his children. Whereas you seem to have attracted a great lover.

Agnes: Max? Well...I wouldn't call him the greatest lover I ever heard about. Few earthshaking fireworks. But he always made sure that I was satisfied. He was very generous, very unselfish that way. He was *my* lover, and I loved him completely.

Jane: Had my husband been like yours, I might have thought twice before leaving him.

Agnes: You were married?

Jane: He was so gorgeous that whenever he entered a room, the women's heads spun around, and conversations ended—often in mid sentence.

Agnes: And yet you left him?

Jane: Turned out that in bed he was boring.

The Choice

Agnes. You left him just for that?

Jane: No, not just for that.

Agnes: He didn't support your art?

Jane: On the contrary, he was one of my biggest fans. Said my art was exciting. Actually helped me with some of the grunt work—stretching canvases, lugging supplies into the studio—that sort of thing.

Agnes: Well then, what was the trouble?

Jane: He liked the suburbs.

Agnes: What's the matter with that?

Jane: I take it you live in the suburbs?

Agnes: I have for years. My gardener's father worked for me, and *his* father before him.

Jane: Kept his family busy, did you?

Agnes: We used all of them—sometimes all at the same time.

Jane: So you must have had manicured lawns and gardens, a tennis court, a swimming pool—all that sort of thing?

Agnes: Yes, all of that.

Jane: Very nice! My ex-husband would have drooled to hear about it. But as for me—no. How long would my career have lasted in the suburbs? Would I have applied for grants there? Could I have made contacts, cultivated them? Could I have been *au courant*, part of the scene—in the suburbs? My career would have tanked.

Agnes: But if he had been willing to live in the city...?

Jane: He *was* willing! He was willing to live wherever I lived. He was a mathematician and could do his proofs just as well in the city as in the suburbs—maybe even better.

Agnes: Then *what was the problem?*

Jane: He wanted children.

Agnes: Ah. I see. There's no compromise on that.

Jane: Even if I could have afforded a nanny to do all the work with the children, I would still have had to *think* about them.

Agnes: You would still have had to *think* about them? And this was an impossible burden?!

Jane: I couldn't afford the distraction. And so, what with the prospect of suburbia, the boring bed, and the tedium of changing diapers, wiping noses, and worse, I walked out on the marriage. It was a no-brainer.

> *A brief silence*

Agnes: You really didn't want them, did you.

Jane: Better to have decided that *before* having them, then afterwards. My paintings—*they* are my children. They have my blood and bones in them.

Agnes: They just don't come and visit you in the hospital.

Jane: Well, in a way they do. I see them in my mind's eye. And I remember the experience of making them. Not unlike your remembering how you and Max conceived Eddie. Pretty much the same, right?

Agnes: Perhaps.

Jane: True, unlike you, I was completely alone. Even if there were others in the house, I put myself in a bunker—a mental bunker that no one else could enter. Well—almost no one. Occasionally I let Debussy in. Sometimes I played a recording of his piano music...

> *Some Debussy piano music plays quietly in the background, and the lights begin to dim to where*

> *we become aware that an image of one her*
> *paintings has appeared projected on the back wall,*
> *and upon her.*

...and occasionally, in my mind, I allowed in the poetry of Verlaine. And gradually, the walls of the bunker dissolved, and I began to *see*.

> *She recites the following, quietly*

Il pleure dans mon coeur
Comme il pleut sur la ville;
Quelle est cette langueur
Qui pénètre mon coeur?

Ô bruit doux de la pluie
Par terre et sur les toits!
Pour un coeur qui s'ennuie
Ô le chant de la pluie!

> *The lights brighten; the music and the image fade*
> *away.*

Agnes: Debussy and—what was his name?

Jane: Verlaine.

Agnes: Debussy and Verlaine kept you company ?

Jane: Two immortals. I had the crazy thought that if I had their music in mind, some of their immortality might rub off on me.

Agnes: And the poetry influenced your work?

Jane: Very much. I did a series of luan panels with those words raining in my heart. All I have to do is to play Verlaine's words in my mind, and those six panels appear before me.

Agnes: Where are they now?

Jane: They were purchased by Middlebury College sometime in the fifties. God knows where they are now—or even if they exist.

Agnes: Why wouldn't they still be in Middlebury College?

Jane: In the fifties, my career was still hot, and they thought they were getting a bargain. I used to get letters from Middlebury inviting me to give them some of my stuff for free. But when interest in abstract expressionism waned, so did interest in my stuff. I haven't heard from Middlebury in years. They could have sold the panels, given them away, or driven them to the dump, for all I know.

Agnes: Why do you suppose that? There's still plenty of interest in Abstract Expressionism. You go to a big museum—like the National Gallery in Washington—and you can see plenty of that stuff on the walls: people like Pollack and Hofmann...

Jane: *Exactly*—Pollack and Hofmann, De Kooning and Kline, Rothko and Motherwell...they're the old masters; they *invented* this métier. I came later; I'm a footnote.

Agnes: A footnote?

Jane: Yeah. Read any good footnotes, lately?

> *Beat*

You seem to know something about art, Agnes.

Agnes: My mother was a painter. She was accomplished—at least enough to teach it in the local school system. She would have loved it if I picked it up, too, but I was more interested in writing. In High School I was very active in the creative writing club. I wrote every time I got the chance, and read everything I could get my hands on.

The Choice

Beat

High school was where I fell in love with Max.

Jane: He was your high school flame—how very sweet.

Agnes: Sweet is exactly what he was. After dating me for eight weeks, he proposed to me.

Jane: And of course, you said yes.

Agnes: No I didn't. Not at first. I was afraid that if I married him, I'd be so consumed with keeping house that my writing would suffer.

Jane: This is starting to sound familiar.

Agnes: And that when the babies came along, my writing career would go out the window.

Jane: This is déjà vu all over again.

Agnes: I knew I would want his children—I was beginning to want them already, and I wasn't even out of High School. But I felt that unless I pursued my writing, I'd be selling myself short. I would never have tried to make it as a writer. I would never have known for sure whether or not I could do it.

Jane: How much of this did you tell him?

Agnes: *All* of it. And he promised me that if I married him, whenever we were both home and I wanted to write, he would take care of the children. He gave me his word.

Jane: Very nice. Did he keep it?

Agnes: He did his best to honor his promise, and in the main he succeeded.

Jane: And did you continue to write?

Agnes: I tried. While Eddie was young I wrote a few things, got a few short stories published in journals nobody's ever heard of. After he went off to college, I worked harder at it. I tried to get publishers interested in my stuff, but trying to sell a collection of short stories is like trying to light a fire on top of Mount Everest. So I self-published a collection, sold a few books to my friends, and stuffed the rest in my garage, where they quietly molder.

Jane: So much for your career as a writer. Do you feel you failed?

Agnes: Maybe I could have tried harder, but I didn't. I suppose *that* was a failure.

Jane: But if you *had* tried harder, if you had given it everything, *if you had never married,* do you think you would have had greater success as a writer?

Agnes: Who knows? I did the best I could under the circumstances. And the chief circumstance was that I didn't want a life without Max. And now that I've lost him, I thank heaven I've a son to remind me of him.

Jane: Very nice.

Agnes: You keep saying that.

Jane: What?

Agnes: "Very nice." Don't you see how that damns with faint praise, and dismisses my life as insignificant—compared to yours? You are the great hero of art, aren't you—all alone, with nobody to tell you whether your life has meant anything. You pick up the paint brush as if the act were an *auto da fé*—an act of faith—

Jane: *(interrupting)* I know what it means—

The Choice

Agnes: *(interrupting)* I bet you do! You are the great martyr, aren't you, giving up everything for your art—husband, children, friends—but the trouble is: There's nobody left to applaud you! Nobody left to weep, even! Nobody but me, that is, and I'm having a lot of trouble applauding *or* weeping. Because, you know what I think?

Jane: I'm afraid you're about to tell me.

Agnes: Damn right I am! Jane, for all I know, you might well have been god's gift to the paint brush, a real genius. But never having seen your art, all I have to go by is what you have told me. And my conclusion is, you are the most selfish person I have ever met.

Jane: Of course I'm selfish! Do you think you can be an artist without being selfish?

Agnes: Johann Sebastian Bach was unselfish.

Jane: He had a wife to do the grunt work—a couple of wives to do it, in fact. That's what every woman artist needs—a wife of her own to free her to follow her genius.

Agnes: So this is why you divorced: you preferred—

Jane: *(interrupting)* Not a bit of it. I used to say—back in the day when I had juices in me—that if I could have found a guy who would throw me a good fuck when I needed it, and get the hell out of the way when I didn't, now that would have been ideal. Oh god. Since then, a whole lot of water has flowed under the bridge—or something.

Agnes: *(smiling)* Or something.

Jane: Did I offend you again?

Agnes: You'll have to try harder.

Jane: I will.

Agnes: See that you do. In the meantime, conversation with you is bracing, to say the least. You do very well—especially for a woman your age.

Jane: I return the compliment—if it was meant as one.

Agnes: It certainly was meant as one. When I arrived in this room, and I saw how you looked, I never expected that our conversation—if we had one—would be so stimulating.

Jane smiles

Jane: Especially compared to the twaddle that passes for discussion in those suburban book clubs of yours, right?

Agnes: Wrong. One doesn't have to live in a walk-up to have an intellectual conversation.

Jane: No, but it helps. Because in a walk-up, you have fewer creature comforts to insulate you from life.

Agnes: Creature comforts are not *ipso facto* evil, nor do they void one's humanity.

Jane: Spoken like a true suburbanite. Talking to you, Agnes, has convinced me all the more that I made the right choice.

Agnes: I wonder.

Jane: What—that I made the right choice?

Agnes: No—that you're all that convinced that you did. In fact—you want to know what I think?

Jane: That I'm selfish; you told me that already.

Agnes: I mean something else besides your being selfish.

Jane: Oh god.

Agnes: Fine, I'll shut up.

Jane: No go ahead, I'm a masochist. Hit me anyway: what do you think?

Agnes: You're jealous of me.

The Choice

Beat

Jane: Bull. Shit.

Agnes: You're jealous because I'm not lonely. Because I have plenty of family to visit me—unlike you. And because I've been able to love *beyond* myself—unlike you, who seem to love only your own work, which celebrates mainly *you*.

Jane: My work celebrates life.

Agnes: So does a six-year-old doing a cartwheel.

Jane: I prefer the painting.

Agnes: I prefer the six-year-old.

Beat

Listen, Jane: I've given birth, and I've nurtured and cared for other living beings. And I will not be told that my life as a wife and mother is inferior to yours.

Jane: Who knows? If in time my work is judged to be of scant merit, then your life will have proved vastly superior to mine, and my life will have appeared...wasted.

Agnes: So, if the market value of your art falls, then your value as a person falls likewise?

Jane: It would have to. My life *is* my art—that's all I've ever done.

Beat

No—wait a minute—I *have* done something else. I bought real estate—decades ago—a loft in the meat packing district. I got it for a song, because in those days, nobody wanted those buildings. Mine didn't even have plumbing in it. Over the years, I installed the amenities, did up a tenant apartment to make some money, and the rest of the loft I used as a studio. I lived in the studio, and the space remaining I used as storage for my paintings. I still own it. When it's sold, my estate will have realized a handsome profit. That's an achievement even a suburbanite might understand.

Agnes: You're impossible.

Jane: I'm very possible.

Agnes: I mean all that anger, all that bitterness.

Jane: What anger? I've no reason to be angry. I chose my life. There was a world of things I could have painted, had I wanted to. On black velour backgrounds I could have painted the faces of children, little angels with huge eyes, weeping glycerin tears. I could have painted crystal bowls of fruit, where the refracted light plays happily within the cut glass, and a lucky ray touches a drop of moisture on a ripe pear—delectable as a woman's breast. I could have made cloud-capped mountains towering over a limpid lake, at whose shore stands a poet in a broad brimmed hat, meditating on the majestic scene. I dare say that at least one of these might be suitable for a living room—provided, of course, that it matched the color scheme, and, for an extra charge, I'd make sure that it did. In fact, my output would be so decorative that by popular demand I'd have to found my own interior decorating business—call it Finishing Touches—and I'd have a whole crew of painters turning out product. My advice would be sought in all matters of interior decorating, and I'd become The Sibyl of Suburbia!

Agnes: But instead of all that you chose Abstract Expressionism.

The Choice

Jane: Maybe more accurate to say, "it chose me." It made me feel that the only valid way to present life was to paint the invisible. I still feel that way although nobody else does. And even though I saw that Abstract Expressionism was out, I kept on making paintings the way I always had. For I felt that at some point it would have to come back, though I might be not be alive to see it And I wanted a legacy of paintings to remind people of who I was, and what I was all about. My loft would be the perfect place to store my paintings, my legacy. I needed a conservator to watch over them, and try to arrange showings for them, and, hopefully, sales. I actually found someone who was willing to do all this for free.

Agnes: He must have liked you a lot.

Jane: He did.

Agnes: Aha!

Jane: But not in the way you think. He was gay. He died last year, and I was forced to hire someone out of my savings. Which are diminishing far more rapidly, let me tell you, now that I have end-stage renal disease, and have had to move into the County Home.

Agnes: But if you had savings, why did you have to move into a Home?

Jane: There was nobody to take care of me.

Agnes: You could have hired a nurse.

Jane: That would mean less for the conservator.

Agnes: *You* need the conservator.

Jane: My paintings need him more. And the longer I live, the less money there is for him. He tells me he's working on a retrospective in the Boston Museum of Fine Art—which might actually come to pass in a couple of years. There's got to be money for that.

Agnes: *(appalled)* What are you saying, Jane?

Jane: I'll give you an oversimplified version.

> *She reaches for a sheet of yellow paper which has been lying on her bed table.*

You see this form? All I have to do is to sign it, to give these quacks permission to withdraw dialysis from me. With any luck, I'll be dead in two weeks.

Agnes: You intend to ...

Jane: Sign it. Just sign it. I'll be out of here, the government can save its money, my estate will have more, and the Conservator will have more time to work for my paintings. It's a win-win, as I see it.

Agnes: You poor wretch. Life is worth living.

Jane: So they say. But I've got nothing to live for except those paintings in my warehouse. I've already given my life to them. There's nothing more I can do for them except pull the plug. And that's exactly what I intend to do.

Agnes: You poor fool. Back in the Home, there are plenty of people who could benefit from someone to talk to, someone to listen to, someone to write letters for them, read them books, do them favors.

Jane: Live for others, is that it?

Agnes: Why not? You might discover you liked it.

Jane: I doubt it.

Agnes: Give it a try.

Jane: I think not.

The Choice

Agnes: Jane, Jane, you have only one life. When it's over, it's over—there's no second chance!

Jane: Don't I know it. I've attended so many funerals that there's nobody left to care what happens to me.

Agnes: Not true.

Jane: Name one.

A long silence

Agnes: *(quietly)* I care.

Jane: Bull shit. I throw at you every insult I can think of, and *you care?!* That's crazy.

Agnes: I know it.

Jane: *Why* do you care?

Agnes: I don't know.

Jane: It's not about me. It's about you: you'd care if you saw *any* human being pass away.

Agnes: Well, wouldn't you?

Jane: I suppose so – theoretically. But during my life I've never let anybody get close enough for me to find out.

Agnes: But all those funerals you went to...

Jane: Colleagues and relatives. I was *supposed* to care, so I attended.

Agnes: And during the funeral service, didn't you care at all about the departed?

Jane: I suppose I did. But my main thought was, *it was their time. When will it be my time? How much time have I left? I have so many paintings in me! I must work harder.*

Agnes: Now I know why I care. It's the artist in you being...being ended.

199

Jane: That's a stupid thing to say, considering you haven't seen one of my paintings.

Agnes: I don't have to. Even if you were completely paralyzed, and couldn't move either of your arms, your imagination would still be full of life. You could still hear the Debussy that has moved you all these years. You could still hear the Verlaine. Someday, that imagination must be snuffed out, and someday, the music in you must be silenced. The world in you must be lost. That's awful, and there's nothing we can do about it. But to lose you sooner than we have to…

She turns away, hiding her face

Jane: You're weeping for yourself, not for me.

Agnes: *(weeping)* **I'm not weeping!**

Jane: Glad to hear it.

Agnes: I'm not my full self, right now. I'm getting emotional, for no good reason.

Jane: Very true.

Agnes: It's just that if you killed yourself, it would… it would…

Jane: It would what?

Agnes: What can I say? It would make me feel bad.

Jane: Oh. It would make you feel bad.

Agnes: *(dabbing her eyes with a tissue)* Yes, it would.

Jane: How bad?

Agnes: Well …

With a brave smile

it would spoil my whole day.

Jane: A whole day?

Agnes: Well, maybe half of the next, as well.

The Choice

Jane: So, offing myself would spoil for you a whole day and a half?

Agnes: Something like that.

Jane: So that you might shed a tear?

Agnes: I wouldn't go that far.

Jane: Not even one?

Agnes: Well, all right: maybe one.

Jane: Oh. Then that changes everything.

Agnes: It does?

Jane: Until this moment I knew of no one who gave a damn whether I lived or died. Now it appears I have a real live mourner.

Agnes: You mean someone who *would* mourn, if you died.

Jane: Yes. I thought I had outlived them all, yet here you are, ready to shed tears if I go.

Agnes: One tear, anyway.

Jane: So my course is clear.

Agnes: And that is...

Jane: To kill myself right away, while you're still in the mood.

Agnes: Oh, you *thing!* You've been playing with me! You're impossible!

Jane: I'm very possible.

> *Enter two men: EDWARD, about 70, son to AGNES, and MATTHEW, about 50, grandson to AGNES. MATTHEW stays by the door, so that AGNES sees EDWARD first, as he strides to her.*

Agnes: Eddie! Oh, you're here! Darling!

They embrace

Edward: *(as MATTHEW strides up to them)* Look who I brought.

Agnes: Matthew!

Matthew: How are you doing, Grandma?

Agnes: Oh sweetie, much better now I see *you*!

Edward: Didn't I tell you, Matthew, that you were the one she really wanted to see?

Matthew: You certainly did.

Agnes: Stop that, you sillies. *(beat)* Oh dear! We have so much to catch up on, but I hate to disturb my roommate, here.

Jane: Don't worry about me; I'm fine.

Agnes: Still: Why don't we get a nurse to bring a wheelchair?

Matthew: I'll take care of it.

And he strides out of the room.

Agnes: *(to Jane)* Jane, this is my son, Edward.

Jane: Pleased to meet you. Your mother has spoken so much about you.

Edward: Uh oh.

Jane: It's all good, all good.

Agnes: Edward, this is Jane Sharpe, a very famous painter.

Jane: Not so very famous.

Agnes: Her work has been shown in the Museum of Modern Art.

Edward: *(to Jane)* Well, isn't that fine! What a pleasure to meet you. My Mom is an artist, too—a writer. Her work has been published.

Agnes: *Self*-published. Don't puff me up, Edward. I'm not in the same league as Jane, here.

Jane: Who knows? You may be in a higher league.

Agnes: Nonsense. I know who I am.

Edward: Which puts you in a high league, indeed, since many people *don't* know who they are.

> *MATTHEW enters pushing a wheelchair, which he maneuvers to the side of AGNES' bed.*

Agnes: Well, that didn't take long!

Edward: Shall I help you into the chair, Ma?

Agnes: No. I want Matthew to do it.

Edward: *(to Matthew)* What did I tell you? She likes you better.

Agnes: Nonsense. Matthew's just stronger.

> *They settle her into the chair, put a blanket over her lap*
>
> *(to Jane) Sorry to disturb you with my funny family.*
>
> ***Jane:*** *Not at all. It's my pleasure—really.*

Exeunt AGNES, EDWARD, & MATTHEW, with MATTHEW pushing the wheelchair. JANE is alone. She sinks back onto her pillow with a smile that slowly fades. She reaches to the yellow form on her bed table, and with conscious deliberation signs it. Then, sinking back onto her pillow again, she reviews the form as the lights dim, the quiet Debussy music begins to play in the background, and the lights are dim enough so that we see the

Paul R. Cooper

image of her painting projected onto the wall and onto her. She lets the paper go, and intones quietly:

Il pleure dans mon coeur
Comme il pleut sur la ville;
Quelle est cette langueur
Qui pénètre mon coeur?

Ô bruit doux de la pluie
Par terre et sur les toits!
Pour un coeur qui s'ennuie
Ô le chant de la pluie!

Blackout

Taking Notes

Scene: The living room of a modest New York apartment. Against one wall is a computer hutch which looks as if it has come from a thrift store. Against another is a couch, in front of which is a coffee table, both of similar provenance. On the coffee table are a few magazines scattered about, and a slim vase with a single yellow rose in it. In addition, here and there, are a couple of chairs, in no better condition than the rest of the furniture. Almost every available inch of wall space is lined with books. There is a door to the outside hall, a hallway to the kitchen, and another hallway to other rooms in the apartment.

At rise, EDIE is discovered sitting on the sofa. She looks to be in her late twenties or early thirties. She's wearing a blue wool turtle-neck sweater and a grey skirt. She wears a simple pendant around her neck. One cheek is disfigured by a port wine stain birthmark, which is sufficiently large to keep the beholder from realizing that if she did not have this birthmark, she would be pretty. But as it is, the birthmark commands your attention.

EDIE holds in her hand a notebook, in which she is busy writing. She pauses in her writing, thinks of the right word, and begins writing again. The front door buzzer sounds. Edie runs to the intercom.

Edie: Hello?

Voice from Intercom: Hello Edie! It's Alex.

Edie: Great! You're right on time.

> *She buzzes him in. Then she runs to the coffee table, and straightens the magazines, after which she goes into the kitchen, and brings out a tray full of nuts and crudités. Then the doorbell rings. She runs to the door, looks through the peep-hole, then opens the door.*

Come on in!

> *In comes a nice looking young man in his mid-twenties. He is hiding a wrapped floral package behind his back. He leans in, intending to kiss her on the cheek with the birthmark, but she turns the other one for him to kiss. Then she examines his face closely.*

You look tired. rough night, I hope?

Alex: Somewhat.

Edie: Good! I want to hear all about it.

Alex: And you will—although I don't know how long I can stay. I'm starved; I need to go out and eat something.

Edie: No need to go out. I put some nibbles out on the coffee table.

Alex: Thanks, Edie. It's a start.

Edie: What are you hiding behind your back?

Alex: *(producing the wrapped floral package)* Not a whole lot.

Edie: Alex! This is special!

She rips open the package to reveal a single, long-stemmed red rose. He takes the wrapping paper from her.

Ohh! Lovely! What's the occasion?

Alex: I figured your yellow rose could use some company.

Edie: Indeed she can. I'll just put him in with her.

As she places the red rose in the vase holding the yellow one, the next couple of lines are spoken:

Alex: Assigned them genders, have you?

Edie: Why not? The yellow one is timid, and the red is passionate.

Alex: Interesting!

Edie: It's awfully crowded in there. Think I should get a bigger vase?

Alex: It's not so crowded. Just cozy. You could use some more water, though.

Edie: Good idea. Give me the paper. I'll dump it while I pour some more water into this.

She picks up the vase, takes the paper from him, then goes into the kitchen, while he goes directly to one end of the couch – his accustomed seat, apparently—and sits, then reaches for one of the crudités that she has set out for him. The sound of running water is heard, and moments later she emerges with the vase filled with water. She sits down on the other end of the couch, reaches for her notebook and pen.

Okay, I'm ready. Shoot.

Alex: Not so fast! Aren't you going to ask me how I am?

Edie: I know how you are. You're hungry. And tired.

Alex: But hungry and tired because of what? You don't know that.

Edie: You're about to tell me.

Alex: But you don't know what I'm going to say, Edie.

Edie: That's true. I *don't* know what you're going to say and I'm being obnoxious. Sorry. Let's start from the beginning. Hello Alex, how are you?

She puts down her pen and notebook

Alex: I'm tired.

Edie: And what's tiring you?

Alex: Everything. The whole dating scene.

Edie: Ah.

Alex: I'm sick of it. As soon as I meet somebody new, I can see, behind all the polite conversation, that she's busy giving me a grade, assigning me a number, which will determine whether she wants to see me again.

Edie: But you're doing the same with her.

Alex: And I hate it. It's pathetic, because all of us have already given *ourselves* a grade, assigned *ourselves* a number. We think, "Well, I'm a seven, seven and a half maybe, but wow, this gal's an eight or a nine—not *too* many points above me—so I'll make a play for her." Or, you could have: "What *is* this? I know I'm a ten; I can do better than *this* dude!"

Edie: The dating calculus, eh?

Taking Notes

Alex: You got it.

Edie: And you've subscribed to it.

Alex: I'm afraid so.

Edie: Then what number have you assigned yourself?

Alex: Doesn't the Fifth Amendment protect me from that sort of question?

Edie: If you want it to.

Alex: Then I decline to answer. Besides, it varies.

Edie: Depending on...?

Alex: Who I'm with. When I'm with a higher number, then I feel that my stock goes up, so to speak.

Edie: And when you're with a lower number, then your stock sinks?

Alex: So to speak.

Edie: Then it follows that every time you visit me, you're in a recession, right?

Alex: WRONG. If anything, it's the reverse.

Edie: But how can that be, since according to the dating calculus—

Alex: *(interrupting)* Please! Enough of that damned calculus, I hate it.

Edie: But you've just said you've subscribed to it, Alex.

Alex: I know, and I hate myself for subscribing.

Edie: Then just cancel your subscription.

Alex: Easy for *you* to say.

Edie: Well, just get away from it for a while.

Alex: That's why I come here.

Edie: I'm honored. But if you're trying to get away from it, would you rather I not ask what brought on all this...fatigue? Maybe you're not ready to tell me?

Alex: If I weren't ready, I wouldn't have come. *(pause)* Well, maybe I would, anyway. I hate to disappoint you.

Edie: I'm so dependent on your visits, is that it?

Alex: No, no, I didn't mean that. But you do seem to like to take notes a whole lot.

Edie: About your doings especially.

Alex: I'm flattered that you find them interesting.

Edie: That's putting it mildly. They're exciting—at least to me.

Alex: Edie, do you think that there's a bit of a voyeur in you?

Edie: More than a little. I feel like I'm peering through a keyhole. Very exciting.

Alex: The door isn't locked. Why not turn the knob, open the door, and come in?

Edie: Too dangerous.

Alex: You could finally stop looking. You could start *doing.*

Edie: I'm not ready for that.

Alex: What would it take to get you ready?

Edie: *(indicating her notebook)* Are you going to give me something to write in this notebook, or should I put it away?

Alex: I'll tell you, I'll tell you!

Edie: Good. *(silence)* So tell me.

Taking Notes

Alex: I'm working up to it.

Edie: You never had to work up to it before. You just jumped right in.

Alex: Well, this one is really embarrassing.

Edie: *(picking up her pen)* Oh?

Alex: Wait. How do I know there's not an audio recorder hidden somewhere?

Edie: Oh, dear Alex! I would never do that to you.

Alex: I want deniability. When your book comes out, I want to be able to contradict anything you've written about me.

Edie: Of course you do. But you've nothing to worry about. First of all, I'm not going to use your real name. And second, I'll show you the manuscript before anyone else sees it.

Alex: Before *anyone?* I get to see it even before Mythical Mary?

Edie: *(smiling)* In my foreword I'll say that although I've told you a hundred times that her name is Mary Evans, you insist on calling my apartment mate "Mythical Mary."

Alex: Well, I've never seen her.

Edie: Yes, and it's a good thing.

Alex: So you keep telling me.

Edie: Because it's true. If she had been in the apartment when you first came to fix my computer, you'd never have bothered with me.

Alex: Apparently because she's so good looking, and you're not, is that it?

Edie: That's it.

Alex: It's nonsense.

Edie: Oh, Alex, don't let's fight about it again.

Alex: I'm not fighting. I just don't like hearing you say how much prettier Mary is. She's no threat to you, trust me.

Edie: She's like a goddess.

Alex: She could be Venus on the half-shell, for all I'd care.

Edie: You're sweet.

Alex: So there's no need to have her clear out before I arrive, no need to keep her away until after I leave. I don't know how she stands for it. Even at the beginning, when you were calling me every other day to fix that desk top, she had to leave each time. She must have been totally pissed.

Edie: Pissed? Maybe a little. But then, when you finally fixed the thing so that it stayed fixed—

Alex: *(interrupting)* What are you talking about? I always fix 'em right the first time. But your computer...well, I always had the impression you were breaking the thing on purpose.

Edie: So I'd have an excuse to call you back? The conceit of the man!

Alex: I didn't say *why* you were doing it. But I did notice that as soon as I started coming on my own accord, your computer stayed fixed.

Edie: Pure coincidence.

Alex: If you say so.

Edie: Hmph!

Taking Notes

Alex: Really, Edie, I believe whatever you say.

Edie: Then please believe this: I've been keeping Mary away not only because of jealousy. It's also because I don't want her to overhear anything you say in this apartment.

Alex: So she knows nothing, right?

Edie: Well, she's not stupid. She works in public relations, so she can put two and two together at least as well as the next person. I'm sure she figures that *something* must be going on, otherwise why would you be coming so often...?

Alex: And why would she have to leave each time? She must be dying of curiosity. She must ask lots of questions.

Edie: She does.

Alex: And do you tell her anything?

Edie: Not a word. Your secrets are safe with me.

Alex: Then in the book, I'll have a pseudonym that nobody can connect with me?

Edie: Of course! Unless, that is, you'd prefer I use your real name?

Alex: Please don't. I'm not proud of that side of me.

Edie: Your name will never leave this apartment.

Alex: Good to know you're looking after my privacy.

Edie: And mine as well. I'm a very private person, in case you haven't noticed.

Alex: I've noticed! The curtains are always drawn when I come here.

Edie: Of course. Being a voyeur, myself, the last thing I need is another voyeur spying on *me*. So don't worry! As I told you, all your secrets are safe here.

Alex: Glad to hear it.

Edie: Good. So then, in the privacy of my living room, with curtains drawn, and nobody here but us two, are you ready to tell me what has brought on all this fatigue?

Alex: I guess so.

Edie: So go ahead, shoot.

Alex: Well, last night I met someone…

Edie: Aha! *(picking up her pen and notebook)* Now we're getting somewhere.

> *She begins taking notes.*

Alex: I first saw her on Match.com. She's from New Rochelle.

Edie: Really! New Rochelle? Did you go all the way up there to meet her?

Alex: Didn't have to. She was coming into Manhattan for shopping, so that wasn't an issue.

Edie: Still, if you two clicked, you'd have to go up there *some* time, and from here to New Rochelle is quite a hike. So for all that she would have had to seem pretty hot—am I wrong?

Alex: No, you're right. She *did* seem pretty hot. Her pictures were *very* hot. But the hottest thing about her was…her prose.

> *He falls silent*

Edie: Did you say her prose? Her *prose* was hot?!

Taking Notes

Alex: Put it this way: she makes her living writing women's porn. You know, the stuff women get off on...

Edie: I know what that stuff is. But how do *you*?

Alex: She emailed me a link to her e-publisher—*Ellora's Cave,* they call it—*Dive into your desires with Ellora's Cave erotic e-books,* it said...so I ordered one of hers. *Eternal Ecstasy,* that's the title.

Edie: I guess that's one way to get read. And I suppose you were turned on by what you read?

Alex: I was astounded! And I'm not exactly a stranger to the world of sex, you know.

Edie: I do know. In my bedroom I've got six notebooks suggesting quite the contrary.

Alex: Oh, God. Maybe you should burn 'em up.

Edie: Lest they spontaneously combust? I don't think so— besides, I've worked so hard on them. They're you.

Alex: The show-off side of me. Maybe half the stuff in there is exaggerated—or non-existent.

Edie: If you did only half the stuff in those books, believe me, that's *plenty.*

Alex: I hope there's more to me than my erotic adventures— such as they are.

Edie: I know there is.

Alex: I'll tell you this: I wasn't prepared to see what this woman put on those pages...it was scorching! How'd she come up with that stuff?! Some of it...embarrassed even *me.*

They say you should write what you know. Well, how the hell did she come to know all that? Where did she learn it?

Edie: I know where you're going with all this. But, as they say, *it isn't necessarily so.* On NPR I heard a woman writer say that the idea is not so much to write what you know *but what you wish you knew.*

Alex: Interesting. But with that face and that body, Viola seemed to me someone who might have learned all that from...personal experience. And if she *did*...and if she could help me make it *my* experience, too...well! I wouldn't have minded driving to New Rochelle. For *some* of that stuff, I'd have driven to Alaska.

Edie: Poor Alex. If *you* feel you are missing out in that way, I wonder if most men don't feel the same thing.

Alex: I don't know about most men. But when I hear about some lucky guy having mind-blowing, cataclysmic sex, I get...jealous, to be perfectly honest.

Edie: You don't think that there are plenty of men who are jealous of *you?*

Alex: There may be, for all I know. Eating your heart out seems to be the universal human condition.

Edie: Not quite universal. My parents have a beautiful marriage. After forty-five years, they're still in love with each other; they're still *satisfied.*

Alex: Nobody would ever accuse me of *that.*

Edie: Not even after an evening with Miss Sex-Bomb from New Rochelle?

Alex: Oh, God! Don't get me started.

Taking Notes

Edie: I hope you finally *will* get started. I've been sitting here with pen poised, and very little to show for it.

Alex: Maybe you've got something better to do than look to me for vicarious pleasure.

Edie: What a mean thing for you to say, Alex. If all I wanted was pleasure of that kind, I could read books by people like that New Rochelle woman, who apparently wants a piece of you.

Alex: Her name is Viola. And there's no need to worry. Nothing happened.

Edie: *Nothing happened?!*

> *As he speaks the following, she takes notes furiously.*

Alex: You heard me. We met at Caruso's. She had told me she loved Italian food, and she wasn't kidding. She was stuffing that pasta primavera into her mouth as if it were…well, something else. Here was this sex-goddess stuffing her face, and all I could think of was…

> *EDIE, still taking notes, shakes her head*

…yeah, you got it. And of course I couldn't touch a bit of my chicken *cacciatore.* I kept staring at her, saying I don't know what. At first she looked at me with a raised eyebrow; I figured she thought I was nuts. But then it turned out that what she really thought of me was worse. She asked me how old I was, I told her the truth, and she said, "Remarkable! Twenty-five years old and still a virgin!" Well, I insisted that I was far from being a virgin, but she said that the more I protested that I wasn't, the more she was

217

convinced that I *was*, and that while in other circumstances a virgin might be a turn-on for her, this time she didn't feel like breaking my mother's heart.

Edie: The bitch!

Alex: Well, after she said all that, I felt frozen; I couldn't eat a thing. Somehow I got out of there, found my way home, turned out the lights and went to bed. Of course I couldn't sleep. I kept staring up into the darkness, watching my misspent life parade before me like last year's Mardi Gras.

Edie: *(as she's writing it down)* "Last...year's...Mardi Gras."

    She looks at him.

Oh Alex, I'm so sorry.

Alex: It wasn't great. By morning I was a wreck. I couldn't eat breakfast, I couldn't eat lunch...

Edie: Poor dear! That horrible woman—rejecting you like that.

Alex: Surely you wouldn't have wanted her to *accept* me?

    Pause

Edie: Would you have *wanted* me to want that?

Alex: I need you to want the best for me.

Edie: Which in this case would have been for her to say *no thanks,* but to say it *nicely,* so as not to hurt your feelings. Wouldn't that have been the best?

Alex: Maybe it would have been best for me to ignore the bait she offered on-line.

Edie: Or for her not to have offered it in the first place.

Alex: I like how you always take my side.

Taking Notes

Edie: There's no one whose side I'd rather take.

Pause

Alex: Look, Edie, how about we go out together for a nice dinner? We'd have fun.

Edie: Thanks, Alex, but I don't think so.

Alex: What's the matter? I'm not presentable enough?

Edie: You're very presentable, but I'm not, and you know it.

Alex: I know of no such thing. And after last night, I'm in no mood to be rejected for a dinner date.

Edie: I'm not rejecting you, it's just that...

She breaks off, hearing a key turn the locks at the door

Oh God, that's Mary at the door. She's come back early.

Alex: Mythical Mary? The Goddess of Public relations? At last I get to see her!

The door opens. MARY enters. She is a very good looking woman. ALEX stares at her. MARY walks toward him.

Mary: So this is the fabled Alex! No wonder you've been hiding him. That was stingy of you, Edie, not like you at all.

Edie: *(frostily)* What are you doing back here so soon, Mary? I thought we had agreed that you'd wait for my text message.

Mary: I got hungry.

Edie: *(stonily)* You could have eaten out.

Mary: I didn't feel like it.

Edie: You didn't feel . . .? **Oh!** You want food, do you?

She rises, furious, and stomps into the kitchen.
MARY, unruffled, takes EDIE'S place on the couch.

Mary: Well, Alex, what have you to say for yourself?

Alex: So…you don't live in New Rochelle after all?

Mary: No, I don't live in New Rochelle after all. And my name is Mary, not Viola. And I didn't write *Eternal Ecstasy*, or anything like it. And I got a friend of mine to hack you into another website, where you'd see *my* thumb-nail, not Viola's. Any more questions?

Alex: *(genuinely bewildered)* What the fuck are you up to?

Mary: The real question is, what the fuck are *you* up to, Alex— whoring around, looking for love in all the wrong places, while right here, under your nose at 170 East 118th Street, you've already found what you're looking for, if only you had brains enough to see it.

Alex: What business is it of yours?

Mary: Let's just say I got a promotion.

Alex: What's that supposed to mean?

Mary: It means that now I can afford to have an apartment of my own.

Alex: I'm not following you.

Mary: Let me draw you a picture. *(as if explaining something to a small child)* Try to understand: I am getting an apartment of my own. Which means that soon I will be moving out. Are you with me so far?

Alex: So far.

Mary: Oh, goody! Now, hang in for the pay-off: When I move out, poor Edie will be *alone*. Right?

Alex: I guess.

Mary: You guess? Oh my god—you'd have hoped that Edie would have fallen in love with somebody *smarter.*

Alex: What? She's fallen in love? With whom?

Mary: With *you,* dodo! Why do you suppose she puts up with your asinine adventures? **She's in love with you!** Now: What are you going to do about it?

Alex: Do about it...?

Mary: Yes, do about it, dunderhead! Edie is in love with you. For some inscrutable reason, the poor thing supposes that only you can make her happy. Now are you going to do anything, or what?

Alex: Well I had thought I might...*(he trails off)*

Mary: Yes, you had thought you might...*what?*

Alex: I had thought I might take her to dinner.

Mary: Bravo, bravo! Excellent start. Not very imaginative, but we don't need imagination here; we need steadiness and resolve. Ask her out.

Alex: I did, but she doesn't want to go. A self-confidence thing. I think she'd rather not be seen in public.

Mary: *Of course.* But that's where you come in. Your job is to love her for herself. And if you do your job well...

Alex: My job, is it?

Mary: If it isn't, you'd better get the hell out of here. I'll tell her you've gone where all her other gentlemen friends went.

    He thinks about it

Alex: I'll leave when I'm good and ready. And I'm not ready yet. I'll stay awhile.

Mary: Good. I'm outta here.

> *EDIE enters with another tray; this one heaped with cheeses, crackers, grapes, and other comestibles.*

Edie: You say you're hungry? Here's some cheese, crackers, a dip, and some grapes. Eat up, Mary. And when you're finished, you'd do us a favor if you'd leave us alone.

Mary: I know when I'm not wanted. I'm leaving *now.*

Edie: I went to all this trouble to fix you something, and you're leaving without eating *anything?*

Mary: Oh, all right! You're so difficult! Look: I'll have this cracker. . . *(she eats it)* Dinner. Delightful! And now, for dessert, this grape . . . *(she takes a grape and eats it)* Gorgeous. God I was hungry. Gotta go. Heavy date. Out of town.

Alex: New Rochelle, by any chance?

Mary: How'd you guess?

Edie: He's got New Rochelle on the brain.

Mary: Why not? Nice place. Bye-bye.

> *Exit MARY*

Edie: The nerve of that woman. I go to all that work and she skips out.

Alex: I'll help you clean up; don't worry about it.

Edie: And to barge in on us—deliberately! How could she?

Alex: Yeah, she's pretty wild. Enough almost to make me forget what I was asking you when she barged in.

Edie: But you didn't forget, did you?

Alex: No. I remember.

Edie: So do I.

Alex: Then what's the story? Why won't you let me take you to dinner—as if I didn't know.

Edie: Well, if you know, then I needn't explain it.

Alex: I need to hear you say the words.

Edie: Do you get everything you want?

Alex: It should've been painfully obvious by now that I get precious little I want. But the reason for that, I think, is that I've wanted the wrong things. But now I want something very worthwhile.

Edie: What—taking me to dinner is all that worthwhile?

Alex: *I* think so.

Edie: Tell you what: Why don't you go to a Chinese restaurant and order out? Then you can bring it back here. By that time I will have cleaned up, and we can have a lovely meal together right here, at home.

Alex: That's good, and we'll do it some time. We'll do it many times, and it'll be great. But not tonight, Edie. Tonight I want you to come out with me. I want to be seen with you. I want my stock to go up.

Edie: You're sweet. But how about *this:* Take my picture, show it to your friends, then your stock may go up—*maybe*—if you take the *good* side, that is.

Alex: Both sides are good.

Edie: You never kiss me on the birthmark side.

Alex: I try to, but you keep turning away.

Edie: My father never kissed me on my birthmark. It was either my forehead, or the side without the birthmark. I'm not used to being kissed any place else.

Alex: Well, you could try getting used to it. Come here…

    He reaches for her

Edie: What are you doing?

Alex: What does it feel like?

    He kisses her on the birthmark

Edie: *(shaken)* You…didn't have to do that.

Alex: I wanted to.

Edie: It's not a turn-off to you?

Alex: Do I act like I'm turned off? Look, Edie, when you were in the kitchen making a snack for Mary, she told me that you…well…that you liked me.

Edie: More than that.

Alex: Well then, let me take you to dinner, for heaven's sake.

Edie: You're making everything so hard!

Alex: *I'm* making everything so hard?!

Edie: Yes! It's not what I planned.

Alex: You had plans, did you?

Edie: Of course. I'd planned to get myself a competence— something I could do from home. So I could *stay* home unless it was absolutely necessary for me to go out. That way nobody would look at me the way they look at a freak, quickly looking away lest I catch them staring. And I'd get myself an apartment mate so I wouldn't be starved for company, and I'd be set. And it was all working out, except my computer broke down, and I needed it fixed, pronto, and I answered your ad, and you came and fixed my computer and ruined everything else!

Alex: Ruined everything, did I?

Edie: Yes! You made me like you, so I kept breaking things on my computer so you'd come back, and eventually you *did* come back without my asking, and that was great 'cause you told me your adventures, and I got to taste that exciting world *and still be safe.* But now you want to take me out of my safe haven, and I don't know how much of all that I'm ready for.

Alex: Well, we can take it real slow. I know a restaurant so dark that the waiters have to tell you what's on the menu. You can barely see your food, let alone anyone else.

Edie: It sounds expensive.

Alex: Don't worry about it. And we'll go in my car, and in the short walk from the parking lot, you can pull up the collar on your coat. Nobody will see you, but my stock will really soar.

Edie: How come?

Alex: Because you'll look like a woman of mystery, someone who doesn't want to be recognized. Everyone will think that you're a movie star, or something. We'll have a great time together.

She thinks about it

Edie: And will you come home with me?

Alex: If you want me to, sure.

Edie: I think I'm up for this.

Alex: Finally, we're making progress. Let me phone in a reservation.

> *He rises to go to the phone, then hears something.*

Edie, there's someone at the door.

Edie: Oh, no!

Alex: Mythical Mary again?

> *Enter MARY*

Edie: Why are you back so soon? I thought you had a heavy date.

Mary: I did. I do. But I forgot something.

Edie: What?

Mary: *What.* It'll come to me. Meanwhile, you two, how's it coming along? Did you get her to go out to dinner with you, Alex?

Edie: *(to Alex)* How did she know about that? Did you tell her?

Alex: *(a little embarrassed)* Well...you were in the kitchen, and I was making conversation...

Edie: But this is a private matter, Alex; it's none of her business.

Alex: So what if she knows we're going out to dinner. It's a small matter compared to everything else she knows.

Mary: Alex, I'd be quiet if I were you.

Taking Notes

Alex: What's the big deal? I simply said that I wanted Edie to let me take her out to dinner, but she was resisting, that's all.

Edie: What business is it of hers where you wanted to take me, or whether I resisted or not? I told you, I want that sort of thing *private,* Alex.

Alex: I know it should be private, but it's a little late for that, Edie. Mary knows a lot more about us than you think.

Mary: That's quite enough, Alex; let's change the subject.

Alex: I don't want to change the subject. This thing is going to hang over Edie and me until it comes out, so let's drag it out right now; I don't believe in secrets.

Edie: You and Mary have a secret?

Alex: You bet your sweet little behind we do, but it won't be secret for long: Edie, I'd like you to meet Viola.

   Silence

Mary: Now you've done it.

Edie: Mary, you are Viola?

Mary: Last night I was.

Edie: For God's sake, ***WHY?***

   Pause

Alex: That's actually a good question, Mary, or Viola, or whatever the hell your name is.

Mary: I've rehearsed two explanations. One is tawdry, venal, and selfish. The other is rather altruistic, in fact almost noble, even a little spiritual. Which would you rather hear?

Edie: I'm more likely to believe tawdry, venal and selfish.

Mary: Okay, here it is: When I sublet the room from you, you made me sign a year's lease. You made me even give you three months' deposit.

Edie: So?

Alex: It means you may be shy, Edie, but not stupid.

Mary: Alex, I've spent days practicing this little speech. Please have the goodness to let me deliver it.

Alex: Sorry.

Mary: Anyway, six weeks ago I learned I was in for a big promotion, with a raise big enough for me to afford my own apartment. I could move out! But I didn't want to lose the deposit. So I thought, if I could just accelerate what was happening between you and Alex then maybe—

Edie: *(interrupting)* How did you know what was happening between me and Alex?

Mary: Oh, please! Haven't you ever heard of an audio recorder? There's one behind the Red Boat.

Edie: *(mystified)* Red boat?

Mary: *(speaking slowly, as if to someone retarded)* The Ruby Yacht. You know: Omar Khayyam? *The Rubiyat?* On the shelf? I put the recorder behind all that poetry. Ever since Alex started coming over here regularly, I turned it on just before you threw me out. It's on now. Wonderful material! Alex's hollow bravado, and your tremulous admiration—you can't make this stuff up!

Alex: So much for privacy!

Edie: *(to Mary)* You...you *thing!* How could you?!

Taking Notes

Mary: I *told* you tawdry and venal. But you haven't let me get to the selfish part yet.

Edie: I'm afraid to hear it.

Mary: Here it is anyway: If I could only accelerate your romance to the point where Alex wanted to move in, you'd be so overjoyed that you wouldn't charge me for moving *out!* But to do that I had to engineer his having dinner with me.

Alex: That must have been some impressive engineering.

Mary: Not really; I had the audio files. Not only did they tell me that you used Match.com, they also told me what you thought you were looking for.

Alex: I've been set up!

Mary: You bet *your* sweet behind you were. My plan was to humiliate you so devastatingly that you'd realize you'd be better off safe at home with Edie.

Edie: You're worse than a thing. You're a manipulator.

Mary: Well, what do you expect? I'm in PR. It's what I do.

Alex: Remind me not to do any work for a PR firm. That's as seamy a tale as I've ever heard. I'm embarrassed to have played a part in it.

Mary: I told you. You wanted tawdry, and I delivered.

Alex: Makes me wonder what kind of noble explanation you could produce.

Mary: That's a lot easier. *(to Edie)* Dear Edie, I'm as unlike you as it's possible to be. I'm self-confident to the point of being obnoxious. Past that point, really. I know I'm insufferable:

it's unlikely I'll be satisfied with anyone who comes my way, and even *less* likely that anyone will be satisfied with *me*. But you, dear Edie, with a little coaxing, could learn to let happiness into your life, and you deserve it. I thought that if I could do that for you, it would give my manipulative life some socially redeeming value.

Alex: It all sounds reasonable to me.

Silence

Edie: I feel so dirty . . . I feel *used*. I don't feel like eating out, tonight. I don't feel like eating, period. Forgive me, Alex, but I'm going to bed.

Alex: *What?!* After all this, you're not going out? Come on, Edie, *please* come to supper. Nobody will see you. The place is so dark, some patrons bring flashlights to see the menu. And once you have something to eat, you'll feel better. *I'll* feel better. Then we can go home. You to yours, me to mine, or whatever you like.

Mary: Not a bad offer, Edie. I'd take him up on it.

Edie: I'm sure you would. But that doesn't mean *I* have to.

Alex: You don't have to do anything. But I *hope* you'll keep me company. Do I have to get down on my knees and beg you?

He goes down on his knees

Please come out with me, Edie. You'll have a great time. You can take notes!

Edie: Get up, Alex, this is silly. I'm sorry to disappoint you, but tonight I want to be alone.

Alex: *(getting up)* Jesus!

Mary: *(to Edie)* Then that's it?

Edie: That's it.

Mary: Your mind's made up? And nothing will change it? Prayers and threats, all useless?

Edie: What are you getting at?

Mary: Well, if you're resolved to stay home, and nothing will change your mind, there's no reason for Alex to eat alone. Because, as it happens, I too am hungry. That cracker and grape wasn't quite enough, as it turns out. So, Alex, if you'd be so kind, we can go together—Dutch treat, of course.

Edie: *(to Mary)* It isn't enough for you to meddle with my life, you have to grab my boyfriend, too?

Mary: Who's talking of grabbing? But if Alex is available, and you don't want him, then what's wrong with my having some nice company at a restaurant? And, Alex, if you agree, this time I won't choose an Italian restaurant, I won't stuff my face, and I won't reject you either.

> *Pause*

Alex: Thanks very much for the offer, but I don't feel like it. If Edie won't come out with me, then I'd rather eat alone.

Edie: You mean that?

Alex: Of course. From the get-go, my whole aim was to get you to come out with me. Failing that, there is no second best.

> *Pause*

Edie: I've changed my mind. I'm coming with you.

Mary: Brava. But how do you know I haven't manipulated you into this, by offering to accompany Alex?

Edie: I assume you have. But there is a limit to stupidity, even mine. I congratulate you on your promotion, Mary, and wish you the best. You can move out whenever you like, and as for your deposit, you can have it back.

Mary: When?

Edie: Tomorrow.

> *In the dialogue which follows, ALEX helps EDIE on with her coat, and they proceed to the door.*

In the meantime, I'm going out with my boyfriend to celebrate my coming to my senses. We'll drink to your health, Mary, and thank you for all your efforts, whether your motives were venal or virtuous...

Mary: A little virtuous, but mostly venal...

Edie: In that case, rest assured that tomorrow morning you'll get your hands on the deposit.

> *Exeunt EDIE & ALEX. After the door closes:*

Mary: Dammit. I'd rather have gotten my hands on the boyfriend.

Blackout

Ten Minutes

Scene: A kitchen table with a few chairs. In one of them sits RACHEL, in her early 60s, looking well preserved and vital. She is wearing a bathrobe, and is sipping a cup of coffee and nibbling on a muffin. Near her is a pad of paper, and a glass of water.

Enter ROBERT, her husband, a couple of years older than she, but likewise youthful looking and vigorous. He is fully dressed, carrying a briefcase, and is on his way out the door.

Rachel: Oh, Robert darling, where are you going?

ROBERT goes to her and plants a kiss on her forehead.

Robert: I'm going to see Hollingsworth, and have him check my math in this last section, here.

Rachel: But aren't you afraid that he'll steal your ideas?

Robert: Hollingsworth? Nah...not enough imagination for that.

Rachel: Will he have enough to appreciate your new theory?

Robert: Not really. I'm going there not to get insights, but some admiration.

Rachel: If it's uninformed admiration you're looking for, you have it already—in your clueless wife.

Robert: Well, Hollingsworth isn't really *that* clueless.

Rachel: I know: nobody could be. However, I do have a saving grace: I appreciate *you*.

Robert: But not my work. To *fully* appreciate me, you'd have to have some background in math.

Rachel: I wish you had told me that before we got married.

Robert: What would you have done?

Rachel: Go to summer school.

Robert: And study mathematics?

Rachel: If that's what it took to get more love lessons from you. You know I'm always up for that. I could do with a lesson this morning.

Robert: Can it wait? I have to see Hollingsworth.

Rachel: You have an appointment with him?

Robert: Not exactly. But he said he'd be in his garden all morning, so that any time would be good.

Rachel: Well then, there's no need to rush.

Robert: I'm eager to show it to him.

Rachel: Well, *I'm* eager to have you show *me* something. Come on. Let's get you some coffee, and some blueberry muffins—you're gonna love them—they came out really well. They'll put you in the mood. Come on, you've got a little time to spend with me.

Robert: Not really…

Rachel: What do you mean, not really? I'm your wife of forty years, for heaven's sake. *You've got time.*

Robert: It's like that, is it?

Rachel: *(coyly)* Maybe just a little.

Robert: Well, if it's only just a *little*…

    He checks his watch

Ten Minutes

Okay—you got ten minutes.

Rachel: Ten whole minutes? As much as all that? I'll set it on the timer. I don't know what we can do in ten minutes, but it will be fun trying.

> *She begins to set the kitchen timer. While she's doing this, the dialogue continues:*

Robert: Maybe we should postpone the pleasure. I want to be at my best for Hollingsworth.

Rachel: What? You've a thing going for him, too?

Robert: Don't be silly! It's just that if he should happen to ask me a penetrating question—if you'll forgive the pun—I want to have enough presence of mind to reply quickly, and not grope for the answer. You know that I'm not as quick as I was when you met me, so it's important not to dissipate my strength before I go over there.

Rachel: Dissipate?!

Robert: You know what I mean. I really ought to go right now.

Rachel: No, no—you promised me ten minutes. I want my ten minutes!

Robert: *(glancing at his watch)* All right, you've got nine minutes left.

> *Silence*

Look Rachel, we've got less than nine minutes. We should talk about *something.*

Rachel: I haven't told you this, but yesterday, I almost got killed in a car accident.

Robert: Oh my god.

Rachel: At the corner of Main and Wall, I entered the intersection because I saw nobody coming. But in the middle of the crossing, I happened to glance to my left and saw this big black truck, heading straight at me—he must have been doing forty-five or fifty! I floored the accelerator and barely got out of his way—just as he ran the stop sign. If I hadn't glanced to my left, he would have broadsided me and killed me for sure.

Robert: And you waited 'til now to tell me?

Rachel: Actually, I wasn't going to tell you at all—I didn't want to worry you.

Robert: What other scares have you had without telling me?

Rachel: Why do you ask? Do you think I'm in the habit of keeping things from you?

Robert: You've been acting a little strange lately; and this morning, *more* than a little strange!

Rachel: Sorry.

Robert: Don't worry about it. At least you were able to act quickly and avoid the truck. That's the main thing.

Rachel: You'd have thought so, wouldn't you?

   A silence.

Robert: Is there anything more to talk about? I have to go in about seven minutes.

Rachel: I give up. You can go *now*, if you like. I'll turn off the timer. Time's up sooner than I thought.

   She reaches for the timer, but he forestalls her.

Robert: Wait—I'll stay if there's really more to talk about. *Is* there anything more to talk about?

Ten Minutes

Rachel: There's Hollingsworth.

Robert: Again with Hollingsworth? What about him?

Rachel: He retired early.

Robert: Because his wife's death took the stuffing out of him. I've told you that.

Rachel: Many times.

Robert: Well, it was so sudden. She didn't even tell him that she'd been diagnosed with cancer—stage 4. Can you imagine?

Rachel: Easily. Stage 4? Hearing that from a doc must be like hearing a death sentence—wouldn't you think?

Robert: I suppose so.

Rachel: The floor drops away from you suddenly, as if you were in an elevator, your gut rises to your throat, and you think, this is only the beginning.

Robert: You've been thinking about this.

Rachel: Doesn't everyone? And some think of getting a little bottle of pills to store away in case of such a death warrant, while others already have the bottle, and when they hear the doc say cancer—that little bottle looms larger and larger as they wonder, when am I going to have the guts to use it?

Robert: Rachel, are you all right?

Rachel: Robert, what I want to know is, do you think Mrs. Hollingsworth went through all that?

Robert: Maybe—I don't know.

Rachel: Wasn't she still holding that bottle when her husband found her?

Robert: Yeah, she was. In the morning, he had left to go to the lab, and in the evening he came home to find—that. I mean, he had no idea!

Rachel: Apparently not.

Robert: What a thing for her to do!

Rachel: Such an angry thing.

Robert: Angry?! What do you mean?

Rachel: Not even to have left him a note! To think what she *could* have said—but didn't.

Robert: Whatever it was, he was shocked to hell. He told me that's when his life ended; he didn't want to touch physics again. Thing is, he didn't *have* to. He had already made his mark, so why bother? He might as well putter in his garden; at his age he wasn't going to do anything else noteworthy in physics. Few of us do at that age.

Rachel: He's your age, isn't he?

Robert: Just about. But I don't have the luxury of not working. What have *I* accomplished?

Rachel: You've been a good teacher, and you've published.

Robert: Nobody will remember me. But if this new paper flies, I may well have overturned quantum mechanics. *That*, I think, will get noticed. *I'll* get noticed. I'll *be* someone.

Rachel: *Look* at me, Robert: I'm telling you that for me, you've always been someone—my genius. You can frustrate the hell out of me, sometimes, but you're always my hero.

Robert: I know it, Rachel, and I'm grateful.

Ten Minutes

Rachel: Show me.

Robert: Show you what?

Rachel: Your gratitude. Show me.

A brief silence

Robert: I know I've neglected you lately, but I feel I have to get these calculations onto the page and into the journals while I still have time.

Rachel: While you still have time? What does that mean?

Robert: Who knows what will happen tomorrow? I want to finish this thing while I still can. But once it's out there, I should be able to have some quality time for you.

Rachel: Without looking at the clock?

Robert: Absolutely.

Rachel: Or your watch?

Robert: I'll take it off.

Rachel: Really?! You say you always feel naked without it.

Robert: It wouldn't matter. I'd start with my watch, and continue until I *really* felt naked.

She looks at him.

Rachel: Look, Robert, do us both a favor: you take that watch off right now.

Robert: Right now? We've only three minutes!

Rachel: You won't be wearing your watch, and I'll stop the timer, and once we get going, I promise you, you won't even think of the time.

Pause, while he thinks about it.

Robert: How about after I get back from Hollingsworth?

Rachel: Oh God. He'll have made some suggestions, noted some problem or other, and you'll tell me, 'just wait until I rewrite the paper," and then, "just wait until I show it again to Hollingsworth," and so on. I know the routine.

Robert: The routine can change.

Rachel: After all these years? I doubt it.

Robert: You should give me a chance.

Rachel: And *you* should strike while the iron is hot. By the time you get back, it may be too late.

Robert: What do you mean, too late?

Rachel: I may no longer be in the mood.

Robert: You're always in the mood.

Rachel: Even for me, there are limits.

Robert: Not that I've noticed.

Rachel: Since when have you given yourself a *chance* to notice? It's been a month!

Robert: I've tried to explain about that.

Rachel: I know—you've been preoccupied with theoretical physics, while my merely physical body seems beneath your notice. Maybe you should check it out anyway— nothing lasts forever... *(darkly)* nor does anyone.

Robert: What does that mean? Are you sick or something?

Rachel: *(smiling)* Why don't you try me and find out?

Robert: *(affectionately)* Always the coquette, aren't you, always the seductress. No wonder I couldn't concentrate on physics when we were young: I was distracted by *you!*

Ten Minutes

Rachel: So it's my fault that you didn't produce in your early years?

Robert: I don't say that; I would never say that. All the same, if you had not been there to love—

Rachel: *(interrupting)* You would have found somebody else, right?

Robert: Probably. But I might not have liked her so well.

Rachel: Look Robert: all I'm asking is that you call Hollingsworth, postpone your appointment and be with me for a while.

Robert: Are you putting me on the spot, Rachel, at my age? Pressuring me to rise to the occasion and perform on demand?

Rachel: I don't need you to perform; I just need you to hold me and crowd out that clock.

Robert: Tonight—when I leave my desk to go to bed—at that time we'll hold each other. And then, when we wake up, and I have some strength in me, we'll make love—with no time limit—none less than an hour, anyway. How does that sound?

Rachel: What it sounds like is **not now**. So what else is new?

Robert: I mean it this time.

Rachel: Of course you do. Don't worry about it.

Robert: But I *am* worried about it.

Rachel: Don't waste your time. I'll be all right. You can take off.

Robert: Are you sure you want me to go? *(checking his watch)* We've got about a minute more.

Rachel: Take it – my gift to you.

Robert: Really? I feel funny about this.

Rachel: No, no—there's no need to feel funny. Just give me a kiss.

He kisses her on the forehead.

My lips need kissing, please.

He kisses her on the lips.

There: was that so bad?

Robert: It was very nice!

Rachel: Thank you.

Robert: See you soon!

He heads for the door and exits.

Rachel: *(after he's gone)* But I may not see you.

She reaches into her bathrobe pocket and produces a bottle of pills, sets it down on the table. She takes a pad of paper and starts writing on it feverishly. She checks what she has written, crosses it out, and tries again on the same piece of paper, crosses the second version out, and tries for a third time. Unhappy with the third try, she rips the paper into little pieces.

You're a bright guy, Robert; you can figure it out.

The timer dings repeatedly, until RACHEL reaches to turn it off.

Time's up.

Ten Minutes

*She gazes at the pill bottle in her hands as **the lights slowly Dim Out.***

The Pessimist

Act One

Scene: The living room of a middle-class apartment in New York City. It is Saturday, at about 2 in the afternoon. On a couch sits WILLIAM HAMMOND, in his middle fifties. He is reading a newspaper, some pages of which lie on the coffee table in front of him. Also in the room is ROSIE, maybe a few years younger than WILLIAM. ROSIE is dusting the furniture, but when she attempts stooping to dust the coffee table, she emits a groan.

William: Rosie! What's going on?

Rosie: Nothing, really. Just a crick in my back. I'll work through it.

William: Why not sit down, take a load off?

Rosie: Diane's boyfriend is coming.

William: I know that. So what?

Rosie: William, you don't want him to see all this dust on the furniture, do you?

William: What dust? I don't see any dust.

Rosie: Do you ever?

William: Well, I thought I did.

Rosie: Don't worry. That's what you pay me for.

William: Oh, that's what it is, is it?

Rosie: Close enough. So if you'll put the rest of your paper in your lap, I'll just—*ouch.*

William: Now you will sit down right now, do you hear? We can't have you falling apart. What would we do for dinner?

Rosie: *(as she sits down, with difficulty, in a straight-backed chair)* What... would you do...for dinner? Poor dears. You'd starve, most likely.

William: Pretty damn close. So you'd better take care of yourself.

He smiles

At least until after dinner.

Rosie: Unless the dust gets off this furniture, you guys aren't *getting* dinner.

William: Oh my! That's a threat if ever I heard one.

Rosie: So will you let me dust?

William: No. I will do the dusting myself. *(he rises)* You just sprits a few drops of this stuff on the surface, and wipe with the cloth—is that it?

Rosie: You got it.

WILLIAM begins dusting the coffee table

Rosie: Did you ever think you'd stoop to this, William?

William: *(as he's dusting)* To dusting? Not to this in particular. But to stooping in general—sure. After a certain point, all life is a falling away. *(he dusts for a moment or two.)* We lose our dignity, our strength, our agility, our sharpness...the ultimate humiliation! As young men, we dream of conquering the world—or, at least, of having our name mean something on every continent. But as we get older, we have an impact on less and less, our world contracts so much that we're content merely to cultivate our gardens, till even the smallest patch of petunias is too much for us, our own house too big for us, until finally our world shrinks to the bed we die in.

Rosie: Oh my god.

William: It's nothing new. In some cultures, a peasant woman, to give birth, merely squats in a field and drops her newborn right onto the earth. But if you take the long view of our little lives, that peasant might as well be dropping her baby into a grave.

A brief silence

Rosie: Didn't I serve you enough for breakfast?

William: Certainly you did.

Rosie: What about for lunch?

William: Look, Rosie, this has nothing to do with breakfast *or* lunch, and you know it.

Rosie: I'd like *not* to know it. Can't you be happy for once? Diane is in love with a wonderful young man who you approve of, and who appears to love her right back. For all we know, he's already proposed to her. You'd think *that* would put you in a good mood, if nothing else can.

William: Oh, I'm in a marvelous mood! My loins are girded with strength. I'm ready for all the bad stuff that may come along.

Rosie: What about the good stuff?

William: *(darkly)* Rosie, as my sainted mother used to say, always expect the worst, and you won't be disappointed.

247

Rosie: Jesus! I hate to contradict your sainted mother, William...

William: Then don't.

Rosie: Well even your sainted mother would say that it's been five years since your wife died, and you have to get over it.

William: What if I don't want to get over it?

Rosie: Then I've been wasting my time here. Gotta go.

William: Rosie, I hope you don't think I've been leading you on, giving you some impression that I might...think of you romantically.

Rosie: Good god, no. It's a challenge to get you really to *look* at me, let alone think of me that way.

William: That would be asking more than I can deliver. I know it has been five years, yet it seems only a few days ago that I saw her in that casket, and saw the casket lowered into the ground. I knew I'd never look upon her face again, yet I kept expecting to see her appearing in a crowd somewhere, crossing the street, or coming around a corner. Sometimes I'd see someone who looked a little like her, and my heart leapt, until I looked closely. Of course my mind knew I'd never see her again, but my heart didn't know it, and I kept looking. But after a few months, there came a day when I knew I had stopped looking. In that cold moment, my life's coffin lid dropped down on me. I'm history, Rosie. You don't want me.

Rosie: You may be right. I certainly don't want a puddle of self pity; I want a man.

She tries to rise.

248

The Pessimist

Ouch.

William: You're not leaving us?

Rosie: I can't!

William: Good. Why not?

Rosie: I seem to have a problem getting up. And when I do get up, I've got to prepare your blessed dinner.

William: Excellent.

Rosie: Then we'll see.

William: I'll think of ways to make you stay.

Rosie: Help me up.

> WILLIAM extends his hands, takes her, and helps her up out of the chair. As she rises, she winces.

William: I'm really sorry about your back.

Rosie: I know that.

William: Where does it hurt?

Rosie: In the small of it.

> He releases her hands, and places his on the small of her back.

William: Right here?

Rosie: A little higher.

> He moves his hands a little higher, and begins massaging her back, pressing her body to him as he does so. ROSIE moans.

Ohhh . . . that's so good. I see what Emily saw in you.

William: I wasn't always a sourpuss.

Rosie: I know; you're not all bad.

William: Glad to hear it. And you're not all bad, either. I saw that immediately.

Rosie: Did you!

William: I certainly did. When you nursed Emily through her final illness, I was very grateful. Especially when you quit your hospital job to stay here with us and give Emily 'round the clock attention.

Rosie: I was just doing my job, nothing more; I left right after Emily passed.

William: True enough. But then you returned to take care of *me* after my bus accident, and you stayed on to look after Diane and me even after I mended—and *that* was beyond the call of duty.

Rosie: Maybe. But what was I going to do? Diane told me that after Emily's passing you had become accident prone, breaking your foot on a curbstone, and then getting a mild concussion by walking into a door. So that when you finally stepped in front of that bus—

William: *(interrupting)* Emily had been gone exactly two years, when that happened—

Rosie: Exactly. In the two years since she passed, you simply had stopped looking where you were going.

William: I no longer cared.

Rosie: I saw that. I also saw that Diane was 16, and needed someone to look after her, which you certainly would not be able to do if you succeeded in killing yourself. No—you simply needed someone to keep an eye on you. Call it crazy, but I moved in.

The Pessimist

William: The world could use more craziness like that.

> *She removes his hands from her back, and steps away from him a little.*

Rosie: Flattery will get you only so far with me, William. I'll go back to the kitchen on two conditions.

William: A conditional employee, are you?

Rosie: First, you gotta finish the dusting here.

William: No problem. And the other?

Rosie: Don't lay your craziness on Diane.

William: It may be too late. I think I already have.

Rosie: I hope not. She's at the beginning of a beautiful new life—full of hope. Don't keep harping on what could happen.

William: She already knows her mother's story.

Rosie: But don't *dwell* on it. Genetics are not fate.

William: So they tell me.

Rosie: *I'm* telling you. If you want to keep me here, then stop with the pessimism thing.

William: I'll try. But look, when you're in the kitchen, if you have a chance, could you bring me a glass of water—but don't fill it up—just bring it half empty?

Rosie: *(in a tone of warning—she's near the end of her rope...)* William!!!

William: Half full, half full! I was only joking!

Rosie: Yeah, right.

> *She starts to leave the living room.*

William: I was only joking!

ROSIE exits. WILLIAM starts dusting, whistling as he dusts. Enter DIANE, nineteen years old, and full of life.

Diane: Listen to you! You seem actually to be in a good mood!

William: Don't worry, it'll pass. Because as you know, Diane—

Diane: I know, I know: Everything good has to come to an end, whereas anything bad goes on forever. I know all about it. But look at you—you're dusting! What's that about?

William: Oh, Rosie hurt her back somehow, and I'm pitching in.

Diane: Good for you.

William: Socially redeeming value—that's me!

Diane: Well, Daddy, you *are* very nice. And if anybody says you're not, I just give 'em the business.

She strikes a pugilistic pose.

William: Giving lots of business, lately?

Diane: Not to people who know you, Daddy. To know you well is to love you.

William: Thanks.

Diane: But with those who *don't* know you, well, you have to be careful.

William: Right, careful. Which means...?

Diane: It means please don't talk philosophy with Brian when he comes here, Daddy. None of that pessimistic stuff. I myself don't mind; I'm used to it. And besides, I understand you—I love you. But Brian might get the wrong idea.

William: I might turn him off, is that it?

Diane: Let's just say he doesn't know you well enough, yet. But he's a wonderful person.

William: I'm sure he must be, else you wouldn't like him.

Diane: I *love* him, Daddy, and I want him—for keeps. I think he's coming over to propose, and I don't want anything to get in the way of that. But once we're safely married, if he says anything derogatory about you, I'll just bop him one.

William: Be sure you do. In the meantime, don't worry. I'll act so normal you won't recognize me.

Diane: Come on, Daddy, you're taking this the wrong way.

William: I'm not, Diane: I know just what you mean, and I'll be good. I want you to be happy for as long as you can.

Diane: That's a qualified blessing, coming from you. You think lasting happiness isn't possible.

William: I fear so, for most people. But it just might be possible for a favored few. I want you to be one of them. So I'll be a good boy and talk about the Red Sox.

Diane: He's a Yankees fan.

William: Then I'll talk about the Yankees. The weather. Whatever. You don't have to worry about me, I'll be good. No philosophy. And if he brings it up, I'll simply steer the conversation to the Yankees.

Diane: Oh Daddy, I love you.

William: Well, you should. I have it on good authority that I'm not all bad.

Diane: Who says so?

William: Rosie told me just now.

Diane: Then it must be true. Rosie is a very good judge of character.

The doorbell rings.

Oh! That must be Brian. I love you, Daddy, but please get lost.

William: *I'll be in the kitchen. Maybe Rosie needs a hand, or something.*

He exits; DIANE runs to the door and opens it. BRIAN enters and embraces her.

Brian: Hi, beautiful!

They embrace ardently.

Diane: I'm so glad to see you!

Brian: I hope so! Otherwise I'd feel pretty lonely.

Diane: That would be silly.

Brian: Oh, I can't be silly—not with a serious girl like you.

Diane: I'm that serious, am I?

Brian: It's one of the things I love about you.

Diane: Then kiss me.

He does

More, please.

Brian: Hm...Business before pleasure. Is your father home?

The Pessimist

Diane: *(pretending innocence)* *Why*, yes—now that you mention it. Why do you ask?

Brian: I want his blessing on our marriage—why else?

> *The following sequence is done playfully, with both BRIAN and DIANE enjoying the game.*

Diane: Don't you think you ought to ask *me* first?

Brian: Haven't I asked you?

Diane: Well, we've *talked* about it a good deal...

Brian: More than that. Didn't I say that maybe we should get married, and didn't you say you agreed?

Diane: I agreed to "maybe." But in a formal proposal, there's no maybe.

Brian: Diane, I don't want to turn you off or anything, but my intentions are so honorable, they're stupefying.

Diane: So you claim. But I haven't received a formal proposal.

Brian: Oh. So you want a formal proposal, do you?

Diane: If it's not too much to ask.

Brian: Is it okay if I'm not wearing a tie?

Diane: You don't have to be wearing a *thing*.

Brian: Now that's an idea.

Diane: Not in Daddy's living room, it isn't.

Brian: Killjoy.

Diane: Sorry. But hold on to that thought.

Brian: I sure will.

Diane: Good. But meanwhile, we were talking about a formal proposal

Brian: Which means, I gather, that now I get down on one knee.

Diane: If you can manage it.

Brian: I suppose I can kneel.

He does.

What I do for love.

Diane: What you do is to make me a formal proposal before I change my mind.

BRIAN produces a ring box, which he does not open.

Brian: My beautiful Diane, You're bossy, superior, and judgmental, but I love you anyway. Will you marry me?

He opens the box, revealing a diamond ring.

Diane: *(smiling broadly)* You come here armed with that rock, and you want to see my father *first?* What's that about?

Brian: Business before pleasure.

Diane: Maybe if my father rejects you then you'll think better of the whole thing, go home and save the ring for someone else?

Brian: Come on, Diane.

Diane: Or maybe you hadn't meant to propose to me at all, but intend to propose to my father, instead?

Brian: Diane, please! Give me a break! Be serious.

Diane: Oh I'm awesomely serious. Isn't that one of the things you love about me?

The Pessimist

Brian: Oh God! Please believe me, Diane: I had intended to propose to you first and speak to your father second, but when I arrived I got rattled. I'm nervous about talking to your dad. I worry about how he might cross examine me. And you know how I am with stuff like that, I think *let's get it over with!* And so I got the order reversed.

Diane: I forgive you.

Brian: Is that a "yes"?

Diane: To what?

Brian: To "will you marry me"? Can I get up off the floor?

Diane: Yes I will marry you, and yes you can get up off the floor, and yes I do love you, silly!

BRIAN rises from the floor.

Brian: I'm glad I'll never have to go through *that* again.

Diane: You had better not.

They kiss. BRIAN is still holding the ring box. When they come up for air, he speaks.

Brian: You should put this thing on, while we both still remember it.

Diane: Oh, I wasn't going to forget it.

She proffers her ring finger, and he slips the ring on.

It's beautiful.

Brian: It's more so now that you're wearing it.

Diane: Darling!

Brian: Now can I speak to your father?

Diane: Certainly. But can I talk to you first, Brian?

Brian: Uh oh.

Diane: It's not that bad. Just...be nice to Daddy.

Brian: He should be nice to *me*. You know how I am with rejection.

Diane: Too well.

Brian: Too well? What does *that* mean?

Diane: It means that if you think someone's going to reject you, you don't give him a chance; you reject him first.

Brian: It makes sense.

Diane: I'm not so sure. But to quote someone I adore, *I love you anyway.*

Brian: Good of you.

Diane: *I* think so. And don't worry about Daddy. He'll be nice to you, silly. He loves me, and he knows I love you. He'll be *very* nice; he *is* very nice. What makes you think he won't be nice? When you've come over for dinner, hasn't he been cordial to you?

Brian: Almost to a fault.

Diane: What do you mean *almost to a fault*?

Brian: Well, maybe he overdoes it a little. Patronizes me just a bit. As if he were saying, look: we both know that I'm a rich economist with millions in the bank, and we both know that you're just a start-out applications programmer, with virtually nothing in the bank. So let's pretend it's not important—not even worth thinking about, much less talking about.

The Pessimist

Diane: Maybe Daddy really feels that way. You see we don't live lavishly. Are these the digs of a rich materialistic snob? Maybe he really thinks that money isn't so important.

Brian: I'm sure he does—in theory. But you don't get to be rich by ignoring these things. And when push comes to shove, he's going to want to know whether I'll be able to support you adequately without asking him for help.

Diane: Brian, I think you may have a self image problem.

Brian: Why not? I learn from the best.

Diane: You're saying that *I* have a self image problem?

Brian: Don't you?

A pause

Diane: Let's not fight, darling.

Brian: I'd be nuts to fight with you. Didn't you slug Hermine James—with one blow, knocking her right down to the cafeteria floor? That's what they say.

Diane: They say right. Except I didn't really hit her that hard. Not hard enough to make her fall. She put on an act, howled as if I were Godzilla Monsoon, and fell to the floor for effect. A regular Sarah Bernhardt, that one.

Brian: How did it start?

Diane: Oh, she had come over to our place for some help in psychology, and I started going over the class notes when Daddy came in to say hello, started talking philosophy, and must have rubbed her the wrong way, because the next day she started bad mouthing him in public, and I couldn't take her talking that way about someone I love, so I bopped her one.

Brian: Wow. I better stay on your good side.

Diane: Well, just be nice to Daddy, and you'll be all right. Okay?

Brian: Okay.

Diane: And don't talk philosophy with him.

Brian: Why? You think I can't hold up my end?

Diane: Of course you can, silly, that's not the point.

Brian: You know: I don't care what the point is; that's the third time you've called me "silly," and I don't like it.

Diane: Please let's not fight, Brian.

Brian: Please stop calling me "silly."

Diane: I'll try. I'm sorry. I apologize.

Brian: Okay. Okay.

    Beat

And now, you were telling me the point of not talking philosophy with Daddy.

Diane: Well, I've told you that Daddy's a pessimist, haven't I?

Brian: You have—and I have to admit, that with the world the way it is, he's entitled to his pessimism.

Diane: Yes, I know. But when I told you he's a pessimist, I wasn't telling you the half. His outlook is really dark—so much so it's almost scary.

Brian: He seems amiable enough.

Diane: It's an act.

Brian: But he's always smiling!

The Pessimist

Diane: I admit that he doesn't match the classic symptoms of depression that you read about—

Brian: *(interrupting)* We can skip the lecture.

Diane: *(wounded)* Oh Brian . . . *(swallowing her hurt)* Okay. All you have to remember is that according to Daddy, there is at best only a dim future for everyone—and every*thing*.

>   *BRIAN takes that in.*

Brian: That *is* extreme. It's as if his god is the second law of thermodynamics.

Diane: Precisely.

Brian: I feel sorry for him—sorry for you, too, having to hear all that from him.

Diane: Well, he tempers it somewhat when he's talking to me—doesn't want me to be as depressed as he is.

Brian: You shouldn't be depressed at all.

Diane: I'm not! I'm loved by someone wonderful; we have our whole lives ahead of us, and we've no need to catch Daddy's depression.

Brian: Right.

Diane: *Still*...to be on the safe side...just don't talk philosophy with him, okay? Don't let him inveigle you into his black hole, okay?

Brian: You know, Diane, you've given me the same lecture every time I've come here. Have I ever slipped?

Diane: No...but this time you might feel more comfortable, and forget.

Brian: I'm not a little boy, you know.

Diane: I know, I know...but it pays to be careful. So will you promise me?

Brian: Okay, Mommy. No philosophy.

Diane: Great. So I'll just go into the kitchen and tell Daddy you'd like to talk to him.

Brian: And I'll check out his library.

DIANE exits into the kitchen, and BRIAN goes to the bookshelves, and, seeing a row of philosophical books, touches each one as he reads their spines:

So, what do we have here? Nietzche? Schopenhauer? Oh boy! Hartmann? Camus? *Dostoievsky?*... What's in Dostoievsky? *(opens the book, turns some pages, reads)* "I am firmly persuaded that a great deal of consciousness, every sort of consciousness, in fact, is a disease." Oh my God!

Meanwhile, WILLIAM has entered, and has been watching BRIAN.

William: Something the matter?

Brian: Just checking out your upbeat library, here.

William: Oh, that. Just a little light reading.

Brian: This is *light?!* What do you do for heavy reading?

William: The daily papers.

Brian: That *is* a dark philosophy.

William: True. But we're not here to talk about philosophy, are we?

Brian: No, no.

William: Very good. *(beat)* What *are* we here to talk about?

The Pessimist

Brian: I love Diane. We want to get married, and we'd like your blessing.

William: You have it. I'm delighted.

Brian: Just like that? Aren't you going to ask any questions?

William: What questions should I ask?

Brian: Well, you could question me on what I do for a living.

William: But I know what you do for a living. You're an applications programmer. Which is what *I* did at your age. I know what it pays. Which is one reason I turned to Economics.

Brian: Then you could ask if I can support Diane on an application programmer's salary.

William: Well, can you?

Brian: Barely. But I have plans.

William: Good.

    Pause

Brian: Aren't you going to ask what they are?

William: Sounds like instead of my interviewing you for the position of son-in-law, you're interviewing me for the position of father-in-law.

Brian: Not a bad idea.

William: Well, how am I doing?

Brian: Very well—and I must say that every time I've come here, you've never seemed as Diane described you.

William: Had I been as described, then I *wouldn't* be doing so well?

Brian: *(a little flustered)* Don't get me wrong—I didn't mean that...exactly...

William: Don't worry about it. How did Diane describe me?

Brian: Very dark, very depressed, very pessimistic about life. But I told her that you seemed very amiable, and she said that it was all an act, and that whatever I did, I must not talk philosophy with you, lest I be drawn into your black hole of depression.

William: With all that, it's a wonder you still want to marry Diane.

Brian: Well, I *am* marrying *her*, you know, not you.

William: Point well taken. All the same, you can't be too careful. When I was your age, I was told to look carefully at my fiancée's mother, since that was a good indication of how my future wife would look in a few years.

Brian: Did you take the advice? Did you check out your future mother-in-law?

William: Well, I couldn't avoid *seeing* her—after all, there she was. But at the same time I tried to avoid *studying* her, if you know what I mean. I felt that if they caught me studying how Emily's mother had aged, it might suggest that good looks meant too much to me, and I was marrying Emily only for her beauty, and would be turned off if she lost her beauty too soon.

Brian: If she looked like Diane, she must have been a knock out.

William: She took my breath away. But I wanted to feel that I was marrying her for her whole self—not merely surface beauty. I hoped that I was the kind of man who would keep on loving regardless how my lover aged.

Brian: And of course, she didn't live long enough for you to find out.

Pause

William: Well, as it happened, soon after her diagnosis she began to waste away noticeably. But rather than love her less, I loved her all the more, if that was possible. I knew I was going to lose her.

Brian: Dreadful. I'm sorry I awakened these memories.

William: You didn't awaken them, Brian, they've never gone to sleep. I think of Emily all the time. *(pause)* All the time.

Beat

Brian: Look, Mr. Hammond, I understand how losing your wife after fourteen years of marriage can jaundice your life...

William: You can, can you?

Brian: A tragedy like that? It would have to be devastating.

William: It would have to be.

Brian: Still it doesn't follow that *all* life is like that.

William: Brian Fellowes, we are at a precipice.

Brian: How so?

William: One step further and we'll be—cue the *Dragnet* music—**talking philosophy**. The very thing that Diane warned against. I owe it to you both to avoid it.

Brian: Very considerate of you, but you needn't treat me like a child. I'm a grown boy; I can take care of myself.

William: Well, after you're married, and you still want to talk philosophy, we can bring it up again.

Brian: There's no time like the present. Let's get it over with.

William: You just got engaged, for heaven's sake. To you, the whole world looks rosy and bright. That's how it should be. This is your moment; why spoil it? There'll be time enough for you to find out.

Brian: Find out what?

William: The truth.

Brian: What truth?

William: I really don't want to talk about it.

Brian: But I want to hear it.

William: Don't force me; I shouldn't.

Brian: Just say it, for crying out loud!

> *Silence*

Sorry for raising my voice to you. I'll just go find Diane, and see if there's somebody in this family willing to talk to me.

> *He starts to leave.*

William: You really want to hear all this?

Brian: Of course I do. Don't worry, you're not going to depress me.

> *WILLIAM sighs*

William: All right; you asked for it. *(hesitating)* The truth is …

Brian: Yes? The truth is what?

The Pessimist

WILLIAM takes a deep breath, and lays it on BRIAN:

William: The truth is that nothing lasts, that everything decays. Which means that whatever you love you are going to lose, and that the price of love is pain.

An appalled silence

Brian: Forgive me for being blunt, Mr. Hammond, but that is sick.

William: We *all* are sick, sick unto death, though most of us are in a state of denial. To get through the day, we sell ourselves a bill of goods. We say that there is a god, or that life has meaning, or that we have the power to *give* it meaning, to give it *purpose,* through our lives, our love, our work, our children. All lies, of course, all ashes. There is no meaning. There is no purpose in this absurd world— nothing but a chance jumbling together of atoms. The only thing that makes sense is to try to get through life with as little pain as possible.

Brian: Oh, come on. There's more to life than grief and loss. There's love. And joy, and beauty, and satisfaction for a job well done. And there's always the chance to help others, and make the world a little better. Our efforts may be weak, and the results small, but they're all worth it. I know you're depressed, but there's a lot to live for, so take my advice, Mr. Hammond, and snap out of it.

William: You don't mince words.

Brian: You've noticed that, have you?

William: You and Diane will have lots to get used to, for however long your marriage lasts.

Brian: Again with the doom and the gloom! Listen, Mr. Hammond, for your information, I intend to stay in this marriage for *at least* fifty years, God willing.

William: Ah yes, God.

Brian: I suppose you don't believe in God.

William: Not particularly.

Brian: Why am I not surprised?

William: Look, Brian, it's not that I want to discourage you, or anything...

Brian: Oh no, heaven forbid!

William: Ah yes, heaven.

Brian: And of course you don't believe in heaven.

William: What's the point, when I don't believe in a god or angels to inhabit it? It's better to stick to the facts, distressing as they are: less than five percent of wedded couples ever make it to their golden anniversary. Some of them simply...die—one hopes of natural causes, though you can't rule out the pernicious effects of a painful marriage. Like murder. Or suicide. As for the rest, the marriages simply...fail, for all sorts of reasons, a common one being that one partner cannot abide the changes he or she perceives in the other.

Brian: Well, that's not going to happen to us. Sure we'll change, but the changes will be relatively small.

William: You know, Brian, that every cell in her body will be replaced in seven to eleven years, as will every cell in

268

yours. The only constant will be the ravages of time: your youthful bloom will wither, your bodies will sag, your arteries will harden . . .

Brian: So what?

William: So this: after forty or fifty years, with every cell changed many times over, will it be the same you loving the same her?

Significant pause

Brian: Yes.

William: But how can that be?

Brian: Because the most important part of a person cannot be seen.

William: I presume you're talking about the soul, whatever that is.

Brian: Yes I am talking about the soul, and I believe in it, unlike you.

William: Well, I'd *like* to believe in it. But after seeing someone succumb to Alzheimers, which robs you piece by piece of everything that makes you recognizably yourself, until at the end you're like a vegetable—when you see *that*, it's hard to see the soul as anything but the collection of inherited and conditioned responses, it's hard to see ourselves as anything but a delicate machine—a marvelously intricate one to be sure—but mechanical, nonetheless. And like machines, we wear out. We break.

Brian: But I don't *feel* like a machine. I feel like a human being. Therefore I am one.

William: You feel, therefore you *are*, is that it? Descartes had it all wrong.

Brian: You think that just because I'm a programmer, I never heard of René Descartes. That's intellectual snobbery of the worst kind, because it's based on class snobbery.

William: Class snobbery?

Brian: Yes, sir. You've had an expensive education, which most of us cannot afford. You stand so high and mighty on your little hill, looking down on us working stiffs...analyzing us, judging us, pretending to be so cool and detached. But cool and detached you are not. You are one of the most passionate people I've ever met. You were deeply in love with your late wife, and even though she's been dead for five years, you ache for her as if she died yesterday. I'd pity you if I weren't so pissed at you. I come here to ask for your blessing, but all you can tell us is, *enjoy your journey to the grave.* My god, to listen to you, we all might as well jump off a cliff right now, and get it over with!

William: I did give you my blessing.

Brian: What you gave us was your sour view of the world, and that sort of blessing we can do without, thank you very much.

William: *(bleakly)* I told you we shouldn't have talked philosophy.

> *Enter DIANE and ROSIE, the latter carrying a silver tray with tea things.*

Diane: So is everything settled? Are you two getting along?

Rosie: We can have tea. I've got the fixings.

The Pessimist

ROSIE goes to the coffee table and begins to set the tea tray down on it, but grunts in pain.

William: Let me do that.

He takes the tray from ROSIE, and sets it down on the coffee table.

Thanks, Rosie, this looks wonderful.

Brian: Nothing for me, thank you. In fact, I have to be going.

Diane: Uh oh—what's the matter?

Brian: We'll talk about it when we're outside. You're coming with me.

Diane: Oh no! Daddy, did you talk philosophy with him?

William: I didn't want to, but he made me.

Diane: What do you mean, he made you? You're an adult, aren't you? Couldn't you just say no?

Brian: *(to Diane:)* Are you coming with me, or not?

Diane: Oh, I'm coming with you, all right.

She goes to BRIAN. They go to the front door and open it. Then she turns to WILLIAM

It isn't enough for you to predict that everything will turn sour, is it, Daddy? Oh no—you have to make *sure* that it does!

Brian: I'll wait for you outside.

BRIAN stomps out

Diane: I'm coming! *(to William, fiercely)* You haven't heard the last of this. *(Looking out the door and calling)* Wait for me, Brian!

DIANE runs out after BRIAN.

Rosie: *(to William)* I can't leave you alone for one minute.

William: There's nothing you could have done had you been here. I told him I didn't want to talk philosophy, but he insisted. Believe me, I tried hard not to.

Rosie: Not hard enough. Poor Diane. Now it will be all she can do to get Brian back.

William: If she has to work that hard to land him, maybe he's not the one for her. There are other fish in the sea.

Rosie: But how many of them would have the stomach to chat with the master of disaster?

Pause

William: It's a wonder *you* do, Rosie; I wonder how you can stand me.

Rosie: I'll tell you something, William: Every time the hospital asks me to return and work full time instead of part time—I do ask myself, how can I stand him?

William: Thanks a lot.

Rosie: Well, what do you expect? Even on the sunniest day: wherever *you* are, it's raining! That can tell on a person.

William: Enough to make you leave me?

Rosie: It ought to. But I don't have the heart to leave you right now. Not like this. I'll wait until Diane is safely married. *Then* I'll leave you.

William: Just when I'll need you the most.

Rosie: Oh, come off it. I can't do you any good. Nobody can— not while you're still pining for Emily.

William: Well, she's a hard act to follow. In fact, she's an impossible act to follow.

Rosie: In *your* opinion.

William: What are you saying?

Rosie: I'm saying that Emily was a human being—she wasn't a saint!

William: Rosie, I will hear nothing bad about Emily.

Rosie: And that's just the problem!

William: Rosie, you watch it.

Rosie: Right. What are you going to do—fire me right now? Then you'll be lonelier than ever.

William: Don't threaten me. I'm telling you I'll hear nothing bad about Emily.

Rosie: Who's saying anything bad? I'm just saying that she wasn't a saint, but a human being.

William: She was a beautiful person.

Rosie: Yes, she was very beautiful.

William: I don't mean just her good looks. I mean she was beautiful on the inside as well.

Rosie: Yes, she was a lovely lady. But she wasn't *perfect,* that's my point, and you don't want to hear it.

William: She spoke up for me when others wouldn't. Diane is just like her mother in that respect.

Rosie: But her mother never had to be prompted.

William: What are you talking about?

Rosie: Do you remember the reunion dinner you gave for your former colleagues?

William: All those programmers—how could I forget it? I wasn't sure Emily was strong enough, but she insisted. For my sake she went through with it. It was the last time she felt able to appear in public.

Rosie: That's right. And do you remember how the programmers laughed at you for having taken so much time on each project?

William: They were drunk, and having a little fun.

Rosie: But *you* weren't having any fun. Your face got longer and longer, until Emily finally spoke up for you—reminded them that your programs were elegant to the point of being works of art, and that elegance takes time. Rather than laugh at you, they ought to improve their own work. That's what she said. Remember?

William: I'll never forget it. For then I knew that no matter what happened to me at the office, I had what they all wished for—a wife who was not only beautiful, but loving and loyal.

Rosie: Yes, she was all of that. But she would never have made that speech if I hadn't prompted her.

William: What?!

Rosie: Don't get me wrong: she was really upset by how they were treating you. But she was frozen. So I was telling her, "Speak up, *say* something." But oh no, it wasn't her place to open her mouth. "But he's your husband," I kept saying. "If you won't open your mouth now, when will you?" So finally, with some effort, she stood up, and without my help walked over to that corner couch where they were sitting, and let 'em have it. Right between the eyes. I was so proud of her.

William: *(a little crestfallen)* So it was your idea, not hers.

Rosie: No, no, she had thought of it, too. She just needed a little encouragement to do something about it.

William: Well, a little shyness is easy to forgive.

Rosie: Believe me, there's nothing to forgive. She was a human being, and nobody's perfect.

William: She came very close to it.

Rosie: For argument's sake let's say that's true.

William: What argument are we having?

Rosie: I'm trying to get you get on with your life. There are better things to do than devote yourself exclusively to worshipping at the shrine of your late wife. I know that comes close to heresy, but there it is. There are better things.

William: What sort of better things?

Rosie: Not letting yourself go to pot.

William: I am not letting myself go to pot.

Rosie: Oh, you certainly are.

William: What are you talking about? I haven't gained one pound. In fact, I may have lost one or two.

Rosie: *More* than a pound or two. You're wasting away. But that's not what I'm talking about.

William: Well then, what *are* you talking about?

Rosie: Well, speaking as a Registered Nurse—speaking *strictly professionally*—I can tell you that five years with no sexual activity is very harmful to you.

> *He looks at her with a curious expression on his face*

I'm just speaking as a Registered Nurse, that's all.

> *Pause*

William: You are, are you?

Rosie: Yes I am.

> *He gives her a more penetrating look.*

William: How do you know I've had no sexual activity?

Rosie: Men send out little signals that they're interested, even though they may not be available. And whether a woman is interested or not, whether or not she's available, she picks up on these signals. I've picked up nothing from you.

William: I'm neither available, nor interested. My aim has been to stay alive until Diane's safely married. Once that happens, well...

Rosie: Uh huh, there you go. As soon as Diane's married, you're just going to jump into the grave to be with Emily—is that it? Just jump into the grave?

William: Well, I won't try so hard to stay out of it.

Rosie: That is the most selfish thing I've ever heard. You've got plenty of energy left. You could use it to make people happy. You could volunteer at a library, a hospital, a soup kitchen; you could teach programming, or economics, or English as a second language; there's a lot of good you could do. But instead of being generous with your energy, you've spent the last five years committing a slow suicide.

William: What business is it of yours what I do with my life?

Rosie: Thrift, William, ingrained thrift. I can't stand to see anything go to waste—especially a man turning away from life because of a delusion.

William: Delusion?! You watch it, Rosie!

Rosie: I call it as I see it.

William: You don't see enough. Okay, in the living room, Emily didn't speak up for me on her own—what does that matter? But in the bedroom, she was a hundred percent for me—and she didn't have to be prompted.

Rosie: The memory of that is a great consolation to you, isn't it?

William: It keeps me going.

Rosie: Then we'll say no more about it.

William: What more is there to say?

    Silence

What more is there to say?

    Silence

You have something to say? Out with it! Speak up! What were you—hiding under the bed?

Rosie: No, I was not hiding under the bed.

William: Then you've got no right to say anything.

Rosie: You're correct. I would have no right to say anything even if I *were* hiding under the bed—which I wasn't—or even if Emily told me everything—*which she did*.

WILLIAM takes this in.

William: She told you . . . ?

Rosie: Everything.

Silence

William: *(with quiet passion)* You get out of here.

Rosie: Out of the room?

William: Out of the house! I'll give you seven days. And five weeks' severance pay—a week for every year you've been with us—whatever! Just so I don't have to see that nosy face of yours ever again!

Rosie: Wow! That was wonderful—the first sign of life I've had from you in years. I may revive you yet.

William: I'm telling you, I don't want to be revived! I'm having a Do Not Resuscitate order signed by a doctor. He's sending it out.

Rosie: Then it hasn't arrived?

William: It's in the mail.

Rosie: Then you're still fair game!

William: Fair game?!

Rosie: Listen, William: when you're dead, you're no use to anyone—including me.

Pause

William: Poor Rosie. I'd be no use to any woman.

Rosie: That's not what I heard. According to Emily you had so much sexual energy she couldn't keep up with you.

William: That was then.

Rosie: And now it's all gone, is it?

William: I really don't know. *(pause)* Listen, Rosie, I told Emily that it didn't matter—my being so much more sexually volatile than she was. I said don't worry about it. But I suppose she told you that, too.

Rosie: She did.

William: I feel like I'm naked in front of you! As if there's nothing you don't know about me.

Rosie: A lot of the less important stuff I do know. Some of the more important stuff I can guess. But some of the *really* important stuff I have no idea about—and I wish I knew.

William: Such as?

Rosie: How you taste.

William: Rosie! Get a grip!

Rosie: *(suggestively)* Really?

William: On yourself, I mean. My god, what's got into you? Is it that new breakfast cereal you've been eating? Maybe they're putting something into it?

Rosie: If that were the case I'd slip some into your oatmeal.

William: Oh god—am I not safe in my own house, anymore?

Rosie: No, you're not safe—there's a threat to your life, but it isn't from me. It's from Emily, who any minute may make you leap into the grave with her.

William: Don't talk rot. She wasn't like that. She wanted me to remarry. I suppose she told you that, too?

Rosie: She did.

William: And I often heard it from her—especially as she got closer to the end. In fact, her last words to me were that she loved me, and she hoped that after I had mourned for her a few months, I'd find someone more able to satisfy me.

Rosie: Oh dear. To saddle you with such guilt.

William: I told her that only she could satisfy me, *only she,* nobody else, and I meant every word of it.

Rosie: And you mean to keep proving every word, until you die. What a crock.

    Pause

William: You wouldn't like the taste of me, Rosie. Too bitter.

Rosie: You could have a different taste, if you gave yourself a chance. Someone could sweeten you up.

William: Not likely.

Rosie: Poor William. I know you don't believe in Heaven.

William: It's a little late in the game for that, don't you think?

Rosie: I know. But for a minute, just imagine that Heaven existed.

William: All these years, Rosie...

Rosie: What?

William: All these years I've been perfecting my pessimism—

Rosie: *(interrupting) Perfecting* it?!

William: Of course. Whatever I do, I want to be the best.

Rosie: Good God.

The Pessimist

William: I've been perfecting my pessimism for all these years, and now am I to be asked to believe in Heaven?

Rosie: No! I'm asking you not to believe, but to *imagine* that it exists. As a thought experiment.

William: What on earth for?

Rosie: For both our sakes—and for Emily's too: Try to imagine that there's a Heaven, and that Emily's up there, and she's looking down on you, right now. Go ahead; I know you can do it.

William: This is stupid.

Emily: I'm the stupid one, for wasting my time on you. I'm leaving.

She starts to rise from her chair

William: No, no, Rosie, don't go.

Rosie: You aggravate the hell out of me, William; did I ever tell you that?

William: No, you never did.

Rosie: Shows you how stupid I was.

William: Stop this, Rosie. You're not stupid.

Rosie: I must be. I figured I could persuade a Ph.D. in Economics, a professor of Game Theory to indulge in a little thought experiment, but oh, no, he's above all that.

William: All right, all right, I'll do the thought experiment. What am I supposed to do—imagine there's a heaven, and Emily's up there, looking down on me?

Rosie: You got it.

William: All right.

He stares straight ahead.

Rosie: Are you doing it? Really imagining it?

William: Yes.

Rosie: What is she dressed in?

A pause while he <u>really</u> tries

William: Why...she's...she's dressed in *light*. There are no wings or anything like that. Just...light. And she's kneeling down—as if she were on the edge of a cloud, or something—and she's looking down. And her auburn hair is falling to the left side of her face, covering her shoulder...you know, the way it did...

Rosie: *(quietly)* I know, William. And what is she thinking?

William: You want to know what she's thinking?

Rosie: Please. Tell me.

William: Well...*(a pause as he imagines it)*...that she loves me...

Rosie: Yes, of course. She loved you more than her own life. But what *else* is she thinking?

Pause

William: This is a very silly conversation, and you, Rosie, are a very silly woman.

Rosie: I couldn't be more serious. You once told me that though Emily's body is in the grave, her spirit is very much alive, and follows you everywhere.

William: And you suppose that's ridiculous.

Rosie: Not at all. I think her spirit is in this room right now. Don't you feel it?

Pause

William: Yes, I do feel it.

Rosie: I know you do. She's with you every day. For all I know, she could be sitting on the other side of you, right here on this couch. Don't you think so?

William: Yes. It could be so.

Rosie: She might be turning to you right now, and placing her hand on your shoulder. Do you feel it?

William: I'm not sure.

Rosie: Well, I'll tell you how you can feel it. Emily's placing her hand on your shoulder, because she's trying to tell you something. Listen deep inside you; you'll hear her speaking. You'll feel her hand. Listen, William. What is she saying?

William: Oh, how would I know?

Rosie: You *do* know. Just quiet down, now, and stop listening to your own voice. Just listen to *hers*. It's deep down. Deep down. What is she saying?

WILLIAM concentrates on EMILY, then breaks away

William: You know, Rosie, it was Emily who encouraged me to change careers, and get a degree in Economics. I was a little afraid to take on something new, but she said *You'll never know till you try.* She encouraged me. That was the way she was.

Rosie: I know.

William: When I wondered whether I should take an unpaid sabbatical to write *Permutations in Game Theory*, she believed in me. She said, *go for it.*

Rosie: What is she saying now? Really listen. What is she saying?

William: She's saying...that...*I'm* the one who...who's silly...for burying myself the way I have been. She wants me to live.

> *ROSIE heaves a big sigh of relief*

Rosie: *(quietly)* Atta boy. The question is: Do *you* want to live?

William: *(looking away)* I don't know.

Rosie: Well, how do you find out?

William: Good question. It's not the sort of thing you can research.

Rosie: Are you sure?

William: Well, I can't just Google it, you know.

Rosie: Not now, anyway. But maybe there are other things you can do. To research, I mean.

William: What are you suggesting?

Rosie: Look around you. Right now. Take a good look. Maybe you'll find something worth living for.

William: Yourself, you mean?

Rosie: Is that so great a stretch?

William: Not at all. *(he considers her.)* You're capable...and good looking...*very* good looking, in fact...I'm surprised that some lucky fellow hasn't snapped you up.

Rosie: To tell you the truth, after three years here without a nibble, so am I.

William: You deserve more than a nibble—a lot more.

Rosie: What are you going to do about it?

William: Whatever it is, I think I better do it fast.

Rosie: You got that right.

William: The thing is...Rosie, do you think that Diane will get Brian back?

Rosie: I sure as hell hope so.

William: So do I.

Rosie: Because if she does, then all kinds of happiness are possible. I will have been right to encourage you.

William: Just like Emily...

Rosie: Perhaps. Maybe like Emily.

William: But what happens if she doesn't get him back?

Rosie: Then all bets are off.

William: That would be...I can't imagine how awful that would be. And I could have done something about it. Emily I couldn't save. But there *was* something I could do for Diane—keep my fat trap shut. And I couldn't even do that. If it's too late, then poor Diane! Where was your father when you needed him?

Rosie: Don't buy trouble. Maybe everything will turn out okay.

The front door bursts open, and Diane enters in great agitation. She slams the door shut behind her.

Diane: Well that's over!

Rosie: What's over, darling?

Diane: The engagement, everything. I broke it off.

William: You what?!

Diane: He gave me the ring around 2:30. I gave it back to him around 3. A thirty-minute engagement. Must be the shortest on record.

Rosie: What happened?

Diane: He insulted Daddy.

William: What did he say?

Diane: He said you were nuts...really crazy. And some more stuff I'd rather not repeat.

William: Well, maybe I *am* really crazy.

Diane: Don't say that, Daddy. You're still grieving for Mommy. I don't blame you. I'm still grieving, too—I don't think I'll ever get over it. Of course, I'm ready to go on with my life, but if you're not—well—to call you crazy is so unfeeling, so uncaring! I don't want to be associated with a person like that, let alone be married to him. So I told him that.

William: In so many words?

Diane: Absolutely.

William: And what did he say?

Diane: Just...*goodbye!*

> *She bursts into tears, and is barely able to keep on speaking*

He just...walked away. I called after him . . . but he kept walking! Forgive me—I can't talk about it.

> *DIANE runs to her room.*

William: This day *has* become a disaster. Naturally.

286

The Pessimist

Rosie: Not naturally. It could have been prevented.

William: I don't think so. I am the way I am, Brian and Diane are the way they are. So it was inevitable; people don't change.

Rosie: Maybe not, but their *behavior* can. Once you learn the results of your behavior, you can take responsibility for it; you can *modify* it. Brian and Diane may still be a little young for that, but what's *your* excuse?

William: *(bleakly)* I have no excuse.

Rosie: There *is* no excuse, William. It's one thing if you want to make your own life a living hell, but to infect others, and make their lives hellish, too—it's a selfish thing to do—self indulgent! Don't you get it, William? *This didn't have to happen! (beat)* I don't know what Diane will do, but as for me, Mr. Hammond, I'm giving you two weeks' notice. I'm quitting. Should have done it three years ago, but I'm a slow learner, what can I say? I told you I was stupid. But now, I'm outta here.

She exits

William: Now I've really gone and done it.

Blackout

The Pessimist

Act Two

WILLIAM'S living room. WILLIAM holds a newspaper in his hands, and he is trying to read it—trying with little success, for he can read only a few sentences of an article before grunting in disgust, throwing the page down, and turning to another—only to repeat the same process. DIANE enters. She is carrying a large, thick textbook.

Diane: I'm returning your Samuelson text, Daddy. Where shall I put it?

William: You can keep it if you like. I know what's in it.

Diane: I know you do. But I *always* return a book. As soon as I save the money, I'll buy my own copy.

William: Aha! So you liked it, did you?

Diane: Very much. It's fascinating stuff. I think I've chosen the wrong major; I should be studying Economics. Why should I waste my time studying Abnormal Psychology when I can get into a *really* dismal science? Just the thing for me.

William: Don't overdo it. We economists can have a light moment now and again, don't you think?

Diane: Not that I've noticed.

William: Don't judge all economists by me. I'd be a sourpuss even if I were a cheerleader. Can you imagine me cheering the home team? *(with low energy)* Rah. Rah. Yuck.

Diane: I see I'm living in the right house.

William: Not that I want to get rid of you, but it would be better if you were living in another house—with Brian, for instance.

Diane: Don't start that again, Daddy. This is between Brian and me—don't interfere.

William: But you haven't even tried to contact him.

Diane: Shouldn't have to. I called after him as he walked away. Should I keep calling after him?

William: Well, no, but—

Diane: *(interrupting)* No "buts", Daddy. If he wants to re-open our relationship, or even if he wants closure, he'll simply have to call me. If he doesn't, well...there's nothing I can do about it, now *is* there?

William: It's been two weeks.

Diane: One week, six days, and twenty hours—but who's counting?

William: I'm really sorry.

Diane: Please stop. I refuse to be an object of pity. And I'm not sure I'd take Brian back, even if he wanted me to. He was rude about you, Daddy; you did nothing to deserve his tirade. And he turned his back on me. How many more such hints do I need?

William: He seemed like such a nice guy.

Diane: He probably is—but not for me, it looks like.

William: Too bad.

Diane: *Will you cut that out?!* Sorry for raising my voice to you, Daddy; you mean well and I love you. I shouldn't get excited; things are the way they are, the way they always have been. You've always said that for the majority of people, lasting happiness just isn't possible. And, as usual, you were right, and I was a fool to think I'd be the exception. It turns out I'm not, and it's better I find it out sooner than later. Which is perfectly okay. What did Prometheus say when that vulture was eating his liver? *To be in pain, and see clearly all the pain to come—is sweet.* How's that for melodrama?

William: Oh, my god.

Diane: Don't make such a big deal of it, Daddy. What was Grandma always saying? *Always expect the worst, and you won't be disappointed.*

William: She had the wrong idea, and so did I, and now I've gone and laid it on you.

Diane: Believe me, Daddy, it's all for the best. Suppose Brian had not walked away. Suppose we had kissed, made up and got married?

William: You would have lived happily ever after.

Diane: Happily, maybe—but ever after? I counted on only fourteen years at the most—if I have mommy's genes. Then as I died of cancer, I would have broken his heart, as Mommy broke yours. He'd have gone on living of course— but brokenly, the way you have been. *(beat)* And the thing is...

William: The thing is...

Diane: The thing is, I love Brian—that's the hell of it—and I don't want to hurt him that way. Better he get away now, with only an ache in his heart, than wait fourteen years and have it ripped out of him.

William: I keep telling you that genetics are not fate.

Diane: Yeah. Until they *are*. You know, Daddy, everyone says I have your looks, your personality, your mind. It'll be ironic if what I get from mommy is her cancer.

William: Don't talk like that. Brian told me that if your mother looked like you, she must have been very beautiful, indeed. "A knock out"—those were his words.

Diane: Yeah, he likes me. One of his more endearing qualities.

> *Enter ROSIE, suitcase in hand, dressed for travelling.*

Rosie: Hi Guys. And goodbye.

William: Oh, Rosie. You couldn't have chosen a worse time to leave us.

Rosie: Can you think of a good time? We've been over this thing till it hurts. Let's not make it worse.

Diane: *(jokingly)* Now come on, Rosie. If you leave there'll be nobody here but me and this horrible curmudgeon.

Rosie: As I've said, you're more than welcome to come with me. We'll get on well, same as we always have.

Diane: I can't leave Daddy—not at a time like this.

Rosie: Your heart belongs to Daddy, does it?

Diane: Well, at the moment, it sure doesn't belong to anyone else.

Rosie: In that case, there's nothing more I can do here.

> *She heads for the door.*

The Pessimist

William: Please Rosie—not quite so fast? We have a little economic matter to straighten out.

Rosie: Always the economist, are you? All right: what do I owe you?

Diane: You don't need me around for this.

> *DIANE turns to go into another room*

Rosie: You don't have to leave.

William: Actually, it's just as well.

Rosie: Oh, it's like that, is it?

Diane: Of course it's like that, what did I tell you? Don't worry: I may be lacking in social skills, but I do know how to make myself scarce.

> *Diane exits*

Rosie: So what is it? Did you give me too much severance pay?

William: Quite the reverse—I didn't give you enough.

Rosie: You gave me a week's pay for every year I worked for you. That was plenty, and you added a little on top of that.

William: Yes, but I didn't include money for the time you spent with Emily.

Rosie: That I didn't do for the money, I did it for love. I won't accept any severance pay for it.

William: Couldn't we discuss it?

Rosie: You're not trying to delay my departure, by any chance?

William: That was my general idea.

Rosie: Poor, dear William, it's a little too late for that.

William: You're making things sound horribly final.

Rosie: *I* am? You've been the one with a foot dangling over the grave, and the other trembling on a banana peel! There's only one thing more final than that, and you've been working on it.

William: I may have been, but the closer you come to leaving, the more slippery that banana peel seems, and the more afraid I am of falling.

Rosie: So it will be all my fault, will it? If I leave, it will be like giving you that big final push into the pit? Sounds like you're trying to guilt me into staying. Are you?

William: If I were, would it work?

Rosie: Nope.

William: Didn't think so. But it was worth a try.

Rosie: You're that desperate.

William: Yup.

Rosie: Then why don't you *do* something about it?

William: Like what?

Rosie: Do I have to draw you a picture?

William: Oh! I get it!

Rosie: At last!

William: You gave me two weeks notice at two o'clock, didn't you?

Rosie: What are you talking about?

William: Until that notice is up, you're still working for me. Is it two o'clock, yet?

The Pessimist

Rosie: *(disgusted)* What difference does it make?

William: Just look at your watch.

> *She does.*

Is it two o'clock?

Rosie: Not quite.

William: Then I still have time.

Rosie: You poor, sweet idiot! You think you have time to persuade me you could change into a man worth living with?

William: Anything is possible.

Rosie: It would take a miracle.

William: Maybe you could work one.

Rosie: Not by myself I couldn't. I tried, but...nothing doing. You'll live the rest of your life in bitterness, and there's not a damn thing I can do about it. And I can't stand to see Diane live the same life.

William: She might not. The story isn't over with Brian.

Rosie: Keep on dreaming.

> *A knock at the door is heard, and Diane rushes in.*

Diane: Did I hear a knock on the door?

William: You certainly did. Will you get it, dear?

Diane: No, Daddy. You get it.

> *Another knock at the door. Both WILLIAM and DIANE look at ROSIE*

Rosie: Don't look at *me!*

William: Rosie, are you still in my employ?

ROSIE checks her watch

Rosie: Technically, yes.

William: Then will you please go to the door and open it? Technically, of course. You don't have to say anything.

Another knock at the door

Rosie: I'm coming!

She goes to the door and opens it.

Well, if it isn't Brian Fellowes!

Brian: Is Diane home?

Rosie: She happens to be home, yes.

Brian: May I come in?

Rosie: Can I stop you? *(to Diane)* Brian's here to see you, honey.

DIANE rises, then makes her way to BRIAN carefully.

Diane: *(soberly)* I'm glad to see you.

Brian: I'm glad, too.

William: Rosie, you and I are *de trop.* Let's get out of here and leave the kids alone.

Diane: No, no, Daddy—you stay right where you are. You too, Rosie. Whatever is said, I want you both to hear it.

Brian: If that's how it's going to be, I'm outta here.

Diane: Well if that's your attitude, you can go!

BRIAN turns to the outside door and DIANE turns go exit into her own room. WILLIAM goes to intercept BRIAN at the outside door, while ROSIE, taking her cue from WILLIAM'S move, stops DIANE from leaving the living room. The exchanges that follow are rapid fire. When an actor isn't speaking out loud, he or she continues to act in "no motion," that is, with full intensity, but without seizing the focus from the actor who is speaking.

William: *(to Brian)* Where the hell do you think you're going?

Brian: What business is it of yours?

Rosie: *(to Diane)* Don't run away.

Diane: Leave me alone!

William: *(to Brian)* Give her a break!

Rosie: *(to Diane)* Hear what he has to say.

Diane: He's had his chance.

Brian: She'll probably call me silly, or stupid.

Diane: *(to Rosie)* How can you call me judgmental?

William: *(to Brian)* You gotta meet in the middle.

Brian: I know that.

William: Then *do* it.

Brian: *Not in public!!!*

> *Pause*

Rosie: *(to Diane)* He wants to speak privately.

Diane: Does he get everything he wants?

Brian: It looks like I'm getting nothing I want.

Rosie: *(to Diane)* Sweetie, you can unbend here, a little. Meet him in private. If you want him, you have to listen to him.

William: Look Diane: Rosie and I have to go into the kitchen to find out something. But if you want us, just give us a shout. We'll come running. Okay?

Diane: You're going to leave me alone with this brute?

William: Well, that was the general idea. But look—if you don't want to be alone with him, tell him so—after we've gone into the kitchen, of course. I don't want to see another scene—I've had enough of those for a while. *(to Rosie)* Come on, Rosie, we've got something to discuss.

Rosie: What?

William: Research.

Rosie: Really?

William: *(as he takes her suitcase)* You have something against research?

Rosie: I'll find out, won't I?

> *WILLIAM and ROSIE go into the kitchen. Diane and Brian look at each other wordlessly for a few moments.*

Diane: You walked away.

Brian: You *sent* me away.

Diane: I called you back, but you kept walking.

Brian: I was afraid you were going to keep haranguing me.

Diane: You insulted my father.

Brian: He insulted *us.* Instead of giving us his blessing, he gave a lecture about death, and the transience of pleasure.

The Pessimist

Diane: He's been through a lot—His inability to save my mother from an agonizing death. His living without her. What have *you* been through?

Brian: Nothing like that. Although being criticized by you wasn't so easy to take—still isn't.

Diane: Should I feel sorry for you?

Pause

Brian: I wonder why I came back.

Diane: Why *did* you come back?

Brian: Damned if I know.

Diane: You do know. You just don't want to tell me.

Brian: Why bother? It's over between us.

A brief silence

Diane: If you say so.

They both stand motionless, looking at each other.

So why don't you go?

Brian: How about you're such a dazzling conversationalist?

Diane: I don't *feel* like a dazzling conversationalist.

Brian: You're not, actually. I made it up to have something to say.

Diane: That's what you said when we met.

Brian: Really?

Diane: You've forgotten? I bumped into you, and my ice cream cone made a big, brown stain on your shirt, and you said *coffee ice cream, my favorite flavor,* and I said, *really?*

and you said, *it's not, actually. I made it up to have something to say.*

Brian: Now I remember. Then you said, *say something real.*

Diane: Yes, I did say that—*say something real.*

Brian: So I said, *I've run out of quarters for the Laundromat,* and you said that you had a washer and dryer in your apartment, so we went over there, and one thing led to another, and I forgot about the stained shirt.

Diane: It got washed though, didn't it?

Brian: Yeah—along with everything else, the next morning, when we got out of bed.

> *Pause*

Diane: What great times we had.

Brian: Yeah, we did.

Diane: We're not having such a great time now, are we?

Brian: No.

Diane: Why did you wait two weeks to come here?

Brian: I thought *you* would call. And I was angry.

Diane: You had no right to be.

Brian: What business have you telling me how I should feel? I can feel anything I want!

> *Pause*

Diane: Daddy was right. Everything turns sour sooner or later. With us it was sooner, that's all; we were lucky to learn it when we did.

The Pessimist

Brian: Yeah, lucky. *(beat)* Look, I gotta go. Do me a favor: tell your Dad that I'm sorry I mouthed off at him—tell him I've a lot to learn.

Diane: We all do. Me especially. When you walked away, I was devastated. Furious at you, but madder at myself for driving you away. I didn't want to look at anyone, speak to anyone. I felt like my life was over.

Brian: Never say that, Diane. Your life isn't over. This is just a rough patch, that's all, and I'm sorry I caused it. I gotta go. Please forgive me.

Diane: I am the one who needs forgiveness—the high and mighty Diane, so quick with the put-down.

Brian: No, no, you were standing by your father, as you should. You once told me that if anyone bad-mouthed him, you'd bop him one. I should have remembered. Your bop hurts!

Diane: Oh Brian, I am so sorry.

Brian: Say something real.

Diane: Darling, it *is* real.

Brian: That sounds like you love me.

Diane: Of course I do, you silly.

Brian: *I am not a silly!* When are you going to stop calling me that?

Diane: Oh, I'm bad!

Brian: What am I going to do about you?

Diane: I don't know. Are you going to leave me?

Brian: How about...a premarital agreement.

301

Diane: Oh, come on.

Brian: I'm serious. You'll agree not to call me silly.

Diane: But what if I forget and call you silly by mistake?

Brian: Uh...then you get to put $5 into the savings jar for our childrens' education.

Diane: That sounds reasonable. But what about your leaving the toilet seat up?

Brian: Same penalty. Five bucks towards college.

Diane: *Ten* bucks!

Brian: $7.50?

Diane: Done! But what happens if I want a kiss and you say you're too busy?

Brian: That'll never happen.

Diane: It happened two weeks ago.

Brian: You're right; I remember now. Okay, if that ever happens again, with either of us, then the slighted party gets to specify how the other will make it up.

Diane: It all sounds good. But how are we going to remember it all?

Brian: We could write it down...

Diane: We'd run out of paper! Why don't we just negotiate as we go along?

Brian: Fine. Let's begin. Shall we kiss now, or later? I say now.

Diane: I say later.

Brian: Oh, no. Why later?

Diane: Are you sure you really want to marry me?

The Pessimist

Brian: My God, of course I'm sure! Why are you saying this? Are you changing your mind?

Diane: Of course not! I want you more than ever, if you'll have me.

Brian: I'll have you, I want you! Why wouldn't I?

Diane: It's no secret; we've talked about it.

A moment while he remembers

Brian: Oh, that.

Diane: Yes, *that.*

Brian: Listen, Diane, just because your mother died young doesn't mean that *you're* going to. Genetics are not fate; your doctor said so himself...

Diane: I know...

Brian: Besides, if, God forbid, you should get sick, medicine has advanced enormously in the five years since your mother died. Every year we live, for heaven's sake, our chances improve that there'll be a cure for us, or at least a treatment, if we should need it. Come on, Diane—what are you thinking? That after a few years with me, you'll *want* to die young?

Diane: No, sweetheart. It's just that if something *should* happen to me...poor you! That will be the biggest bop of all. I'd like to spare you that, if I could.

Brian: It's too late, way too late for sparing me anything. I love you, for God's sake. I'll take my chances. Besides, who knows, it might be the other way 'round. *I* might be the one dying young.

He kisses her.

Diane: Because I'm so disgusting?

Brian: Of course. What else?

Diane: Darling! When shall we marry?

Brian: As soon as possible.

Diane: Wonderful! Daddy and Rosie will be so happy.

Brian: I'm not so sure about your father. After all, it's a happy ending—it goes against his philosophy.

Diane: Now you be nice. Daddy loves me very much, and if you give him a half a chance, he'll love you, too.

Brian: I'm sure I'll get used to it.

Diane: Oh, you! *(beat)* Let's get him in here. *(Calls out loudly)* Oh, Daddy! I need you!

> *The kitchen door opens. Enter WILLIAM and ROSIE. Their arms are around each other's waists, and they both are smiling.*

William: What's the matter, baby? Is this brute being mean to you?

Diane: Terribly mean. He wants to marry me right away, with no time to plan a big wedding or anything.

William: Well, what do *you* want? Might you want to put it off until you graduate college?

Diane: I want what he wants, Daddy; I submit to fate.

Rosie: That's wonderful, darling!

> *The two women embrace.*

You have the right idea, you two: don't put *anything* off.

> *WILLIAM goes to shake BRIAN'S hand.*

The Pessimist

William: Congratulations, young man, you're getting a peach.

Brian: Don't I know it!

William: Take care of her.

Brian: I will.

William: How beautiful this is. It almost makes me envious of your happiness.

Brian: You? Envious of *happiness?!*

William: Oh yes. I've been researching the matter, but it's a big topic—too big for me—and I've gone looking for assistance.

Brian: Where are you going for that?

William: More properly, you should ask, *to whom* am I going.

Diane: Uh-oh.

William: I've been consulting with Rosie.

Diane: Rosie?!

William: Yes, and the results are promising.

Diane: *(with wonder—she is really surprised)* Oh my god!

William: *Very* promising. Splendid, in fact. But I need more research to make sure.

Rosie: *(smiling)* Your father is a thorough researcher.

William: Rosie has made it a pleasure. So much so, in fact, that if things continue at this rate, we might get married ourselves.

Diane: *(Overjoyed)* Rosie and...? Daddy?! That's wonderful! *WILLIAM and DIANE embrace.*

William: We mustn't leap to conclusions. Rosie and I must verify our results with even more research.

Rosie: *(to Diane)* Your father is a *very* thorough researcher.

Diane: I'm so glad to hear it! And if your researches, as you call them, continue positively, you might consider a double wedding with us!

William: Oh no dear, that's *your* day, I wouldn't want to detract from it.

Diane: You wouldn't. I'm so proud of you! I want to show you off!

William: As the bride of the hour, you can still show me off.

Brian: Besides, as Mr. Hammond says...

William: You can call me Dad, if you like.

Brian: Sorry. As Dad says, all this may be a bit premature.

Diane: But Brian, if it should turn out that Daddy and Rosie are ready, and we're not married yet, you wouldn't mind a double wedding, would you, dear?

Brian: Of course I wouldn't mind—though we might want to take care that this double happiness wouldn't undermine your father's constitution.

Diane: Brian, **don't start!**

William: *(with a broad smile)* No, no, Diane, Brian is perfectly correct, here. It is quite true that to a mind like mine, acutely tuned as it is to every possibility of disaster, an occasional happiness must come as a shock—as it did to me when I was doing my researches. But I've decided to be philosophical about it.

Diane: Oh, no.

The Pessimist

William: Oh, yes. *(with an air of stoic resignation)* I've decided that into every life some happiness must fall. To deny it, to pretend that happiness doesn't exist, would not be mature. We must face this possibility with steadfast resolve, we must gird our loins with strength, and learn to deal with it.

Brian: And just how do you intend to deal with happiness, Mr. Hammond?

William: I intend to enjoy every minute of it!

BLACKOUT

www.ingramcontent.com/pod-product-compliance
Lightning Source LLC
Chambersburg PA
CBHW031249170626
46807CB00001B/59